The TARNISHED GARDEN

The TARNISHED GARDEN

ALYSSA COLMAN

Farrar, Straus and Giroux
New York

Farrar Straus Giroux Books for Young Readers
An imprint of Macmillan Children's Publishing Group, LLC
120 Broadway, New York, NY 10271 • mackids.com

Our books may be purchased in bulk for promotional, educational,
or business use. Please contact your local bookseller or the
Macmillan Corporate and Premium Sales Department at
(800) 221-7945 ext. 5442 or by email at
MacmillanSpecialMarkets@macmillan.com.

Library of Congress Cataloging-in-Publication Data
Names: Colman, Alyssa, author.
Title: The tarnished garden / Alyssa Colman.
Description: First edition. | New York : Farrar Straus Giroux, 2022. | Sequel
to: The gilded girl. | Audience: Ages 8–12. | Audience: Grades 4–6. | Summary:
When Izzy O'Donnell saved the students at Miss Posterity's Academy for
Practical Magic her courage caused the Mayor of New York to allowed new
"kindling schools" to open, and open them to any child who wanted to apply,
even if they are poor, and that is how Maeve O'Donnell ended up with her
older sister at the Manhattan School for Magic; but unlike Izzy, Maeve is
terrified of magic because she feels its wildness, and fears that she will never be
able to control it—and when Maeve's magic goes rogue it will take both sisters,
and the help of the school house dragon to stave off complete disaster.
Identifiers: LCCN 2021009017 | ISBN 9780374313951 (hardcover)
Subjects: LCSH: Magic—Juvenile fiction. | Sisters—Juvenile fiction. | Schools—
Juvenile fiction. | Dragons—Juvenile fiction. | Self-confidence—Juvenile
fiction. | New York (N.Y.)—History—20th century—Juvenile fiction. | CYAC:
Magic—Fiction. | Sisters—Fiction. | Schools—Fiction. | Dragons—Fiction. |
Self-confidence—Fiction. | New York (N.Y.)—History—1898–1951—Fiction. |
LCGFT: Historical fiction. | Novels.
Classification: LCC PZ7.1.C644925 Tar 2022 | DDC 813.6 [Fic]—dc23
LC record available at https://lccn.loc.gov/2021009017

Designed by Aurora Parlagreco
First edition, 2022
Printed in the United States of America by Lakeside Book Company,
Harrisonburg, Virginia

1 3 5 7 9 10 8 6 4 2

For my dad, without
whom this wouldn't have been possible.

The TARNISHED GARDEN

The Snuffing

Maeve hadn't sparked magic yet, but she knew how to effectively disappear. She hurried toward her best hiding spot as the counting began. Though hide-and-seek was a frequent pastime for the kids on Rust Street, no one ever found her crouched behind the snuffing bucket on the corner. On a cold December day like this, the steam rising from the magically warmed water was either too much of a threat or a promise of snuffed magic for anyone to get too close. But for Maeve, there was no better place to hide.

Jimmy Pickett counted loudly behind her. *Twenty-eight, twenty-nine* . . . Maeve had until the count of fifty to get to her spot but couldn't risk running on the slick, frozen pavement. The tread was nearly gone from her too-big boots, and the rags stuffed into the toes poked out through the holes.

She ducked around a display of half-frozen turnips in

front of Murphy's Grocery. A glance behind her revealed a handful of other kids fanning out to their hiding spots along Rust Street.

A hand shot out from behind the turnip display and grabbed Maeve's skirt.

"Hide with me," her older sister, Izzy, said as she tugged Maeve down next to her. Their knees knocked together, but the thick stockings that Mam had knit protected them from pain.

The street vendor on the curb leaned over his pushcart full of men's hats. "Well, if it isn't the O'Donnell sisters."

Maeve put her index finger to her lips. "Don't tell anyone we're here, Mr. Green."

Their downstairs neighbor didn't take the hint. "I didn't know Murphy's was getting in a shipment of red hair and freckles this morning!" He put his hands on his hips and laughed at his own joke. Fortunately, two women with shopping baskets came over to browse the hats and Mr. Green shifted his attention to bargaining with them.

"Ready or not, here I come!" Jimmy Pickett had the loudest voice in the Tarnish.

Maeve looked out at the street. "We're too exposed here." She hesitated. Did she dare reveal her best hiding place? For Izzy, she decided she would. "Come on, I know a better place to hide—"

"Stay with me." Izzy swept her hand to indicate the bustle in front of them. "We get to be entertained by everything happening here. Besides, hide-and-seek is for little kids and I get bored."

"Jimmy's twelve and he still plays," Maeve pointed out.

Her older sister rolled her eyes. At eight years old, Izzy fancied herself very grown-up. Too grown-up, Mam often said with an exasperated shake of her head. But Maeve was six and not only did she want to play, she wanted to win. She could see the corner with her snuffing-bucket hiding spot from here. Right behind it, there was a little cranny in the wall that perfectly fit one small-for-her-age girl. Maeve bit her lip, torn between staying with her sister, her favorite person in the whole world, and moving on to the best hiding spot in the whole world.

Down the block, Jimmy shouted. Maeve tensed. He'd probably found Josie Kern. Everyone always found Josie first because of the bright blue coat she had received from some uptown charity. It was the kind of color that either came from money or magic, and it stuck out in the Tarnish.

A breeze whistled down the street, tugging at shawls. A strand of Izzy's hair blew across Maeve's face, casting the busy street in a rosy hue.

Maeve pushed the hair out of her face. "Izzy, we should—"

But Izzy's attention was on the tiny gold sparks dancing between her fingertips. Maeve's eyes widened at the sight of her sister's magic. Even a year after Izzy had started sparking, Maeve still hadn't gotten used to seeing it.

"It's the Kindling Winds," Izzy said in a reverent tone.

As if to prove her point, a second and stronger gust

whooshed through the block, flinging icicles from awnings and sending ladies' skirts swinging.

Jimmy shouted again. But it wasn't a cry of triumph.

Mr. Green glanced away from his customers. Lines of worry appeared on his dark brown forehead. "Jimmy Pickett's ignited."

"Come on." Izzy stood up. She grabbed Maeve's hand and pulled her to her feet. "Let's go watch."

Maeve knew that twelve-year-olds' magic either snuffed or kindled when the Winds began to blow, and that no one in this neighborhood knew the secrets of kindling. But she'd never witnessed a snuffing before.

Down the block, there was a thin pillar of black smoke above dark-haired, blue-eyed Jimmy Pickett. He stood in the middle of the street and stared at the rings of flame around his wrists. Izzy gasped with awe, but Maeve felt sick to her stomach. She and Izzy had pretended they were kindling so many times, but Maeve had never fully understood that when the Winds blew, she would be *on fire*.

"It's beautiful," Izzy whispered.

It's terrifying, Maeve thought.

"Clear the way to the bucket for the lad," Mr. Green shouted. His customers clutched their baskets and stepped aside.

But Jimmy wasn't heading toward the bucket. Instead, he swung his arms through the air.

"He's going to try to kindle his magic," Izzy said, right before the people around them started shouting.

As Jimmy pumped his arms, the flames grew into whorls

as big as barrel hoops and the crowd that had gathered stepped back, forming a circle around him.

"Does he know how to kindle or is he making it up?" Maeve's knuckles were white from clutching her hands together so hard. Neither sister could take her eyes off the flames.

"Dunno," Izzy whispered. "Maybe he's an Ember."

Maeve recoiled. "Mam says the Ember Society's not real."

The skin of Jimmy's fingertips had reddened like he'd touched a hot stove. He coughed and smoke came out of his mouth.

"Get to the bucket, boy!" Mrs. Murphy shouted from the front door of the grocer's. "The longer you wait, the worse the burning gets!"

"I don't wanna snuff. I love my magic too much," Jimmy said through gritted teeth.

Maeve watched, and wished the world was a different place, one where love didn't have to hurt so much. She whimpered. Izzy's face softened and she wrapped her arms around her little sister.

The crowd rippled as someone pushed their way through. It was Jimmy's father, with a snuffing bucket tucked under his arm.

The water sloshed as Mr. Pickett held out the bucket. "It's time, son. I know it ain't fair, but neither's the world."

The girls clung to each other.

"There you two are," Da said, and Maeve felt his hand on her shoulder. He gently spun his daughters around and

Maeve looked up at his bright red beard and worried eyes. "You're too young to see this."

"But I want to watch," Izzy protested. Behind them, there was a splash and a sizzle.

Maeve felt nauseated and she was thankful when Da led them away to where Mam was waiting on the outskirts of the crowd. Their mother must have run downstairs in a hurry because she wasn't wearing her shawl.

Mam put her arms around the girls' shoulders and gave them a quick squeeze. "It's scary, I know. As long as we have each other, we'll be all right."

Maeve's mind raced as she and Izzy followed their parents toward the front door of their tenement building. Izzy would suffer that horrible burning when she was twelve and it would happen to Maeve not long after that. Behind them, she heard Jimmy's da consoling him. The ghosts of flames still danced a sickening green in Maeve's vision when she blinked.

"That's never going to happen to me," Izzy whispered to Maeve.

"Me neither," Maeve agreed, relief pouring out of her like a too-long-held sigh.

"Yeah, when we kindle, we'll do it right," Izzy said.

Maeve slipped on a patch of ice and fell. She was too stunned for it to hurt. How could Izzy see things so differently?

"You all right?" Izzy offered Maeve a hand up. Gold sparks flickered at her fingertips.

Maeve stared at the hand but didn't take it. How could

Izzy want to kindle after what they'd witnessed? Could magic ever be worth going through that?

Maeve burst into tears.

"Oh, Maevers. Let's go inside," Da said, scooping her up.

She wrapped her arms around Da's neck and pressed her face against the boiled wool of his coat to block out the world.

Maeve thought again of her hiding spot. When the Kindling Winds blew for her, she'd head straight for the bucket—even if she had to do it on her own.

ONE

The Rotten Egg

MAY 1907

Maeve

Maeve slipped her feet into the stiff ankle boots of her school uniform. She'd been in New York and at the Manhattan School for Magic for two weeks, and everything about her new life pinched worse than the boots.

She tied the laces and let her heels clunk against the wooden bed frame. How long could she dawdle before Cook expected her downstairs for her shift on kitchen duty? She looked around the room for an excuse. Her roommate, Antonia Sabetti, was brushing her glossy black hair for what Maeve estimated was the third time that morning. Antonia's older brother, Tom, was friends with Izzy. Apparently, this meant that Maeve and Antonia were supposed to be friends too.

Antonia caught her eye in the mirror and Maeve pretended she'd been looking at the pink paisley wallpaper. There was far too much pink in this room. Both of the beds had pink and cream bedding, and the pink wardrobe that stood in the far corner contained a bunch of new dresses for Maeve—some pink as well.

Maeve was uncomfortable here, and not only because she didn't like pink. She didn't feel like she deserved any of this. Not the lovely study desk—thankfully, cream colored—or the textbooks with their new, store-bought scent. She felt guilty every time she put her school-issued crystal into the pocket of her pinafore to go to class because she knew the terrible truth: She shouldn't be at the Manhattan School for Magic at all.

Maeve was terrified of magic.

She raked her fingers through the tangles in her red hair and wove it into a single braid down her back. It wasn't the tidiest braid she'd ever done, but her mind was distracted. She wanted to love her magic the way that Izzy did, but every time she tried to do magic, the word *dangerous* sizzled in her mind. Yesterday, their teacher Miss Lawrence had given each pupil a glass of water with the instruction to channel her magic into the water until it steamed. When Maeve had searched down inside herself and felt the raw edges of her magic, she'd panicked and dropped her glass. It shattered into so many pieces even Miss Lawrence couldn't magic it back together.

The school year had started in April instead of January because the new school had still been under construction. The headmistress, Miss Clementine, was always reminding the students that the shortened school term meant they needed to work extra hard. But working harder was exactly what Maeve was afraid of, and she knew today would be no different.

At the thought of trying to do magic again, fearful silver sparks shot from Maeve's fingertips.

"*Bleeding stones*," Maeve cursed, as a few of the sparks fell on the pink paisley carpet.

"You should be more careful." Antonia paused her hair brushing. She eyed the spot on the carpet where Maeve's sparks had landed. "You know what happened to the last school that was here, don't you?"

"Right. Sorry." Of course Maeve knew. Everyone she met here told their own rendition of the courageous Isabelle O'Donnell's dramatic kindling amid the burning of Miss Posterity's Academy for Practical Magic. It had been an amazing story the first two dozen times Maeve heard it. Izzy had saved the students at Miss Posterity's when the school caught fire during last year's kindling in December. The mayor of New York had been so inspired by her actions that he'd enacted a law that permitted new kindling schools to open, and that allowed anyone to apply, no matter whether they were rich or poor. He'd named the law the Isabelle O'Donnell License after Izzy, who wasn't afraid of anything. Izzy, who was incredibly brave and had learned to kindle against the odds. Izzy, who everyone loved and Maeve could never match.

"I've got kitchen duty this morning. See you at breakfast," Maeve said to end the conversation as she opened the door.

Antonia stood up. "We're *both* on kitchen duty this morning. It's Wednesday, remember?"

With no option to escape Antonia's presence, Maeve led the way out into the hall.

There were seven other bedrooms on the second floor, their varnished doors identical and matching the wood-paneled hallway. The other half of today's kitchen crew, Ida and Minnie, came out of the door opposite theirs. Ida was Black, tall, and carried herself in a graceful way that made her seem even taller. Minnie was even paler and shorter than Maeve and had already busted a hole in the knee of her stockings. Both girls greeted Antonia warmly and mumbled hellos to Maeve before they all started down the hall.

"It's a good thing we don't have to do magic on kitchen duty if *she's* on our shift," Minnie whispered to Ida, but everyone heard her.

"Shh. Don't be rude! She's Izzy O'Donnell's sister," Ida shushed her.

Maeve's shoulders rose up to her ears. She wondered what the penalty would be for missing kitchen duty if she turned around now.

"We should probably hurry," Antonia said, a little louder than was necessary. "Hey, last one down to the kitchen is a rotten egg!"

The other girls took off, laughing as they ran toward the stairs. Maeve hesitated only a split second before she raced after them. Two weeks at the school had taught her that she did *not* want to be the rotten egg. Zuzanna had been the rotten egg heading to their Everyday Enchantments class two days ago, and it had made her dress smell so bad they had to open every window in the classroom.

Maeve's heart pounded in time with her boots down the stairs. *Not last, not last, not last,* it said.

The main hall on the first floor was lit by a huge magicked skylight. Despite the fact that there were three more floors of the school building between the skylight and the actual sky, it always accurately displayed the weather. Gray clouds drifted in the glass above as Maeve and the others ran past the library toward the dining room. She could see the closed kitchen door at the end of the hall.

She gained on the others, her residual strength from farm work winning out over their head start. But as she was about to reach them, her shin twinged where she'd broken it last summer and her new boots skidded on the floorboards. She lost a length and then another behind the girls. When she made it to the doorway, the other three were panting and pointing at her.

Last.

"You're the rotten egg!" Minnie declared. She gripped her crystal and pointed at Maeve's uniform.

Instinctively, Maeve thrust her hands into her pockets and ducked. Her fingers brushed against her own crystal and she felt her magic surge at the same moment Minnie's enchantment hit her.

The stink was immediate and unbearable. The other girls danced away from her, shrieking while pinching their noses in disgust. Maeve had somehow deflected the enchantment and had made the whole kitchen reek of rotten eggs.

Ida gagged. "Why did you do that?"

"I—I didn't mean to," Maeve protested.

She wished she knew a good invisibility enchantment, but she'd undoubtedly mess that up too. Every time Maeve tried to do the pretty magic they taught at the school, it came out wild and uncontrollable. *Her magic is dangerous,* a dozen voices whispered in her memory.

Cook chose that moment to enter through the door from the dining room. She peered at them through the silver-framed spectacles perched on her pointy nose. "Morning, girls. Are you ready—*Stones alive,* what is that smell?"

Minnie pointed at Maeve with the hand that wasn't holding her nose. "She did it."

"It was an accident." Maeve took her hands from her pockets, determined not to touch her crystal.

"Go and open the windows. Thank goodness you're unkindled and the smell won't last long." Cook pointed first at the row of windows near the stove and then at four aprons hanging on pegs by the doors. "Put those on, the rest of you. We're making eggs this morning." She winced. "On second thought, toast sounds better."

"No more rotten eggs when Maeve's around," Ida whispered to Minnie.

Minnie wasn't very good at keeping her voice down. "It's not my fault. You would think Izzy O'Donnell's sister would be good at magic but she's . . . not."

Maeve ducked her head so no one could see how much those words stung. She opened the first window. Spring-morning air rushed in, smelling of motorcars, carriage horses, and the faintest hint of the flowers blooming across the street in Central Park. She reached into her other pocket and rubbed the embroidered sachet again. It made her feel calmer.

After all, she was used to being on her own. Maeve didn't like to talk about her time out West, and there were parts of it she didn't like to think about either. Years earlier, when Mam and Da had died and Maeve was sent away, the matron on the Orphan Train had predicted that her sparks would make her tricky to place. The harder Maeve tried to hide her sparks, the worse the consequences got, right up until she sparked in surprise when a goat butted her and she almost burned down the Taylors' barn. *She's dangerous. Magic is a liability on a farm,* they said as they dumped her back into the matron's frowning care. Maeve had tried her best to never make a mistake and let her sparkings show, but with few options left, Matron dropped her off at a stock-yard where the rancher gave orphans room and board in exchange for work. Maeve hated it from the first moment. The cattle were huge and their frightened lowing kept her on edge. The other orphans there were mostly older boys. When they saw Maeve sparking, they told her to meet them in the back field after supper and they'd teach her how to hide her magic. Maeve had gone, but she'd found the field empty—or so she'd thought.

Now, whenever she closed her eyes at night, she smelled the salt and grass scent of the bull. She felt the rush of air as it tossed her up high, and heard the *crack* of her leg as she came back down. The rancher sent for the doctor and

Matron, and Maeve spent the next three weeks alone in a hospital room with only a bouquet of prairie roses for company. One of the nurses gave her a spare bit of fabric and embroidery thread to pass the time, and Maeve made herself a small sachet filled with the dried prairie roses from the bouquet. As she stitched, she told herself she was better off on her own. She kept the sachet to remind herself whenever she doubted it. Like now.

By the time Maeve got the kitchen windows open, the other girls were occupied with the toasting bread and frying sausage. The *thump* of boots overhead signaled the other students were awake. Maeve busied herself with the breakfast preparations and when Cook said it was time, helped carry the food through the swinging door into the dining room.

One long rectangular table with twenty chairs took up most of the space, but the pressure of where to sit wasn't the only thing that made Maeve uncomfortable. The robin's-egg-blue-and-white frescos on the wall, depicting exotic flowers and women in Grecian gowns, gave Maeve the impression that she was standing in a cameo brooch. It was elegant, but the frescoes could be bossy.

As if on cue, a voice from a figure in the closest fresco, a woman with a water pitcher, whispered, "Stand up straight."

Maeve rolled her shoulders back and spotted Izzy and Emma sharing a newspaper in their usual spot by the window. Izzy saw her sister and waved. Maeve couldn't wave back because she was holding a serving bowl full of fruit, but it warmed her heart that her sister looked so happy to see her. Izzy looked different than she had when they were growing up in the Tarnish. Older, obviously, but now she also wore her red hair in the same style as Emma's golden curls: pulled back from her face with a ribbon tied in a bow. Maeve thought self-consciously of her own messy braid.

The headmistress, Miss Clementine, entered the room, deep in conversation with a sleek black cat. Miss Clementine was a tall woman who wore her orange hair in a softly swirled pompadour that wobbled like a gelatin mold when she walked. The cat, however, was not a cat at all, but Figgy Pudding, the powerful house dragon whose magic protected the school. Maeve had never met a house dragon before she'd arrived at MSM. Izzy said they were exceptionally rare.

The headmistress nodded at something he was saying. "You're right, Figgy. I'll—" Miss Clementine reeled back. "*Great gems,* is that smell coming from the kitchen?" Her eyes widened with realization. "Not again. I'm officially banning that rotten egg enchantment from this school. We are learning proper, practical magic for young ladies here." She waved her hand in front of her face.

Figgy hopped up onto his usual chair. "It's lasting oddly long. I scented it even before they started frying the sausages." He licked his lips and eyed the platter in Antonia's hands.

"That is odd," Miss Clementine said with a frown.

Maeve looked at the floor. She knew there was something wrong with her magic.

She tried not to meet anyone's eyes as she and the other

girls on breakfast duty rounded the table, dishing out fruit, toast, and sausages. In the center of the table there were big pats of butter shaped into swans and brass toast racks with curlicue decorations that matched the curves of the chandelier.

When she was done serving, Maeve sank down into the chair next to Izzy.

"Morning," Izzy said with a smile. "Did you sleep well?"

Izzy didn't know about the bull and the nightmare that had kept Maeve staring at the ceiling for hours on end. Maeve shrugged. "Not bad, you?"

"Well enough." Izzy yawned and covered her mouth with her hand. "Emma and I were up too late talking again."

Maeve bristled. When she had arrived at MSM, she'd thought she'd be sharing a room with Izzy, since they'd shared everything growing up. But Izzy already had a roommate.

Emma leaned forward. "Good morning, Maeve."

Maeve mumbled hello. Emma had on her sage-green dress-uniform for the Briolette School, which she attended—though she stayed at MSM when she wanted to be with Izzy and when her father traveled, both of which meant she spent more time at the school than not. Izzy was studying privately with the headmistress, Miss Clementine, but her green dress was a curiously similar shade to Emma's uniform. It was disorienting how in sync the two of them were. When they were little, Izzy and Maeve had been *the O'Donnell sisters* wherever they went. Now everything was *Izzy and Emma* and Maeve didn't know where she fit in.

"Izzy, did you see this? They mention you—well, the Isabelle O'Donnell License, at least." Emma pointed to something in the newspaper. "It's about Glint Kindling Academy."

"Our rival, you mean," Izzy said.

"The fact that they're the only other kindling school that has opened under the license doesn't automatically make them our rival." Emma took a sip of tea, holding her cup so that her pinkie finger extended ever so elegantly.

"So what does the newspaper say about our rival?" Izzy asked through a big bite of toast.

"Don't talk with your mouth full," the woman in the fresco whispered, and Izzy rolled her eyes at it.

Emma frowned. "Looks like their school won some kind of grant from the city council."

Maeve caught sight of the newspaper. Next to the article, there was a picture of a woman with a long beak of a nose. "Who is that?" she asked, in an attempt to be included.

Izzy swallowed her toast. "Mrs. Katherine Nimby. Glint Academy is our rival, but she's our nemesis."

"She's on the city council and tried to oppose the O'Donnell License," Emma explained to Maeve.

"Fortunately, Mayor Slight is on our side and he outranks her," Izzy said, and grinned at her sister.

For a moment Maeve felt the bright light of Izzy's love and attention. She lived for moments like this, when the two of them connected and it felt like old times again.

"Oh, that reminds me. Frances wants to have lunch with us this weekend, Iz," Emma said.

Izzy and Emma began to make plans for their weekend, leaving Maeve in darkness.

Maeve looked down the table. Antonia was chatting with Mary, who Maeve had heard met Emma while selling flowers on the street. The other girls were a mixture of kids from middle-class neighborhoods around the city. She wished there were more students from the Tarnish where she and Izzy had grown up, but few had applied. Though the school offered scholarships, a life uptown was still too far out of reach for many in the Tarnish.

While everyone else at the table chatted happily, Maeve pushed her fruit around her plate with her fork.

"Don't play with your food," the bossy woman from the fresco whispered.

Maeve stopped. She was about finished eating when Izzy turned to her again.

"Don't you think so, Maeve—" Izzy looked down at Maeve's plate and frowned. "Why are you eating your toast like that?"

"Is there something wrong with it?" Maeve looked from her plate to Izzy's. She'd cut her plain toast into rectangles while Izzy's and Emma's were triangles. Was there something wrong with rectangles?

"Not even butter?" Izzy stuck out her tongue. "You should magic some jam on it or something." Izzy lifted her toast and, to prove her point, the blackberry jam on it doubled in thickness. "Magic is delicious. Try it."

Maeve's throat went as dry as her toast. If there was one person she wanted to keep her wild magic secret from, it was Izzy. What if she tried to magic jam onto her bread, and instead caused the chandelier to start oozing jam or the entire tablecloth to become a sticky mess?

Luckily, Miss Clementine chose that moment to stand up at the end of the table. Her brooch winked with magic and everyone's water glasses dinged for attention. Maeve exhaled in relief as Izzy turned to listen.

Miss Clementine cleared her throat. "Before we dismiss for class, I'd like to remind you that some important visitors from the Board of Magical Education will be touring the school during your art lesson with Mr. Harris." She nodded at Emma, who smiled at this mention of her father. "I'm counting on you to be on your best behavior and do your *best magic*."

Was Maeve imagining it, or did the headmistress's eyes linger on Maeve when she said that last part?

Maeve set her uneaten jam-less toast on her plate. She had to find a way to get control over her magic before something bad happened. Something *dangerous*.

She lifted her pinkie finger as she took a sip of her tea— and spilled the tea in her lap.

TWO

The Manhattan School...for Magic

Izzy

Izzy paced up and down the middle of the library. The Board of Magical Education officials were due to arrive any moment. Miss Clementine had reassured the students that the Board officials routinely toured all new schools in the first weeks of operation, but Izzy was still nervous. Outside, it had begun to drizzle and the light coming through the windows took on a grayish tone.

When he built the school, Mr. Harris had used a cozying enchantment to make the library always feel warm and snug. The walls were painted the pale pink of sunset clouds, and Izzy thought the color made the tall bookcases look like skyscrapers.

Figgy Pudding napped on one of the plush purple love seats. He had a paw draped over his eyes, and his furry side rose and fell in contented slumber. Izzy wished he would wake up and talk to her. She missed the days when she,

Emma, and their friends Frances Slight and Tom Sabetti were together, learning to kindle. Now Emma and Frances were off at Briolette, Tom went to the boys' school, Trilliant Academy, and Izzy had stayed behind. Sure, it had been her choice. The thought of sitting in class next to the girls whose toilets she'd scrubbed last year and enduring the inevitable stares and snubs at a magical school made Izzy feel like an impostor.

Plus, she'd reasoned that she'd get to spend more time with her sister if she stayed at MSM. But Maeve was different than Izzy remembered. She had tried to ask Maeve about her time out West, but it was clear that she didn't want to talk about it.

A smudge on the nearest floor-length window distracted her. Izzy couldn't have their guests seeing that. She gripped her school-supplied crystal and made a scrubbing motion toward the smudge. With a flash of her magic, the window gleamed, and she attempted the mental exercise to *sear* the enchantment.

No one had told her how hard it was to make magic permanent. She'd thought after she kindled, *poof*, any enchantment she did would last forever, but that wasn't the case. Searing was like mentally catching the strings of the enchantment and tying them into a knot. Izzy had yet to get the hang of it.

The window's shine faded as the smudge reappeared. Izzy wiped it off with her sleeve.

She caught her reflection in the glass and touched the spot over her heart where she hoped her school pin would go. Would it be the kite of Briolette, the teardrop of

Pendeloque Prep, or the shield of Cabachon Day School? She promised herself that she'd be ready to go to a school when the next term began in January. Izzy pictured herself searing enchantments left and right while her school pin gleamed for the world to see that she, Isabelle O'Donnell, was an accepted member of magical society.

Out in the hall, the doorbell rang.

Figgy's head popped up and he blinked his yellow eyes. "They're here."

"Ready, Izzy?" Miss Clementine poked her head into the library. "You know what to do, Figgy?"

Figgy bowed his head. "I shall do my part for the school and continue my nap in this highly visible location." He curled up and was asleep again in seconds.

The bell rang again, less patiently than before. It was enchanted to ring in a way that matched the ringer's mood, so as to warn the person answering the door. Izzy had found it especially helpful when it rang shrilly with false cheer so she knew to expect a traveling salesperson.

"See you in a bit." Miss Clementine ran a hand over her frizzy hair and hurried down the hall.

Izzy was supposed to be reading in the library when the Board officials passed through, but she couldn't sit still. She heard Miss Clementine's heels click on the floorboards as she hurried to the front door. Izzy crept over to peer out the library doorway.

The storm in the magically accurate skylight cast the hallway in a gloomy gray full of shadows. Miss Clementine opened the front door to reveal a gentleman wearing a long black coat. Though it was pouring rain, his coat and umbrella were dry.

"Mr. Rote! I'm sorry, but now's not a good time for a visit," Miss Clementine said, and Izzy's brow furrowed as she tried to place his name.

Mr. Rote nodded stiffly and stepped inside the foyer, despite not being invited. He was so tall that he had to duck his head so he didn't hit his even taller top hat on the doorframe. When he took off the top hat, Izzy saw that his hair was as white as whipped cream, but there was no sweetness about him. "Yes, I know about the Board's visit. My patron, Ms. Glint, is a member and said I might join their tour. I assume that's not a problem."

Izzy's breath caught as she realized who this was. What was the headmaster of Glint Kindling Academy doing tagging along on the Board's tour? Was he trying to spy on them?

The doorbell rang with a saccharine sweetness that set Izzy's teeth on edge. Miss Clementine opened it to reveal two men and two women, also dressed for rain but magically dry.

Izzy immediately recognized the woman in front from the newspapers. Gems sparkled in Gladys Glint's earrings and necklace, befitting of the wealthiest woman in New York. She was so fancy that her hair could only be called silver, never gray.

"This place is absolutely precious. It's a Harris design, yes?" Ms. Glint craned her neck up to look at the skylight.

The bland-looking gentlemen quietly introduced themselves to the headmistress, but Izzy couldn't hear their names. She turned her attention to the woman standing at the back of the group at the same time that Miss Clementine did.

The headmistress's eyes widened. "Oh, I didn't realize anyone from the city council would be joining us, Mrs. Nimby."

Izzy froze in horror. *Nimby?*

The woman Izzy called her nemesis gave a trilling little laugh. "Perhaps you haven't heard, but I've recently been appointed the Acting Commissioner of the Board of Magical Education. Hopefully to be fully confirmed soon."

Izzy gripped the doorframe. This was the woman who had tried to block the Isabelle O'Donnell License. The woman who believed that people like Izzy shouldn't be allowed to kindle because they weren't rich. This couldn't be happening.

Miss Clementine also appeared to be at a loss for words.

Mrs. Nimby opened her handbag and removed four tea bags. Or at least, Izzy thought that's what they were, but with a flash of Mrs. Nimby's gem, they became four clipboards. She handed one to each of the Board members along with a pen. Mr. Rote took a notepad out of his lapel pocket.

Izzy watched Miss Clementine struggle with the visitors' coats. She squared her shoulders. Their rival and their nemesis on the same tour? She couldn't let Miss Clementine face this alone.

She stepped into the hall. "Miss Clementine, let me help you with those things."

The visitors turned and Izzy suddenly understood how the animals in the Central Park menagerie felt.

"The famous Isabelle O'Donnell," Mr. Rote said.

"Some would say, *notorious*," Ms. Glint added with a wink. She handed Izzy her umbrella. "Nice to meet you, dear."

Mrs. Nimby handed Izzy her coat without a word and Izzy resisted the urge to hand it back.

"Will Miss O'Donnell be joining us?" Mr. Rote asked.

This was her school and Izzy was prepared to do anything to make sure it shone. "Sure, I can." She took the men's umbrellas.

"Thank you, Izzy," Miss Clementine said, and Izzy got the sense she wasn't just talking about coats and accessories. "We'll see you again momentarily."

The group headed off to the dining room while Izzy stumbled to the hall closet feeling like a human coatrack.

When she joined them in the dining room, Miss Clementine was in the middle of explaining the frescoes to the guests. "They're enchanted to watch for common lapses in manners to help our students learn how to behave in magical society." She gestured at the frescoes. "Since he financed much of the project himself, Mr. Harris was able to try out experimental and whimsical enchantments like this."

"It's rude to point," the fresco woman pouring water whispered.

"It's also rude to stare," a figure from a part of the fresco to the woman's left added.

That's when Izzy noticed that the visitors were looking at her, not at the wall.

Miss Clementine cleared her throat for attention and strode over to a black stretch of wall. With a dramatic flourish, she pushed a tiny brass button halfway down the wall. "Let me show you another one of Mr. Harris's magitectural inventions: the relevator."

"An elevator?" One of the men raised a skeptical eyebrow. "That's hardly an invention. They have passenger lifts in the new skyscrapers downtown."

"This is a *rel*evator," Miss Clementine said, putting the stress on the first syllable. "Elevators go up and down using pulleys and cables, but a relevator will magically take you to any room in the house where one of these buttons has been installed."

On cue, a bell dinged and two brass doors appeared in the wall. They slid open to reveal a wood-paneled car with a brass handrail at waist height. Mr. Harris had tried to explain how it worked, but Izzy's eyes had glazed over within the first thirty seconds of his technical-jargon-filled answer. Magitecture was definitely Emma's thing, not hers.

"Can we ride it?" Ms. Glint asked hopefully, and Miss Clementine quickly agreed.

Mr. Rote put a hand on his stomach. "I get motion sickness. Perhaps Ms. O'Donnell can walk me to the next stop on the tour?"

Miss Clementine watched Izzy to gauge her reaction. Izzy shrugged. They were only going across the hall. She'd be fine.

"Oh, this will be fun," Ms. Glint said as the men followed her inside.

"Be sure to hold on," Miss Clementine cautioned as the doors shut.

Izzy heard one of the women *whoop* in surprise and then there was silence.

"We can go this way." Izzy pointed toward the hall.

Mr. Rote bobbed his head in appreciation. "I'd been hoping I'd get to speak with you, Miss O'Donnell. I find you fascinating."

"Thanks?" Izzy walked faster. The way he said it didn't sound like a compliment.

"You've started quite the controversy about the future of magic in New York, especially now with the Extinguishings going on."

"I didn't mean for any of this to happen. I just wanted to get my magic." Izzy didn't know what the Extinguishings were, but they didn't sound good. She made a mental note to look into that later and pushed open the door. Figgy was still sleeping on the love seat by the fire where she'd left him. "This is the library."

Mr. Rote stopped by the door to admire the collection of framed newspaper articles on the wall. "These are very interesting."

Izzy had forgotten about those. Emma and Miss Clementine had framed several articles about last year's kindling—well, the ones that were nice about it, anyway. The papers that catered to the upperest-upper class of magical society had not been thrilled about the idea of expanding magical education to the lower classes. Izzy's favorite article was the one with the headline: "Diamonds in the Rough: Students Kindle in the Snow." It featured a large black-and-white photograph of Izzy, Emma, Frances Slight, and the other girls from the school on that night last December. With blankets around their shoulders and proud grins on their faces, it was impossible to tell the difference between the servants and the students. Izzy liked to look at the picture and remind herself that she belonged in this magical world now. Plus, she liked the phrase *diamond in the rough*. She'd sparkle brightly one day, she just needed to polish herself a little more.

Mr. Rote studied the articles. "A bit of a skewed selection, isn't it—" He started to say something else, but the bell dinged again and the doors of the relevator slid open. An exhilarated Ms. Glint and a queasy Mrs. Nimby stumbled out, followed by the men and Miss Clementine.

"I'm telling Harris that I want one," Ms. Glint announced.

"That thing should be illegal." Mrs. Nimby made a note on her clipboard.

Miss Clementine quickly began talking about the number of books in the library and the vast range of subjects available to students. The men wandered off to study the shelves, but the rest of the group's attention was on Figgy, who had woken up when the relevator bell dinged.

"Hello," he said, and blinked at them sleepily.

Ms. Glint's eyes sparkled with delight. "Is that a house dragon?"

Figgy sat up. "Figgy Pudding at your service, ma'am."

"My grandmother had a house dragon." Mrs. Nimby's brow furrowed. "This one's rather scrawny, isn't he? Are you sure you're feeding him enough?"

Figgy's ears flicked to the side. "I don't know whether to be insulted or to say thank you."

"House dragons come in many different sizes and shapes. One of my buildings has an elegant longhair. In firelight, his scales are a magnificent blue," Ms. Glint said wistfully. "I'm a bit of a collector of house dragons and try to entice them to live in all of my properties."

Mr. Rote looked between the framed articles and Figgy. "Are you the same house dragon who failed to prevent the fire at Miss Posterity's?"

The air in the room chilled ten degrees. Maybe literally. House dragon magic was mysterious like that.

"That inferno was beyond the ability of one house dragon," Figgy said, sitting very straight and stiff. "House dragons used to operate in families, or at the very least, in pairs, but our once great numbers have been depleted. Still, we dedicate our lives to protecting humans and magic. *Some* people are grateful for that."

His tail lashed the couch in agitation, and the air above him shimmered with magic. Across the room, Izzy saw his shadow move in unison, but the tail on the wall was heavy with scales.

Mr. Rote either didn't notice or didn't care. "I'm well aware of house dragon powers and their *limitations*—"

Mrs. Nimby pressed a hand to her chest and spoke over him. "Personally, I find house dragons temperamental. They're outdated, especially with the city's top-notch firefighting capabilities."

"But they're so cute." Ms. Glint wiggled her fingers in Figgy's direction.

Figgy flexed his talons and the shimmering above him

intensified. At the sight of this, Miss Clementine hopped into the center of the conversation. "Why don't we let Figgy continue his nap and we'll move on to the classroom? Izzy, you've been very generous with your time, but I know you need to get back to your homework."

Izzy barely had time to be grateful before the flurry of goodbyes was complete. Mr. Rote and Ms. Glint looked back as they followed Miss Clementine out of the room, but she couldn't tell if they were looking at her or Figgy.

When they were gone, the unspoken words Izzy had kept bottled up came out in one loud, frustrated *"Arrrrrrgh,"* as she sank down on the love seat next to Figgy.

"I quite agree," the house dragon said. On the wall, his shadow shrank back to its normal size.

"Are you all right?" Izzy asked.

"I've been gravely insulted, but I'll live." Figgy licked his paw and wiped his ear. "That Glint woman saying she's a collector of house dragons! Like we're prizes! She and the headmaster are still sore that no house dragons want the post at Glint Academy."

Izzy glanced at the hall, but Mr. Rote and the others must have already gone into the classroom. "Why do you think no house dragons want to go to Glint Academy?"

"I don't know. Frankly, there aren't enough house dragons to take every post these days. Once, we numbered in the thousands, but there're only a little over a hundred of us in the city now. More and more people think like that Nimby woman, that we're simple firefighters. Magic's getting so scarce that I can't even recall when the last litter of house dragon kits was born." His ears drooped. "I'd hoped that your kindling and opening this school would help."

"It will," Izzy said, and Figgy hopped into her lap. "Figs, you're going to shed on my dress."

"House dragons do not *shed*. We honor you with our fur." Figgy leaned in for a pet. She stroked his head. He purred and continued pontificating. "Additionally, perhaps no one wants the job because house dragons are creatures of habit. We don't like to leave our post unless we must."

A worry formed in Izzy's mind. She sat quietly while she tried to figure out how best to voice it. "Is it true what you said about house dragons working best in families or pairs?" She swallowed. "Are you lonely, Figgy?"

His ears swiveled back and forth as he considered the question for a long moment. "Sometimes I wish I'd been fortunate enough to have a companion of my own kind. But I love my friends. I'd walk through fire for you."

"That's easy for you to say, master of flame." But still, Izzy's heart warmed. "I love you too, Figgy. Don't ever leave me, all right?"

"Leave? And miss out on Cook's gravy?" Figgy licked his lips. "Apparently, I need fattening up."

They were both still laughing when the screaming started in the classroom.

THREE

May Day

Maeve

Maeve took a deep breath and squared her shoulders to her easel.

The classroom's buttery-yellow walls were paler in the rainy gray light. Ten easels stood in three neat columns facing the blackboard at the front of the room. A palette had been clipped to the side of each easel, but instead of a rainbow of colors, each palette only held a generous dollop of white paint.

Maeve dabbed her paintbrush in the paint and peeked at the other canvases. Antonia was painting a cake, Mary a bouquet of sunflowers. On Maeve's right, Felicity was enthusiastically painting something brown that might have been a dog or a cat but it was hard to tell. Everyone was supposed to be painting something they loved but Maeve had yet to begin.

At the front of the room, Mr. Harris had magicked

himself a temporary wooden stage under his wheelchair so that the students could watch him demonstrate painting on his own easel. He always wore a crisp suit and bow tie to their weekly art lesson. "You must hold the image of the colors in your mind as you reach for your magic and tint the white paint. Start with one color. Once you've mastered that, begin layering in others," he instructed as he painted.

With delicate sweeps of his paintbrush, an image of the Brooklyn Bridge filled his canvas. Sometimes, multiple colors came out of the brush at once, twisting together to create sky or clouds. It was very impressive and very intimidating.

Maeve had to paint *something* but she was afraid she'd mess it up. Maybe she could paint clouds. They were already white and she wouldn't have to do any magic. Maeve went to dip her paintbrush into the paint, but she used the wrong hand and accidentally dipped her crystal. She was trying to scrape it clean on the side of the palette when the door to the classroom opened.

Miss Clementine entered in mid-spiel. "This is our larger classroom. We have a second classroom located on the fourth floor that we'll use when we expand. Our current enrollment only includes eleven-year-olds. As they move into their kindling year, we'll add a class below and then expand to two grades."

Maeve tried to concentrate on her canvas, but it was even harder now with the tour group there. Out of the corner of her eye, she saw them approach the stage and heard Miss Clementine introduce each one to Mr. Harris. Maeve nearly gasped when she recognized one of the women as the very same that Izzy had called the school's nemesis that morning.

"Oh, hello there," Mr. Harris said as Ms. Glint hopped onto the stage next to him and shook his hand enthusiastically.

"I'm Gladys Glint, sir. So wonderful to meet you in person at last. I'm thrilled with your work," Ms. Glint said. "Next time I'm bringing my photographer. I'd love to have a picture with my favorite magitect."

Mr. Harris stared at their still shaking hands. "I'm sorry, Ms. Glint, but I'm getting paint on you." Indeed, she'd grabbed his hand with the paintbrush still in it and her skirt was now covered in multicolored polka dots of paint. Ms. Glint shrugged, though her dress was clearly expensive.

Mr. Rote cleared his throat and spoke in a low, polite tone. "I apologize, Mr. Harris. We don't mean to disrupt your lesson."

"Not a problem!" Mr. Harris said. "Please, feel free to look around. I'm sure our budding artists would be happy to display their work."

"Indeed." Mrs. Nimby frowned at the nearest canvas, where Mary's vibrant yellow sunflowers had returned to white paint. "Perhaps you can tell us a little about your admission standards and coursework, Miss Clementine?"

Maeve felt bad for Mary, who was awkwardly fiddling with her paintbrush while Mrs. Nimby and two very bored-looking gentlemen inspected her easel.

"Certainly." Miss Clementine smiled, but it seemed

strained. "Our school's motto is: *Anyone worthy.*" She pointed to where the words were, in fact, painted above the blackboard in swirling blue letters. "Any student who believes they are worthy of magic may apply. In addition to the usual kindling coursework, we have weekly lessons on magical manners, and extra Magical History classes to close any gaps in their knowledge. With increased staff and funding, I'd like to give the students more freedom to explore their different magical talents."

Mr. Rote's brow creased in concern. "At Glint Kindling Academy, we've found that students learn best in a small and rigidly structured environment. We even schedule the length of time our students brush their teeth."

He walked down the column of easels and the students he passed leaned away from him, like they might accidentally get stuck on his teeth-brushing schedule if they got too close.

Mr. Rote reminded Maeve of the people at the Gemstone Society for Orphan Welfare, who had made decisions about her life because they were rich and she wasn't. He made her feel nervous and angry at the same time.

She faced her canvas, but her palms had grown sweaty. Her crystal slipped from her grasp and fell to the tile floor with a *crash*. Maeve quickly scooped it up.

It wasn't until she stood up again that she discovered it had cracked. The two pieces fell apart in her palm. Horrified, she shoved her hand into her pocket where the pieces settled next to her prairie rose sachet. What was she going to do? The tour group was getting closer.

For a moment, she thought about raising her hand and asking for a new crystal, but she pictured the way the other students would whisper to each other: *She's so bad at magic she can't even hold a crystal.* No, she had to get through this on her own. Maeve thought of the purplish-pink prairie roses in her sachet. She would paint them.

Miss Clementine and the tour group were getting closer. Maeve's hand shook as she slipped it into her pocket. *Please work*, she pleaded silently to her magic as her fingertips found the end of her broken crystal.

Maeve didn't know that her sachet had settled between the two halves of her broken crystal. Magic flowed from her fingertips into the crystal and straight into the seed-filled sachet. Not realizing what she'd done, Maeve lifted her paintbrush.

The floor rumbled.

Felicity looked up from the easel next to Maeve. "What was that?"

Thick, green branches ripped from Maeve's skirt pocket. She tumbled backward in surprise, and Felicity leaped away screaming.

"Watch out!" Mr. Harris shouted.

The sachet fell from the tear in Maeve's pocket, branches sprouting from it and spreading like overgrown stitches, taking on a life of their own. Waxy, serrated leaves unfurled toward the stage. Pink buds with starburst centers formed along the branches and burst into bloom unnaturally fast. Antonia screamed as vines wrapped around her easel, toppling it to the ground. It disappeared from view almost instantly as the branches climbed up and over it. Students shrieked as the branches reached the walls and grew upward. A crack spread across the ceiling, sending down a shower of white plaster.

Maeve didn't know how to make it stop. She squeezed her fists tight and wished with all her might that it would end.

With one final shudder, the vines stopped growing and went still. Maeve took a shuddering breath. Had she done that too? Magic was terrifying and she didn't understand it at all.

She surveyed the destruction. Branches hid the floor and stretched high up over the cracked blackboard. The prairie roses had taken down most of the easels. Several of the students were coated in plaster dust from the ceiling. Ripped canvases and blobs of white paint littered the ground among the twisted vines. The chaos had lasted less than two minutes, but the classroom looked like an ancient, overgrown ruin.

The other students picked their way through the branches, their expressions a range of shocked, frightened, and curious. The adults from the Board stood at the edges of the room, staring at the vines like they were snakes that might strike.

"Is everyone all right?" Miss Clementine asked. When murmurs came in the affirmative, she ordered the students to head to the drawing room. "Carefully now," she said, eyeing the crack in the ceiling above them. Maeve started to follow her classmates, but Miss Clementine held up a hand. "Not you, Maeve. You stay right here."

Maeve looked away so she wouldn't have to see the curious or frightened way her classmates looked at her. She longed for the comfort of her sachet to rub.

Miss Clementine turned to the members of the Board of Magical Education. "I don't think this is as bad as it looks."

As if it wished to disagree, a giant piece of the ceiling fell into the center of the floor with a *crash*.

"Ow! Someone help me!" Mrs. Nimby cried from the side of the room. She tugged at the branches wrapped tightly around her ankle. "What are these weeds anyway?"

"They're prairie roses," Maeve said. When they looked her way, she wished she hadn't spoken.

"What did you do, girl?" Mrs. Nimby snapped.

Maeve was on the edge of tears. "I was trying to paint."

"Mrs. Nimby, she is my student and I will handle this," Miss Clementine said, but Maeve didn't have any time to be relieved.

Izzy appeared in the doorway with Figgy at her side. Her face had gone pale behind her freckles.

"What happened?" Figgy asked. "It sounded like—" He looked up at the hole in the ceiling. "Well, that's exactly what it sounded like."

Izzy gaped at the room. "Are you hurt, Maeve?"

Maeve wanted her big sister to hug her and tell her everything would be fine, but there were too many brambles between them.

"I'm fine," she said, but inside she was in turmoil. Now Izzy would see that Maeve was dangerous. Would she send her away?

Izzy's brow furrowed with concern, but she wasn't looking at Maeve anymore. She picked her way through the roses to where Mr. Harris was still onstage, staring at the cracks in the ceiling with horror.

"You're safe, Mr. Harris." Izzy crouched beside his chair. She rested her hand on his.

He started and blinked rapidly, like he was waking up from a nightmare. "Izzy." He wiped his forehead. "The earthquake—a flashback. I thought the building was going to collapse."

Mr. Rote and one of the other men succeeded in detangling Mrs. Nimby from the branches. She draped an arm over each of their shoulders and whimpered dramatically whenever her left leg touched the ground.

"Why don't we go into the drawing room for some refreshments?" Miss Clementine suggested in a strained voice. "Lemonade, or perhaps something a little stronger to steady our nerves?"

Ms. Glint shook her head. "We must be going."

"Come visit us at the academy if you'd like to discuss your school's entrance requirements." Mr. Rote shot a glare in Maeve's direction. "I have suggestions."

"We will address this at the next Board meeting," one of the men said gruffly.

But it was Mrs. Nimby who made everything worse. As she limped from the room, she shouted in a voice loud enough to be heard by the entire school, "Can you imagine if she'd been attempting more than a simple enchantment?

It is my professional recommendation that she should be expelled and sent back to wherever she came from immediately. That girl is dangerous."

Dangerous. The word echoed in Maeve's head.

The quiet that followed the Board members' departure was excruciating.

"I fear they'll hold this calamity against my powers as well," Figgy said at last, studying the ceiling.

Miss Clementine frowned at the branches. "This isn't your fault, Figgy. Truthfully, I'm not even sure what kind of magic this was." She scanned the room until she found Maeve, still in the corner. "Maeve, come here and give me your crystal."

"I'm sorry—" Maeve started to apologize.

"Maeve, why did you do that?" Worse than mad, Izzy sounded sad. Disappointed, even.

"I didn't mean to do it," Maeve protested, but she bit her lip. She had wanted to lash out at them, hadn't she? Maybe she *was* dangerous. Maybe she deserved to be sent away. She wished she was a year older and the Kindling Winds would blow right now, so she could snuff her magic and never worry about being dangerous again.

"Your crystal, Maeve," Miss Clementine reminded her. Numbly, Maeve picked her way through the branches to hand it over. The headmistress frowned at the two pieces. "We're going to discuss this. Go to my office and wait for me there, please. I may be a while."

Maeve looked at Izzy again, but her sister was talking

to Mr. Harris in a reassuring tone. She headed to the doorway, but she had no intention of going to Miss Clementine's office.

They were going to send her away, just like everyone else did. Why had she ever thought she might be worthy of magic, or that she might be able to fit into her sister's new life? She knew she was better off by herself.

She couldn't disappoint anyone if she was already alone.

So when she fled the chaos in the classroom, she went straight upstairs to pack.

FOUR

Mr. Harris's Offer

Izzy

Miss Clementine sealed up the classroom until they could figure out what to do with the brambles. Figgy, Mr. Harris, and Izzy stood in the hall and watched her magically lock the door with a sweep of her hand and a flash of her brooch.

"I should have built it stronger," Mr. Harris said.

"I should have protected it better." Figgy hung his head.

"I . . ." Izzy didn't know what she could have done, but she felt like she should have done something.

"Nonsense. None of you are to blame. We couldn't have foreseen something like this." Miss Clementine pointed down the hall toward her office. "I'm going to have a chat with Maeve."

"I'll go with you—" Izzy started.

Miss Clementine shook her head. "Let me handle this for now, Izzy."

"Are you going to expel her like they said?" Izzy asked nervously. "Maeve wouldn't do something like that on purpose, I know she wouldn't." But did she really know Maeve anymore? She thought of the way Maeve had bit her lip when she apologized, like she was trying to stop herself from saying something. There had never been secrets between them before.

Miss Clementine exhaled loudly. "I'm not sure what I'm going to do yet, Izzy. Why don't the three of you join the students in the drawing room and enjoy the refreshments? No sense in letting them go to waste."

Izzy did not feel like going to a party, but she dutifully followed Mr. Harris and Figgy into the drawing room. The students were clustered around the dessert table where Cook had outdone herself again. Several were still visibly shaken, but the desserts were helping with any remaining nerves. There were spun-sugar nests with chocolate eggs, rectangular shortbread cookies that had been piped with icing to resemble the school's town-house exterior, and even a foot-tall maypole wrapped with fondant ribbons. Sometimes Izzy forgot that Cook didn't have magic because she made such beautiful things even without it.

"Let's get this party started, shall we?" Mr. Harris pulled his chair up to the piano and taught the students the words to "All Gems Bright and Beautiful."

The tension melted from the room but stayed firmly stuck in Izzy's shoulders. The words *Please don't expel my sister* repeated in her head to the tune of "All Gems Bright and Beautiful." If Maeve got expelled, that would be it for her kindling. Maeve would never get her magic. The thought gave Izzy a hollow feeling in her stomach and she couldn't enjoy any of Cook's delicacies.

By the time Miss Clementine returned, the party was winding down and most of the students had already drifted off toward their rooms. Izzy went straight to the headmistress.

"So? How'd it go?" Izzy couldn't stop from bouncing on her toes. "You were gone awhile."

Miss Clementine surveyed the desserts. "Maeve was not in fact waiting for me in my office. I finally found her in her room, packing her suitcase."

Izzy felt like the floor had shifted under her feet. "She was running away?"

"No, she was under the mistaken impression that we were going to expel her—"

"So she's not being expelled?" Izzy sighed with relief.

Miss Clementine smiled. "No, Izzy, she's not. I believe today's incident was an accident, though, as I discussed with her, Maeve will have detention. I'd like for her to help Mr. Harris restore the classroom when the roses have been cleared and his schedule allows time for repairs." The headmistress picked up a shortbread town house and bit off the first floor. "I gave her back her crystal, or shall I say, the two halves of it, and told her to come see me when she is ready for a new one."

Mr. Harris came over to join them. "Everything all right?"

Izzy nodded. "I should go see Maeve—"

The headmistress put out a hand to stop Izzy. "I'm sure she will want to see you soon, but Maeve asked to be alone for a while. I know this is rough, but be strong, Izzy. When things get dark, we must shine brighter."

"Well said." Mr. Harris swept his arm toward the punch bowl. "Would you like a beverage?"

As soon as their backs were turned, Izzy headed for the door. She wanted to see her sister and was sure that when Maeve had said she wanted to be alone, she didn't mean *Izzy* should stay away.

Maeve's room was at the end of the hall on the second floor. Izzy knocked on the door, but there was no answer. She knocked again. "Maeve?"

It seemed to take ages before Maeve opened the door a crack. Her eyes were red like she'd been crying. "Are you here to yell at me?"

"No." Izzy swallowed. She didn't know exactly why she was there. She was mad, sad, and curious about what had happened, and hadn't sorted out what she wanted to say yet. "I wanted to make sure you were all right."

The corners of Maeve's lips turned up the tiniest fraction, and she loosened her grip on the door.

Izzy smiled. She knew that Maeve would want to talk to her. "Tell me what happened, Maeve. Why did you do it? *How* did you do it?"

Maeve's smile disappeared. "I don't know." Maeve tightened her fingers on the door like she was about to shut it. "I'd like to be alone for a little while, Izzy. I have a lot to think about."

Izzy put her hand on the door to stop it. "I can help you. That woman who got hurt today was Mrs. Nimby. She has a new job and could probably get us shut down, so we have to figure out what happened so it can't happen again."

Izzy hadn't meant to say all of that, but it came out in a rush. She realized that the truth was that she was scared. Scared of what might happen to Maeve. Scared of what might happen to the school. Scared of what might happen to the license.

"It won't happen." Maeve's expression was closed off. "I told Miss Clementine that I won't do magic anymore. It's too dangerous."

Izzy was so surprised she let go of the door. Without her resistance, it shut with a *boom* that reverberated down the hall. Izzy stared at it for a moment in shock. "What do you mean you're not going to do magic anymore? You have to do your classwork and learn how to kindle!" she shouted through the door.

There was no reply from the other side. Izzy tried the doorknob and found it locked.

Fine, she'd give Maeve some time to cool down. Izzy pressed her palms to her forehead as she waited for the relevator to take her upstairs to her room. Maybe she should have listened to Miss Clementine and stayed at the party.

Maeve didn't come down to dinner that night. Emma poked her head into the dining room just as the students on cleanup duty were clearing the table.

Izzy looked up, glad to see her friend. "Hi, Em, are you hungry?"

Emma shook her head. She'd changed out of her Briolette uniform and was wearing a white blouse and burgundy skirt. "Papa and I ate after he picked me up at school." She pointed behind her into the hall. "Might he and I have a word alone with you, please?"

Izzy followed. "Is something wrong?"

"On the contrary, or so I hope," Mr. Harris said from the drawing room doorway.

Well, that wasn't reassuring. Izzy followed the Harrises into the drawing room.

The party table was still out, but the crumbs had been swept away and the dirty dishes carried to the kitchen by the students. If this had been Miss Posterity's, Izzy would have been cleaning up from a party like that for hours.

"Come and sit with us a moment, Izzy." Mr. Harris had wheeled himself over to the fireplace and pointed at it. His watch winked with magic and a fire crackled to life in front of the wood-framed sofa. It felt cozy after such a rainy and challenging day.

Izzy sat, and Emma joined her. Emma put her hands in her lap. A bright red stone on her finger caught Izzy's eye.

She gasped. "Your ruby ring! You got it back!"

They'd traded Emma's ruby ring to a pawnbroker in exchange for kindling flints last year, but it had been a trap to catch kids kindling illegally. Emma had been so sad it was gone. The sight of that ring warmed Izzy's heart.

"Papa tracked it down." Emma looked at her father adoringly.

"I'm so glad," Izzy said. "I hated when you had to give it up. It meant so much to you."

Mr. Harris looked between the two of them fondly. "You two have been through a lot together." He cleared his throat. "Which reminds me. I want to thank you for your kindness to me today," Mr. Harris said. "The flashback was a strong one and your gentleness got me through it. There are many things I wish hadn't happened the way they did last year, but one I'd never change is having you in our lives, Izzy."

Emma bounced with excitement. "Papa and I have been talking about this for a long time, but when he told me what you did today, we knew it was time to ask you."

"Ask me what?" Izzy felt nervous.

Mr. Harris put his hand on his daughter's shoulder. "Emma always says that you're as dear as a sister to her, and I thought, with your parents gone, you might want someone to look after you. If you would consider it, I would like to adopt you, Izzy."

Great stones. Izzy didn't know what to say. She'd never expected this.

Mr. Harris pulled a small rectangular box out of his coat pocket. "A month or so ago I asked you what kind of gem you would like, if you could have any in the world. Do you remember what you said?"

Of course she did. They'd been lounging in the Harrises' living room, enjoying the leftover mashed potatoes that they'd magicked into ice cream sundaes and playing would you rather when Mr. Harris asked the question. They'd teased him that he wasn't playing the game right, but Izzy had answered honestly anyway. She'd thought about the "Diamonds in the Rough" headline when she answered. Like the gold school pin, having a diamond of her very own would show that her kindling had been just as real and her magic just as good as those of any other girl who had been at Miss Posterity's. But she thought they were playing a game. She never thought he might actually get her a diamond.

Mr. Harris opened the box to reveal the most beautiful bracelet Izzy had ever seen. It had a delicate gold chain and three round-cut diamonds lined in a gold setting like glittering peas in a pod. Izzy stared at it openmouthed.

"I don't know what to say." She gulped.

Emma clasped her hands over her heart. "Say yes, Izzy! We could be real sisters. *Isabelle Harris.* Doesn't that sound wonderful?"

Izzy glanced at Emma's ring. She thought about something else she'd thought was lost that Mr. Harris had located. "What about Maeve?"

Mr. Harris pulled out another box and opened it to reveal a second bracelet. "I don't know your sister very well yet, so I thought perhaps you would like to be the one to discuss it with her. The offer is open to Maeve as well."

"Look!" Emma pulled up her sleeve to reveal a third matching bracelet. "Three diamonds, three sisters, get it? We'll be one big happy family!"

Tears formed in Izzy's eyes. *Oh stones,* they were going to think she'd gone soft at the sight of the diamonds. How would it feel to be Isabelle Harris? A name like that and a father like Mr. Harris would open doors. What would it be like to have a family to enjoy dinner with at the end of the day and a place to come home to? Amazing, probably.

She opened her mouth to speak, but no words came out. "Thank you," she finally managed to squeak. "I'll talk to Maeve about it. I'm sure she'll be thrilled!" But as she said it, she worried. Her conversation with Maeve this afternoon hadn't exactly gone well and her sister barely knew the Harrises. "How long do we have to decide?"

"Take as long as you need. The bracelets are my gift to the two of you regardless of what you decide." Mr. Harris handed her the boxes. "Thank you for taking such good care of Emma and me."

Izzy swallowed. The Harrises were generous and genuine. It would feel so nice to be taken care of by family again.

Later that night, after Emma had gone home with her papa, Izzy slid the bracelet boxes out from under her pillow. Across the room, Figgy snored and rolled over on Emma's empty bed, his breath rising and falling in the rhythm of sleep. Izzy's room—or *their* room, as Izzy thought of it, even though Emma was only here part-time—was on the third floor and a far cry from the attic full of broken furniture they'd shared at Miss Posterity's. On either side of the large window, they each had a canopied bed piled with lace-covered duvets and silk pillows. Mr. Harris had thoughtfully provided Figgy with a matching house dragon–size bed, but he ignored it in favor of stealing their pillows.

Izzy watched the stones in her new bracelet sparkle in the moonlight. The thought of being sisters with Emma made her smile brightly in the dark. She loved her friend as much as any family she'd ever had.

Which made it complicated.

She wanted to talk to Maeve about it, but she also didn't. What if Maeve said no? Or worse, what if she exploded again and destroyed something bigger than one of Mr. Harris's rooms: What if this wrecked Izzy's relationship with the Harrises themselves?

Izzy couldn't imagine a life without Emma in it. Just like she couldn't imagine a life without Maeve.

She really hoped she wouldn't have to choose between the two of them, but as she closed her eyes, she had a terrible feeling that she might.

FIVE
Foxglove's

Izzy

Izzy kept an eye on Maeve on Thursday. As far as she could tell, Maeve avoided speaking to anyone. Even Izzy. Maybe especially Izzy.

On Friday after breakfast, Miss Clementine stopped Izzy on her way to the library.

"I'm concerned by how hard Maeve's taking this. I feel like she's punishing herself even though I assured her we believed it was an accident," Miss Clementine said, with a worried look over her shoulder at the sealed-up classroom door. "Maeve declined to do any magic in both Miss Lawrence's and my classes yesterday."

Izzy had forgotten that part of their conversation. She hadn't thought Maeve was being serious when she said she wasn't going to do magic anymore. "I want to help. What can I do?"

Miss Clementine rubbed her temples. "Perhaps there's a

way to lift her spirits? You're her sister, I'm sure you know best how to cheer her up."

"Absolutely," Izzy said, determined to follow Miss Clementine's advice this time. Izzy racked her brains and came up with something that never failed to cheer her up when she was down. She was sure that Maeve would come around to wanting to do magic again once she'd relaxed. Izzy tore a page out of her notebook and quickly wrote a message asking Maeve to meet her in the foyer after class.

That afternoon, Izzy pushed open the door of Foxglove's Bakery and inhaled the sweetened air. Inside, fashionable residents of Manhattan's Upper East Side queued in front of a glass counter showcasing the finest magically made cakes and pastries. Izzy's mouth watered at the sight of the perfectly sculpted sugar butterflies and honey-dipped strawberries on puffs of cream. Foxglove's was exactly what the elegant sign on the wall proclaimed: THE SWEETEST OF MAGIC.

Maeve surveyed the interior with her arms crossed, but at least she was smiling. It was the first time she'd done that since she'd met Izzy in the foyer and noticed that Emma was coming with them. It might have been a rough start, but Izzy was sure her plan was a good one. She could cheer up Maeve and help her get to know Emma better at the same time.

"So, what do you think?" she asked Maeve. "Isn't magic wonderful?"

"It smells good in here," Maeve said in a tiny, hopeful voice.

Izzy adjusted the strap of her lavender leather purse. It had been a birthday gift from Miss Clementine and wearing it made her feel very grown-up. She'd tucked Maeve's bracelet inside, still in its box. She was hoping she'd cheer Maeve up enough to tell her about Mr. Harris's offer today.

"Come on, let's get in line." Izzy rounded the gold stanchion and joined the small queue waiting between the velvet ropes.

There were several people ahead of them. As each customer reached the front, they used their magic to ring a tiny bell on the counter before ordering. The bell was unnecessary, really, since a white-aproned teenage clerk was already standing behind the counter waiting to take their order, but it served a more important purpose—it showed the customer had magic.

"What should we get?" Izzy pointed into the glass display case. "Anyone know what's in a millionaire shortbread?" She pointed at the label for the apple mille-feuille. "I'm not sure how to say that, but I'd bet it's delicious."

Emma tapped her chin thoughtfully. "Frances got the glazed strawberry éclair last time we were here, right, Izzy? Maybe I'll order one of those."

They busied themselves with admiring their options. Maeve admitted that she didn't have much of a sweet tooth—a shocking revelation to Izzy—but said she thought she'd order a lemon tart.

Two teenage girls ahead of them in line whispered to each other. Both of them wore the shield-shaped pins of Cabachon Day School. Izzy touched the spot on her chest where her pin would go. One of the girls saw the motion out of the corner of her eye and squinted at Izzy like she was trying to figure out how she knew her.

Izzy ducked her head and her gaze landed on a stand by the door with copies of the day's *Gem Herald* on sale. The headline above the fold read "Bezel Opera House Is Nineteenth Extinguishing."

"Hey, Emma, what's an Extinguishing?" she asked.

"You should really read more news, Izzy. Not just articles about our own school and Glint Academy," Emma chided. "The Extinguishings are places around the city where magic has been burned up. Bezel Opera House, Cannetille Cultural Center, Gerlot's Department Store, and several more." She ticked a list off on her fingers.

"You mean, they burned down like Miss Posterity's?" Izzy asked.

Emma's golden curls swished side to side as she shook her head. "No. They look like they've been burned, but it's not fire that's causing it. Papa says it's like reverse magitecture. Something's happening that's drawing magic out of buildings, reducing them to their raw materials from before they were magicked—something dangerous."

Izzy glanced at her sister. Maeve's back was stiff and straight but her brow was wrinkled in concern. She regretted bringing up the Extinguishings. They were supposed to be cheering Maeve up today, not stressing her out.

"D-dangerous? Do they know what's causing all this?" Maeve asked.

"No one knows for sure. Some people"—Emma fidgeted

with the clasp on her purse—"well, some people are blaming the new kids that can learn magic. No offense."

Izzy tried to change the subject. She picked up a wrapped rectangular box and waved it. "Look at these little chocolates. What do you call these again, Emma?"

"Why do they think we're causing them?" Maeve asked Emma in a small voice.

"They're called truffles, Izzy," Emma said without turning away from Maeve. "They think the new people using magic are causing it to dry up, but Figgy says that can't be true. Magic comes from within." Emma looked over her shoulder as the next customer dinged the bell. "I'm sorry, I'm not doing a very good job of explaining it. You should read the articles for yourselves. You live in the world and should know what's happening."

"That sounds like something Tom would say," Izzy teased, and Emma blushed like she did whenever someone mentioned Tom Sabetti. Tom had kindled with them last year and gotten into Trilliant Academy on a scholarship. He still sold papers in the mornings to support his family and sometimes talked like he was already a journalist.

Izzy put the chocolates back on the shelf, glad that the conversation about Extinguishings had ended. A mother and her two whining young boys finished at the counter and sat at a white iron table at the front of the shop. One of the boys bit into his spun-sugar bow without so much as a look. Izzy cringed. She'd never take even the tiniest bit of magic for granted like that.

The Cabachon girls dinged the counter bell and moved

up to place their order with the clerk. Izzy, Maeve, and Emma shifted forward a few paces as the door to the shop opened.

"Oh no," Maeve muttered when she saw who had entered.

Mrs. Nimby hobbled into the shop with a large bandage on her ankle and a crutch under her arm. The two girls following her were clearly her daughters. Both had their mother's blond hair and their noses were equally high in the air. They were so busy looking at the coffee menu on the chalkboard over the clerk's head that they didn't notice the Manhattan School for Magic girls as they queued directly behind them.

"That's Pearl Nimby," Emma whispered. "She's a year ahead of me at school and a terrible snob. Let's avoid her." She mouthed the word *Nimby* like she'd just realized what she'd said. "Should we leave?"

Izzy had been wondering the same thing. But what would that accomplish? Slinking out before they got their dessert would hardly cheer up her sister. "We have just as much right to be here as they do. Come on, we're next in line."

Izzy stepped up to the counter. She gathered her courage, but before she could summon her magic, the bell rang. Izzy froze.

The clerk looked from Izzy to Mrs. Nimby like he wasn't sure what he was supposed to do.

"The usual, please, Charles, and make it quick. My ankle

hurts terribly," Mrs. Nimby said, and hobbled pathetically on her crutch.

Izzy wished she knew an enchantment that could make them invisible and spare them this embarrassment. But a glance at Maeve's cowering form made her realize that she needed to be extra solid in this moment.

"Excuse me, Mrs. Nimby, but we were next," she said.

The clerk shifted his weight. "They were waiting, ma'am."

"Mother," Pearl whined, and twisted a lock of her silky hair around her finger. "Make them go away. This is taking too long."

"I'm trying, sweetheart." Mrs. Nimby faced the clerk. "We have been loyal customers of your family's shop for many years, Charles, and have you ever known me to make a fuss?"

"Um." The clerk bit his lip.

"No, because I am a reasonable woman, but I have been pushed to my limit." The Acting Commissioner of the Board of Magical Education put a hand over her heart like she had been wounded. "As everyone knows, I have dedicated my life to improving this city, but this school for teaching magic to unworthy children has landed in our neighborhood and I, will not stand for it." She pointed at Maeve. "This girl's dangerous magic is the reason I'm forced to hobble about." She demonstrated a wobbly step on her crutches. "People like that do not belong in a fine establishment such as this."

Emma put her hands on her hips. "It was an accident."

Izzy put a hand on Emma's shoulder. "She's my sister. I'll handle this."

Mrs. Nimby's eyes widened. "Oh, isn't this perfect? My assailant is Isabelle O'Donnell's little sister."

Izzy heard her name being whispered around the shop along with the word *license* as the patrons pieced together what was happening. By this point, every eye in the store was on the MSM girls. She wished they'd left when they had the chance.

The clerk turned to Izzy. "I don't want a scene. You can go around back to the servants' pickup if you want to order."

"I have magic," Izzy protested. "We're not the ones who are causing a problem."

"You *are* a problem wherever you go," Mrs. Nimby said.

The clerk crossed his arms and looked at Izzy. "Please leave or I'll have to summon the police."

"But . . ." Izzy tried to find the right words to say and failed.

Maeve's face pinched up like she was about to cry. When she was five, Maeve had stood up to bullies twice her size to protect the ants they'd been frying with a magnifying glass. Where was the strong sister Izzy remembered? Resisting the urge to take one last look at the display case, Izzy ducked her head. "Come on. Let's get out of here."

Maeve didn't need any urging. She was out the door before Izzy even finished turning around.

"I'm never ordering from here again," Emma fumed under her breath as they headed to the door.

Behind them, Mrs. Nimby raised her voice like she wanted to make sure Izzy heard her. "It's not your fault, Charles. There've been too many problems with magic since that school opened. The O'Donnell License won't stand if these Extinguishings keep happening. I, for one, will be using my new position and authority to ensure that we put aside these foolish notions that anyone can kindle. Then magic can go back to normal. Now, we'll take two of the lemon tarts—"

Feeling like she couldn't breathe, Izzy pushed open the door. Maeve was leaning forward with her hands on her knees in front of the haberdasher's shop next door. Motorcars zoomed down Fifth Avenue, filling the air with the scent of oil and hot rubber.

"I'm sorry," Izzy said to Maeve. "I wanted so badly for this to be a nice day."

Izzy was angry at Mrs. Nimby, but she was even angrier at herself. It was as bad as when she tried to stand up to the Board for Figgy. She'd wanted to defend her sister, but she'd cracked worse than spun sugar. Why couldn't she find the right words?

Emma paced the sidewalk, hands in fists by her sides. "What a horrible snob," she fumed. "Now I see where Pearl gets it. I can't believe she's in charge of the Board of Magical Education."

"Can we please get out of here?" Maeve said. "I never want to see that woman again."

Izzy had a feeling they were far from done with Mrs. Nimby. But she had to salvage this day with Maeve.

There were too many other important things at stake. She touched the lavender purse holding Maeve's bracelet. She'd do whatever Maeve wanted to right now. Anything to cheer her up.

"Where do you want to go?" she asked.

To her relief, Maeve smiled shyly. "Well, I do have one idea, but it's a little far."

SIX
Rust Street

Maeve

An hour and a half later, Maeve and Izzy sat on a bench on Ludlow Street with pickle juice running down their cheeks. The deli they had known as Wasserman's Best had new owners and was now called Schneider's Best, but it had the same delicious pickles sold straight out of the barrel.

The sidewalks in front of the stores were already filled with people selling fish, produce, hats, stale bread rejected from the shops uptown, and just about anything a person could want. Children too young to work and too unlucky to have a place in school wandered the streets. Customers from the local Jewish community hurried in and out of Schneider's, trying to get their shopping done and be home before sundown.

Izzy and Maeve relaxed on their bench, an island of calm in the midst of the hustle and bustle. Maeve felt better there, without magic and its expectations. That bakery had been awful.

Emma had blushed as red as a beet when she told them she was supposed to go for a walk with Tom that afternoon and couldn't go downtown with them. She'd handed Maeve some money and told them to have fun. Maeve couldn't believe her luck—five whole dollars, a trip back to their old neighborhood, and Izzy to herself for the afternoon. In fact, she knew it couldn't be luck. There was a catch here and she was waiting to find out what it was.

Maeve took another bite of her pickle, relishing the sour taste of the brine and the sweet dill. Da used to bring these pickles home for the girls as treats.

"They taste as good as I remember," she said.

"Next time, we'll each get two." Izzy slurped on her pickle.

Maeve wiped her face with her handkerchief and looked around the bustling sidewalk. "You know, our old building isn't far from here."

Izzy frowned. "So? We don't know anyone there anymore." Still, Izzy looked south toward Rust Street.

Maeve shrugged. "It'd be nice to see it. Like seeing family." It was more than that, really. She felt like if they saw the place where they'd been so close, it might make them close again.

"Family, huh?" Izzy put a hand on the purse she'd been carrying all day. "If it would make you happy, let's go."

The sisters cut through the familiar alleyways, stepping around puddles and uneven paving stones. On either side of them, tenement buildings slouched together like they needed one another for support. Izzy and Maeve passed several stark-white signs bearing the circular emblem of the Registry's magical enforcement unit. KINDLING WITHOUT A LICENSE IS STILL ILLEGAL. REPORT ILLEGAL KINDLERS TO THE REGISTRY FOR A REWARD, the signs read in bold, weather-proof enchanted letters. Beneath one of them, someone had painted the word EMBER in large red letters.

The Ember Society. Maeve hadn't thought about that in a long time. Not since—

"There it is." Izzy gestured upward at 55 Rust Street.

Maeve gasped. She hadn't recognized their old home. The brick exterior was crumbling, and the five-story tenement house had a distinct tilt to the right. A faded blue quilt hung on the fire escape outside their old third-story window and a woman who was not Mam leaned out to pull it back inside.

The street itself seemed rougher—or had it always been that way and she'd never noticed? Murphy's Grocery was run-down, and the empty storefront next to it had a broken window that no one had bothered to repair. There was trash on the ground and huge potholes in the street. The snuffing bucket that had been Maeve's favorite hiding place was now across the street on a more prominent corner.

Maeve's breath hitched in disappointment. A part of her had hoped for a sign of what she should do about her magic, but all she saw was an actual sign in the window of Murphy's that read FRESH FRUITS AND VEGETABLES AVAILABLE HERE with a pile of withered apples underneath. Not very helpful.

"Well, I've seen enough," Izzy said.

So had Maeve. She turned, but found their way blocked by two ragged street urchins. Clearly brothers, the boys had the same oval face and gaunt, dirt-streaked cheeks. Maeve felt the hair on the back of her neck rise. She didn't like the way their gazes kept straying to Izzy's lavender purse.

"Are you lost?" the boy on the left asked.

Izzy pointed at the tenement behind them. "No. We lived here."

To her surprise, the boy laughed. "With clothes like that? You aren't from here."

Maeve realized how they must appear: Izzy in her cream silk dress and Maeve in her school uniform. The clothes were new and made the girls stick out like sore thumbs.

Three other kids, two boys and a girl, climbed out from behind a stack of crates on the street. These were decidedly not siblings, but they moved with the practiced desperation that said they worked together. The girl pointed at Izzy's purse and the boys nodded.

Maeve began to sweat. Like Tarnish novices, Maeve and Izzy had stumbled right into the clutches of a street ring.

Izzy clutched the strap of her purse. In doing so, her sleeve slid back, revealing a delicate gold bracelet with three tiny diamonds in a line.

Maeve's mouth dropped open. Where had Izzy gotten a bracelet like that?

The street kids seemed to be wondering the same thing.

"Give it to us or we'll have to take it." The boy held out his hand.

"Run!" Izzy shouted.

The sisters took off. They dashed around the corner while the street kids gave chase. Maeve pushed her way through the crowded market street after Izzy, muttering *excuse me* with every step. The world was a blur of dark clothing and the musty, salty scent of people. For a moment, it smelled so similar to the bull of her dreams that Maeve nearly gagged.

She glanced over her shoulder to see the kids from the street ring threading their way through the crowd behind her. They rounded another corner and Maeve spotted the Tarnish Varnish, a barbershop she remembered from growing up. She knew a shortcut.

"This way," Maeve said, and pointed down a street to their left.

Izzy followed, panting and still clutching her purse.

Maeve realized she'd turned the wrong way. She should have gone right. Tenements rose up in front of them like a wall. It was a dead end.

She heard a shout and knew the kids would find them at any moment. Maeve was a split second away from panicking when she saw a break between the buildings on her right. A wooden fence ran in front of the gap, so she couldn't see inside, but a loose board in the middle beckoned to her. *Hide in here,* it seemed to say.

It was as good a sign as any. "Come on, Izzy."

Maeve ducked between the boards and found herself in a different world.

Or at least, that's what she thought at first. She rubbed her eyes and tried to catch her breath.

She stood at the edge of a lush green garden. A field of knee-high grass stretched out twenty feet in front of her. Beyond that, she could see a dense cluster of flowering shrubs and a winding path leading through them. There were fruit trees of some sort farther back.

"What in the *stones*?" Izzy gasped beside her and Maeve knew she wasn't imagining it.

They waited for the kids to come bursting in after them, but heartbeat after heartbeat, nothing happened. Finally, Maeve's racing pulse calmed and she knew they were safe.

The bare bricks of tenement buildings surrounded the garden on three sides. The fence they'd come through appeared different from this side. Shinier, somehow. A gentle breeze blew through from the back of the garden, a breeze that shouldn't have been possible because there was a wall there. It seemed to Maeve like a sigh or an exhalation that the garden itself had been holding in for a very long time. But that was silly.

"Maeve, you're sparking," Izzy cautioned.

Green sparks rained from Maeve's fingertips to the soil. As soon as she spotted them, they stopped.

"Sorry," she said.

After she spoke, she noticed the quiet. She couldn't hear the shouts of the pushcart peddlers, the crunch of the carriages on the stone streets, or the rattle of coal chutes. It was as if the noise from the street had been sealed off when she went through that loose board. The longer she looked, the more she observed that the garden was overgrown. The flower bushes bled together and vines threatened to overtake the fruit trees. It appeared that no one had been there in a long time.

"This place is so strange," Maeve said.

"I never heard about a magic garden in the Tarnish before," Izzy said.

"A *magic* garden? How do you know it's magic?" Maeve asked.

Izzy took two steps forward onto the grass. "Can't you feel it?"

Maeve paused. Now that she tried, she did feel it. There was a hum about the place, like the soil beneath her and the sky above were buzzing with energy. Her magic felt like it was lingering below the surface of her skin.

"We're probably trespassing," Maeve said.

"As soon as those kids are gone, we'll go." Izzy dropped down on the grass and lay on her back. She draped an arm across her face and the diamond bracelet sparkled in the sunlight.

"Are you going to tell me where you got that now?"

"Oh." Izzy sat up. "I have a bracelet for you too." She pulled a rectangular box from her purse and opened it. "Hold out your wrist."

Maeve did as her sister asked. Izzy fastened the delicate clasp and held her wrist next to Maeve's so they could admire them side by side.

"It's beautiful." Maeve stared at the bracelet. She loved it immediately. Her magic seemed to purr at the feel of the gems on her skin. "Thank you, Izzy."

Izzy tugged the neckline of her dress. "It's not from me. They're a gift from Mr. Harris and Emma."

"Why are the Harrises giving us presents?" Maeve stared at the tiny sparkling diamonds on her wrist and felt her magic rise up again. Desperately, she pushed it back down.

"They want to adopt us," Izzy said in a rush.

Maeve listened, growing increasingly upset while Izzy got more and more excited as she explained the offer from Emma and her papa. What about Mam and Da? Did Izzy want to cast them aside for a fancy family to match her fancy new life?

Izzy's cheeks were flushed with excitement when she finished. "Don't you see what a great opportunity this is for us, Maeve? We'll be part of a respected magical family. A real family again, with a real home."

"We are a real family." Maeve crossed her arms and the bracelet's clasp scraped against her skin. "They're trying to buy us, Izzy. They'll tell us what to do, where to go, and how to be, and even how long to brush our teeth."

"Brush our teeth? What are you talking about, Maeve?" Izzy blinked in surprise.

But Maeve was too upset to explain. She fiddled with the clasp on her bracelet, trying to take it off. It felt like a handcuff now. "We have a family, Izzy. Mam and Da—"

"They'd want this for us, Maeve, I'm sure they would.

Da always told us to go after the best life we could get, didn't he? They'd want to make sure we're taken care of and together." Izzy took Maeve by the elbow, but she wrenched her arm away.

If the Harrises adopted them, it would always be *Emma and Izzy* and Maeve would be cast to the side. She knew she would.

"We can be together, just the two of us. We don't need anyone else and we'll take care of each other." Maeve spun around to face the trees. Out of the corner of her eye, she thought she saw something moving again, but decided it was a squirrel or a blowing leaf.

Behind her, Izzy sighed. "I tried to take care of you before and look where that got us. Split up for two years and now we're practically strangers."

Maeve's heart thumped painfully. "We're not strangers. We're sisters."

"I want to take care of you, Maeve, but I need help. Things are so . . . unpredictable right now," Izzy said.

Maeve heard the deeper meaning in her words: *You're unpredictable.*

Izzy picked up the rectangular box and put it back in her purse. "Keep the bracelet. You don't have to decide right now. Get to know the Harrises better."

Maeve fiddled with the clasp of her bracelet. She didn't want the gift. "Will you still say yes if I say no?"

Izzy closed her eyes. "I don't know."

A gentle breeze rustled the leaves in the garden. Despite the sunshine, Maeve shivered. She turned her face so Izzy wouldn't see the tears in her eyes and saw a blur of movement high above the garden fence. It was a boy, standing on the rickety iron fire escape of the tenement building on the left. He had untidy black hair and his wrinkled white shirt was untucked. His back was to her, but she could see his shoulders shaking with silent sobs.

Maeve blinked in surprise when she saw that the boy's hands were wrapped in thick, wet rags. What was that about? She felt like she was watching something private, but she couldn't tear her eyes away.

Izzy didn't seem to notice the boy. She pointed at the fence. "The coast will be clear by now. We should get back to the school," she said, sounding defeated.

Maeve hesitated for a second, watching the boy and fiddling with the clasp on her bracelet. Why were his hands wrapped like that? She'd never seen anything like it.

Izzy cleared her throat and Maeve came back to herself. Maeve thought she saw something sparkle on the ground in her peripheral vision, but Izzy was already holding the board in the fence open, so she didn't stop to investigate.

There was no sign of the street kids as the girls found their way back to the elevated line. They took the train uptown in silence, each lost in her own thoughts. Rust Street, the magical garden, and the boy with the rag-wrapped hands . . . what a strange day this had been. Maeve didn't know how she felt about any of it, especially Mr. Harris's offer. She unconsciously reached for her bracelet and her heart lurched when her fingers found bare skin.

Her new bracelet was gone.

SEVEN

Cadenza, Forte, and Treble

Maeve

That night, Maeve lay awake, staring at the ceiling of her bedroom. The pillow beneath her head was soft, but her insides were a hard knot. She'd lost the diamond bracelet, the nicest gift that anyone had ever given her, even if it came tangled in emotional strings.

Thinking about the Harrises made Maeve's breath tighten. She'd once heard Mam tell Da that Maeve dealt with problems like bread dough. She mixed everything up until she couldn't tell one feeling from the next and then kneaded it over and over until she was exhausted. Da said that maybe Maeve, like bread dough, needed time to relax and rise on her own. Maeve wished her problems were already fully baked and she knew what to do.

She barely even knew the Harrises. How could she become part of their family? Were they only taking her because she was connected to Izzy? Maeve shivered, though it was warm under her covers. What would happen when they found out she was dangerous? Would they send her away like the farmers had done? Would they separate her from Izzy?

One thing was certain: She had to find her bracelet. What if Izzy thought that Maeve had thrown the expensive bracelet away on purpose to spite the Harrises? Whatever happened, she wanted Izzy on her side. The idea of going back to the Tarnish alone and encountering that street ring again terrified her, but she needed to be strong if she was going to find her bracelet.

The sun peeked in around the edge of the bedroom curtain, glinting with the promise of a new morning. The golden glow reminded her of the sparkle she'd seen at her feet in the garden. She'd been fidgeting with the clasp while watching the boy. The bracelet must have fallen off then.

Maeve sat up. She still had money left after buying the pickles. There was more than enough for subway fare to get downtown and back.

She got out of bed and opened her armoire. As quietly as she could, she took out a well-worn paisley dress she'd brought from Omaha and a small leather satchel that she'd been given by one of the other farmhands. Those would blend in downtown.

Antonia grunted and opened her eyes. "What are you doing? Is it time to get up for class?"

"It's Saturday. Go back to sleep," Maeve said.

"Sounds good," Antonia said, rolling over.

Maeve's awake-at-dawn farm habits served her well, and no one else was up yet as she left the school through the back door in the kitchen, grabbing a few of last night's dinner rolls and a big handful of beef jerky from the jar in the pantry. She wrapped them in her handkerchief and tucked them into her satchel. Maybe, if she had a few moments to spare, she could explore the garden. She had to admit that she was curious.

Outside, several of the street sweepers cleaning away yesterday's refuse nodded politely at her as she ducked her head and hurried past.

There were no trolleys or subways along Fifth Avenue because the wealthy residents disliked the noise, so she crossed over to Third Avenue to take the elevated train like they had yesterday. The man in the ticket booth yawned as she paid the nickel fare.

A clock on the platform showed that it was just past six thirty in the morning, and the handful of people waiting for the train had their noses in their morning newspapers. The front page read something about Extinguishings and the Bezel Opera House again, but Maeve was distracted by a photo of an elegant calico cat. Even in the black-and-white image, her eyes seemed to pierce Maeve to her very bones.

The man next to her fluffed his paper and the headline became clear: "Opera House Search Reveals No Sign of Missing House Dragons."

An express train rattled past on the upper level and Maeve covered her ears. A moment later, the local train arrived and she climbed on board the half-empty car.

Maeve found a seat by the window as the train lumbered

through the streets of Manhattan. Some of the buildings were so close, she could see into people's living rooms. Though it seemed impossibly loud to Maeve, the residents must have been so used to the trains clattering past their apartments that no one even looked up. A lump formed in Maeve's throat when she spotted a mother lovingly braiding her daughter's hair. She turned away from the window.

A middle-class couple on the bench seat across from her were sharing a newspaper. "Shame about those house dragon kits," the husband said.

"I'd almost forgotten about house dragons. They're adorable, aren't they?" She leaned against his shoulder. "Do you think they're dead?"

Maeve stared at the haunting picture of the house dragon on the front page again.

The man scanned the paper. "Don't fret, dear. If the kits are alive, someone will find them. Look at this!"

The woman's eyes widened as she read whatever the man was pointing to. *"Great gems."* She stood up as the train pulled in to Thirty-Fourth Street. "Darling, this is our stop."

Maeve rode in silence, wishing they had left their newspaper behind so she could read the article. She got off the train at Grand Street. While uptown had been sleepy, the streets of the Tarnish teemed with energy. Weekends meant little to those who worked in the city's factories, workshops, warehouses, and thoroughfares. Maeve let herself float along with the current of adults and children headed to work.

Maeve turned at the Tarnish Varnish barbershop again.

When she spotted the fence, her step felt lighter. In a few moments, she'd have her bracelet back and all would be well.

She was nearly to the fence when metal clanged loudly above her head. Maeve instinctively covered her head with her arms, but the only thing that came at her were angry words.

"You! Stop!" a boy shouted.

It was the boy she'd seen on the fire escape yesterday, but his tears were long gone. His curly black hair almost obscured his straight eyebrows. He wasn't particularly tall, but his arms and legs were long and gave him a funny, coltish look. But what drew Maeve's attention were the wet rags wrapped around his hands again.

He gripped the fire escape railing with his rags and shouted at her. "I saw you making sparks in my garden yesterday. I know you're the one who did it."

His garden? Maeve stopped in her tracks. "Did what?"

She peered up at him on the first story of the fire escape. He was as unkempt as he had been the day before and his breeches had a stain on the knee.

"*Magic*," he said like the word tasted bad. She was afraid he'd jump down and chase her, but he stayed on his perch.

Maeve pointed at the fence. "I dropped something in there. I need to get it and then I won't bother you again."

He crossed his arms and the rags left wet marks on his shirt. "You can't go in there. No one's allowed in there. That's why it's invisible."

Maeve was confused by his statement. She looked back and forth from the boy to the boards. "I could see it. It's a beautiful garden."

His frown deepened. "Then why did you destroy it?"

"I didn't destroy anything." Prickles of fear ran down Maeve's spine. *Dangerous*, the voices in her head hissed.

"Go on, then." He jutted his chin toward the board. "Go see for yourself."

Maeve stepped backward toward the loose board. *He's trying to scare you*, she told herself. Forget exploring. She'd grab the bracelet and get out of there. She pushed the board aside and entered the garden.

Ash was everywhere, strewn about as if a massive fire had ripped through the lot. The plants that had been so lush and green yesterday were blackened and burned.

Maeve felt like she couldn't breathe. Had her magic caused *this*? She remembered the green sparks raining down from her fingertips into the soil. It had only been a little sparking, right? Then she thought about the prairie roses ripping from her pocket and gulped. *That* had only been a little painting.

Maeve walked deeper into the lot, scattering ash with every step. The garden was much deeper than it was wide. Two charred and gnarled trees interlaced their branches to form an archway into the back of the lot. They looked like the apple trees Maeve had tended at one of the farms, but it was hard to tell. One had the remains of a squirrel's nest tucked into the crook of a branch.

Maeve walked back to where she thought she'd dropped

her bracelet yesterday. She crouched down and brushed the ground with her hand, hoping to see the glitter of gold, but though she made a wide circle where she thought she'd been standing, nothing turned up.

It had to be there. Unless whatever her magic had done to the garden had somehow destroyed her bracelet too.

There were no scorch marks on the brick walls or smoke stains like there should have been from a fire this size. It was like the whole garden had—a word came to Maeve's mind, something she'd seen on the paper that morning—*Extinguished*. But how was that possible? Emma had said no one knew what was causing them.

You're the one who did it, the boy had said.

Maeve's head jerked up. There were voices coming from the back of the garden, behind the burnt apple trees.

"Give it back or I'll tell Mother!" a small boy whined.

"Mother isn't here. You'll have to catch me if you want it," a second boy's voice, gruffer than the first, taunted back.

Maeve stopped. Were there children here? What if it was another street ring?

She was contemplating fleeing when she heard a third voice, this one a girl, say, "Give the bracelet back to him and don't be such a pest. I'm trying to take a nap."

Whoever it was, they had her bracelet! Her heart thumped and her limbs wanted to run away, but Maeve took a deep breath and made up her mind. She had to get the bracelet back.

She headed toward the voices. She hadn't taken more than three steps when something small came prancing out of the underbrush. At first she thought it was a squirrel, but then she saw it was a chubby tabby kitten with a white blaze on his chest. He tripped over a branch and fell face-first onto the ground.

"Ouch, that hurt," the kitten said. He sat up and rubbed his nose with a white-socked paw. As he did, he caught sight of Maeve and froze.

Another kitten swaggered up behind the first. This one was an inch taller, lean, and an orange marmalade color. A delicate gold band dangled from his mouth and three tiny diamonds winked in the sunlight.

Maeve stared in shock. The voices she'd heard were . . . kittens? If they were talking, they couldn't be ordinary kittens. But what were house dragon kits doing in a garden in the middle of the Tarnish?

"Hide!" The marmalade kit gave the tabby a shove with his head. "Go!"

They scrambled away through the undergrowth, leaving tiny paw prints in the ash.

"Wait!" Maeve shouted after them, more confused than scared now. "That's my bracelet!"

Maeve tried to follow in the direction they'd gone, but the underbrush was thick and burned branches scratched at her legs. Forced to go back to the path, she lost sight of the kits, but she could still hear them rustling as they raced toward the back of the garden.

She rounded a bend in the brambles in time to see an orange-and-yellow-striped tail disappear under a cracked stone bench. Maeve leaned forward to see where it had gone and saw three pairs of golden feline eyes blinking at her. The orange and gray kits were there along with a long-haired calico.

They stared at Maeve and Maeve stared back.

"I'm not going to hurt you. Please, I need my bracelet back," Maeve said. She crouched down and held out her hand in an offer to let them sniff her like she had with the skittish barn cats. She was reasonably sure that house dragons didn't bite. Then again, she'd only met Figgy, who was rather sophisticated.

"How did you get in here? No one's supposed to be able to get in here," the calico said warily.

"There was a loose board in the fence. I think the garden let me in," Maeve said, though she felt silly hearing herself say it out loud.

The kittens had a quick whispered conference under the bench. To be polite, Maeve pretended she couldn't hear.

"She was here yesterday too. I saw her," the gray tabby whispered. "That's how I found the sparkly bracelet."

"But Mother told us no one could find us here," the marmalade kitten said. "She said no one could get in."

"She *said* that the garden was invisible and would protect us against anyone with bad intentions," the calico corrected. She studied Maeve with uncertainty in her golden eyes.

So the garden was invisible. Maeve almost asked a question about what had happened, but stopped herself when she remembered she wasn't supposed to be eavesdropping.

The orange kitten stiffened like he was ready for a fight.

"Maybe Mother was wrong. Look what happened here. The garden couldn't even defend itself."

Maeve cringed. She felt terribly guilty about what her magic had done.

"Mother is never wrong," the calico said loyally.

"Do you think she has any food?" the gray tabby whispered to the others. "I'm ever so hungry."

If she fed them, they might give her bracelet back. "I have some rolls and a bit of jerky. I'd be happy to share them," Maeve called.

The gray tabby started to creep forward but the calico batted him on the head to stop him.

"I'm hungry!" the kitten whined. "We've been here for days and days. Mother should have been back by now."

At this, the kittens went quiet. Their golden eyes reminded Maeve of another pair she'd seen that morning, but in black-and-white—*wait a second*.

"You're the missing house dragon kits from the papers," Maeve exclaimed.

The kits ducked like she'd thrown something at them.

"I'm hungry," the gray tabby whined to his siblings.

There were plenty more questions that Maeve could have asked, but she saw the way the kits' eyes were dull with hunger. They needed food more than she needed answers or her bracelet at the moment. She spotted another stone bench opposite the kittens' hideout. After sweeping off the ash with her hand, she sat down on it and opened her satchel. She spread out her handkerchief and broke the rolls and jerky into tiny pieces.

"You can come out. I won't hurt you. I've been hungry before too."

As she broke up the rolls, she told them about the times she'd been hungry. There was the long string of days when Mam had been too sad to do anything after their da died and there was no food in the house. She told them how Izzy had turned their hunger into a game that helped them get through, and how little Maeve thought her big sister was the bravest and smartest person in the world.

The kits crept forward, as enticed by her words as by the smell of the food. She set the handkerchief on the ground and they crowded around it to eat. The gray tabby seemed like he intended to eat until everything was gone, so Maeve waited until the calico and marmalade kit paused to lick their whiskers before introducing herself.

"I'm Cadenza. I'm the oldest," the calico replied.

"I'm Forte. I'm the biggest," the orange kitten bragged.

The gray tabby swished his tail. "I'm Treble and I'm hungry."

"Your name is Trouble?" Maeve asked, confused.

"No, but that would certainly fit." Forte laughed.

The gray tabby stuck his small pink tongue out at him. "*Treble*. We're named after musical terms."

"Of course. The papers said you were born at the opera house that Extinguished," Maeve recalled.

This was apparently news to the kits. Treble choked on a piece of meat and coughed.

"It Extinguished?" Forte jumped up like he was ready for a fight. "Like it did here?"

"No!" Cadenza gasped. "But Mother might be there!"

"I'm sorry. I thought you must have known," Maeve said. "I saw it in the papers yesterday. Has she been gone long?"

"She left us here three days ago." Cadenza's whiskers drooped. "She said something bad might happen at home and we couldn't stay there. She said to wait here while she went to check on something." Cadenza gulped. "I'd never seen her afraid before."

Maeve scooted closer. She wanted to pet the kit but worried that she might run away. "What was she afraid of?"

Treble wiped a crumb off his whiskers. "She said someone was after her. After us."

"Who? And why?" Maeve wished again that she'd read the article about the Extinguishings for herself.

Treble shook his head. "We don't know. She said she'd tell us more when she got back."

"I'm not afraid. We should go find her." Forte pounced on a drifting bit of ash.

"Mother said not to leave the garden until she got back. Not under any circumstances." Cadenza rolled her eyes. It was a funny expression to see on a feline face and Maeve hid a laugh by eating a bite of a roll.

"*Mrow!*" Forte tackled Cadenza and they rolled around in an adorable orange-and-calico blur, kicking and play-biting at each other's necks.

Treble scooted closer to Maeve. "Mother told us not to leave, even if someone offered us sausages. I like sausages." He leaned over and hooked another piece of jerky with his claw. An idea lit up his golden eyes. "But you can leave the garden. You could help us find her!"

"Yes!" Forte stopped fighting his sister and scurried over. Cadenza followed and their whiskers quivered with excitement.

Maeve shook her head. She had enough on her plate to deal with, especially if her suspicions were correct and her magic truly was dangerous. "I only came for my bracelet."

"What if you promise to help us in exchange for the sparkly?" Cadenza offered.

"I can't. I'm sorry. In fact, I should probably go. May I please have my bracelet now? I can leave the rest of the jerky for you." She stood up.

The kits' ears drooped in disappointment.

Treble lifted his chin. The bread crumbs stuck to his whiskers ruined the regal effect. "We will accept your offer of jerky, but when you go, we must shield the garden against you. Forever. Farewell." He puffed out his cheeks like he was holding his breath and stared at Maeve. Nothing happened.

"He's trying to do magic," Cadenza explained.

Forte sighed. "I warned him that if he doesn't learn soon, he'll appear like a squirrel instead of a cat."

Treble threw his head back and wailed. "I don't want to be a squirrel!" He stuck out his lower lip. "I miss Mother. She would teach me how to be a proper house dragon."

"We all miss her. But at least we have each other." Cadenza began to groom Treble and he leaned in to his sister for a cuddle. Giving up his tough act, Forte snuggled up against them.

Maeve felt the ache of missing her own family. She told herself that she had enough to worry about trying not to lose what was left of it. Someone else would find the kits soon and then . . . what would happen? Maeve hesitated. What if whoever found them was like the Gemstone Society and split the kits up like Izzy and Maeve had been? Would they too become *practically strangers* instead of siblings?

They looked up at her with round, questioning eyes and Maeve made up her mind. No, she wouldn't let that happen. She couldn't mend her own fractured family, but she would prevent this one from breaking.

Plus, maybe fixing one family could fix two. Izzy would be so proud of her when she heard that Maeve had located the missing house dragons on her own. She imagined a framed article hanging next to the ones about Izzy's kindling. "Maeve O'Donnell Saves the Day," the headline read in her mind. Then Izzy would see that they could take care of themselves and they didn't need the Harrises.

Maeve sat down on the bench again. "I'll help you find your mother."

The kits cheered and trotted over to rub their cheeks against her ankles in thanks. They purred and puffs of steam rose from their ears. Maeve bent down to stroke their backs.

"I saw her picture in the paper so I know what your mother looks like, but do you know where she might have gone?" Maeve asked.

The kits shook their heads.

"We thought she was home in the opera house until you showed up," Forte said.

Maeve bit her lip. This wasn't going to be easy. "I'll do some digging and figure out where to start."

"Promise you won't tell anyone about us." Cadenza's tail swished back and forth. "Whoever's after Mother could come searching for us."

This suited Maeve's plan fine. "I promise I won't tell," she agreed. "Will you be safe here alone? You could come back to school with me if you like—"

"We told you, Mother put an enchantment on the garden to protect us." Cadenza's whiskers quivered. "If we leave, we lose her protection."

Forte sat up. "One thing. We're keeping the sparkly bracelet until we know you'll come back."

Maeve hesitated. She didn't like this answer, but she accepted it. At least she knew where the bracelet was. "I'll come back tomorrow morning and bring you more food."

After three more questions about what she *might* be able to find in the kitchen and two more promises to return, Maeve headed to the fence. When she emerged on the other side of it, she realized what she'd forgotten.

"I hope you're happy with your handiwork," the boy shouted from his fire escape.

Maeve ducked her head and hurried down the street. She didn't know what to say to the boy. How was she going to help the kits with him patrolling in front of the garden?

EIGHT

In the Kitchen

Izzy

At least the kitchen *smelled* like baking bread, even as Izzy's freshly magicked loaves turned back into blobs of dough.

"*Stones,*" she cursed, and smacked the counter with the heel of her hand. Would she ever get the hang of searing enchantments?

Figgy glared at her as his porcelain food bowl rattled. His whiskers were covered in gravy. It was late afternoon on Sunday and the kitchen was a little warmer than was comfortable, thanks to Izzy's constant magic and the large iron stove in the corner.

"Why aren't Tom and Emma here yet?" Izzy asked, and flopped down on the nearest stool. "We're supposed to practice searing together."

Figgy shot her a sideways look, his yellow eyes gleaming. "Lovely mood you're in today."

Cook bustled past carrying a burlap sack of beans. The

worry lines on her forehead had lessened in the months without the former headmistress, Miss Posterity, around, and her mole-like squint had disappeared after Miss Clementine had her fitted for spectacles. Her vision had sharpened and her manner had softened—though she still insisted on being called Cook instead of her given name, saying the title was a sign of respect.

"What are you sitting around for, Izzy? Miss Clem said to make sure you finish the bread and read the section on expanding enchantments on page 87. Those loaves have got to feed fifteen by dinnertime."

Izzy crossed her arms. "It's too hard."

Cook *tsked*. "Do you know what's too hard? Listening to you complain while I do this without magic. You had the privilege of kindling, now learn to use it."

Thoroughly chastened, Izzy stood up and started working on the bread again. Cook opened the windows as the room warmed further with her magic. Soon, Izzy had three golden loaves in front of her. Now for the expanding enchantments on page 87. She reached for her textbook. As soon as she was distracted, two of the loaves turned back into dough. Izzy cursed and fidgeted with her bracelet.

"So, did you ask her?" Figgy eyed the diamonds. "How did it go?"

"About as poorly as you can imagine." Izzy buried her face in her hands and told him about the awful encounter at Foxglove's and the conversation with Maeve. "Why is it so much easier to talk to Emma or to you than my own sister?"

Figgy put a paw on Izzy's arm. "We've been through a lot together recently. Give it time with Maeve. We don't know what *she's* been through."

"It would help if she would tell me, but every time I ask, she clams up." Izzy sighed. "I feel like I never know what to say these days, to Maeve or in general. I say nothing or I say the wrong thing." She met Figgy's gaze. "When the Board members insulted you during the tour, I wanted to stand up for you, but my tongue got twisted up."

"Fortunately, I was able to speak for myself, but not everyone is so lucky. Like it or not, last year's kindling made you a leader. You have a voice and you must learn to use it." He sat up straighter. "Perhaps I could give you some public speaking lessons?"

A leader? Izzy didn't think she deserved that title. "No, thanks, Figs. I'm not really one for making speeches. Besides, no one wants me in charge. I can't seem to do anything right lately."

The last loaf turned back into dough.

"ARGH!" Izzy shouted, and Figgy's ears twisted backward in alarm.

"Patience," Figgy cautioned. "Important things can take time."

"I don't have time," Izzy said, gesturing at the lumps of dough. "I have to get Maeve to see why this is best for both of us, figure out what to do about Mrs. Nimby and the Board, and I have until dinnertime to sear an enchantment so I can feed—wait, how many was it?"

"Fifteen," Cook called from where she was sorting beans.

"Fifteen!" Izzy groaned.

Laughter out in the hall made Izzy's back tense. A moment later, Emma and Tom entered, chuckling at some private joke.

"You're late," Izzy snapped, and they both blinked at her in surprise.

"Sorry." Emma set the stack of books she was carrying on the counter next to Figgy.

Tom leaned on the end of the counter and smiled at Emma, revealing the small gap between his front teeth. "Pelicans," he said, and whatever that meant made Emma burst into fresh giggles.

Izzy sighed as dramatically as she could and flipped open her textbook. Where was Frances Slight when she needed a fourth wheel?

She'd opened her textbook to a section entitled "Translucence: The Strange Phenomenon When Invisibility Enchantments Become Visible." That was silly. If an invisibility enchantment became visible, it wasn't an invisibility enchantment anymore, was it? She rolled her eyes and flipped to page 87 and skimmed the section on expanding enchantments.

Expanding objects was about as basic as magic got, and boring too. It wasn't like she could turn a bowl of water into a swimming pool. With her recently kindled magic, she might be able to make a bathtub. These pages suggested turning clothespins into table legs. What a waste of time.

Her ears perked up when she heard her sister's name. "What was that about Maeve?"

Emma nudged Tom with her elbow. "You tell her. It was your idea."

"Well, when Em told me what happened with Maeve and the prairie roses, it made me wonder if maybe her magic got changed when she was out West, you know? Emma said we should ask Figgy about it."

Izzy felt a rush of relief. That could explain what had happened with the prairie roses. "Is that possible?" she asked Figgy.

Figgy wiped a drop of gravy from his whiskers. "Potentially." He tilted his head. "Remember how last year I told you that there were many different paths to magic, only people had forgotten them? It's also possible that Maeve is on another path. Perhaps something newly reopened and unexplored."

Izzy hoped it wasn't a path straight out of the school. "Well, that sounds harder to fix—"

The kitchen door opened again.

"Hello, Maeve," Cook said loudly, and Izzy's mouth snapped shut. "Have you come to help or to join the chatterboxes over there?"

"Antonia said her brother was here?" Maeve squeaked.

Cook muttered something about the kitchen being too crowded and headed for the scullery. Izzy looked up in time to see Maeve grab one wrist with her other hand. Her sleeves slid up to reveal disappointingly bare wrists.

"Hi. You're not wearing your bracelet," Izzy said.

Maeve seemed to shrink two inches. Her gaze traveled between Izzy and Emma. "I, uh, haven't made up my mind yet."

Emma smiled. "Hello, Maeve. Did you need help with something?"

Maeve ducked her head. "I was wondering if Tom had any of yesterday's papers that I could buy?"

Tom's eyebrows rose. "Sure do." He reached into his bag and pulled out a paper. Maeve offered him a penny but he waved it away. "Naw, take it. Not too many people wanting Saturday editions on Sunday."

"Thank you," Maeve said, taking it and turning to go.

Izzy wanted her sister to spread the paper out and join them. To chat with her friends and become one of them. But Maeve was like a scared bird that longed to take flight.

Figgy leaped up, nearly upending his bowl of gravy. "Wait! It's Aria!"

"What's an aria?" Izzy was concerned. She'd never seen the unflappable Figgy so shocked.

Figgy sat down on the counter. His eyes were wide like he'd seen a ghost. "May I see that newspaper, please?"

Maeve set the paper down in front of him, and Izzy studied the picture of a long-haired calico with piercing eyes.

"Do you know this house dragon?" Maeve asked.

Figgy scanned the article. "She's my cousin. I haven't seen that face in too many years." He pressed a paw to his heart. "My goodness! She's had kits! Why didn't she write me?" Then his eyes narrowed. "Oh no."

Izzy read over his shoulder. "The whole family is missing. Figgy, I'm so sorry." She quickly scanned the page. "That's odd. Why is Gladys Glint offering a reward for the kits' safe return? And why just the kits and not the whole family?"

"There's a reward?" Maeve asked. Her eyes widened as Izzy showed her. "That's a lot of money. Why would someone offer that?"

Figgy bristled. "House dragon kits are increasingly rare these days. It's been years since the last litter was born. They'd be a crown jewel in her *collection*. I bet she thinks they're *so cute*." Disgust thicker than gravy dripped from his words.

"Well, they probably are," Izzy said, and Figgy shot her a look.

"Maeve, you've gone pale. Is everything all right?" Emma asked.

Izzy turned her gaze from Figgy to her sister.

Maeve's shoulders rose toward her ears. "I was wondering how someone would find a lost house dragon."

Figgy sighed. "If you're thinking of the reward, I wouldn't waste your time. With this amount on the line, many people will already be looking for them. Frankly, they'd be better off asking a hou—" He paused and his whiskers quivered with excitement. "Of course! Why didn't I think of it immediately? Does anyone have a small scrap of paper? A thin strip will do."

Tom dug into his satchel and produced a scrap of paper. Figgy set a paw on the paper and closed his eyes. Heat rose from him, and the air above his shoulders shimmered with magic. Words appeared in a cursive script on the paper.

Maeve's eyes widened. "I didn't know house dragons could do that."

"Me neither. Figgy never explains his magic," Emma said with a chuckle. "There are probably a hundred things he can do that we don't know about."

"Now, to send this." Figgy trotted across the counter to the window and made an odd chittering sound. Izzy was about to ask what he was doing when a pigeon landed on the sill. Izzy watched, astounded, as the "pigeon" puffed up its iridescent chest feathers with self-importance and saluted Figgy with the tip of its wing.

Cook chose that moment to exit the scullery. "Figgy Pudding, don't you dare let that thing inside my kitchen!"

"This will take but a moment, madam," Figgy said. He held out the paper and the pigeon took it in its beak. The pigeon saluted Figgy again before it flew out the window.

Izzy looked at the stunned faces of the other humans. "Does someone want to tell me what just happened?"

"Pigeon Post. It's how we house dragons communicate. Didn't you ever wonder how I always have the latest news but never leave the house?" Figgy answered, trotting back over to them. "I assure you that my paws are very clean," he said to cut off Cook's protest and sat down on the counter between where Emma and Izzy were standing. "I sent a note to the Wigglebottoms. They protect the Lariat Library on Madison Avenue. If anyone knows where Aria went, it will be the Wigglebottoms."

"Are the Wigglebottoms named after the ice cream parlor?" Emma asked.

"Other way around," Figgy said with a wink.

"I've had enough of the pigeons and chitchat in my kitchen," Cook cut in. "How's that bread coming, Izzy? The rest of you lot, either pitch in or clear out. I've got a meal to make."

Emma and Tom offered to peel vegetables for the soup and followed her to the other side of the kitchen, where a pile of potatoes and carrots waited. Izzy looked at the bread she'd forgotten. The dough had risen on its own. At least her expanding enchantment would be a little easier to sear. Thinking about searing reminded her that she had something else she still needed to change.

"Maeve!" Izzy called, and caught up to her sister, who was halfway to the door. "Maybe we can do something together next weekend? Emma and I were talking about getting ice cream."

"Um, maybe." Maeve eyed Emma's back as she inched toward the door. "I might be busy."

"All right, just let me know—" But before Izzy could say anything else, Maeve was gone.

"Is it me or was she acting strange?" Emma asked, coming up beside Izzy with a half-peeled potato in her hand. Her ruby ring winked with magic and a few more strips of potato rolled themselves up into tidy scrolls. "It looked like she had ash under her fingernails."

Izzy hadn't noticed. "She's been strange since she got back from out West."

"It's a good thing she didn't want today's paper." Tom strolled over to his satchel. He pulled out another newspaper with a picture of the school on the front page. Above the picture, the headline read "Mayhem at Manhattan School for Magic." "Mrs. Nimby says some pretty upsetting things. She's blaming you and the school for the Exings—that's what they're starting to call the Extinguishings. Saves print space."

Izzy crossed her arms. "We're making magic better, not worse. It's getting harder to control because the magical elite keeps hoarding the magic for themselves."

"*We* know that, but that's not what they're reporting." Tom sighed. "I wish they'd let me write for the papers. I could set them straight."

Emma leaned against the counter. "Speaking of setting things straight, Papa went over to patch things up with Ms. Glint. He was afraid the prairie roses might cost him the art gallery project he's been working on for her."

"Wait, the art gallery he's been talking about is for *Glint*?" Izzy had not put that together.

"Yes, the *Glint Art Gallery*." Emma nodded. "It opens in mid-June and there's going to be a big party. Papa's asked us if we want to come."

Izzy perked up. "A party?" She'd always wanted to be invited to a fancy society party. Though the fact that this party was for Ms. Glint lessened the appeal somewhat.

Cook came out of the scullery, struggling under the weight of the full pot. "You lot are stickier than toffee and teeth! Every time I turn around you're back together."

Water sloshed over the side of the pot and Izzy and Emma hurried over to help her. As soon as her hands were free, Cook pointed at the loaves of dough. "Izzy, the bread!"

Izzy dragged her feet back to where the lumps of dough were waiting to intimidate her. As she passed the giant iron stove, she noticed it was hot already, waiting for the soup.

When no one was looking, she opened the oven and slid the bread loaves inside. She'd work on searing later. There was enough to think about at the moment.

NINE
The Boy with Rag-Wrapped Hands

Maeve

The thought of the kits, hungry and alone in the garden, propelled Maeve from her bed at dawn on Monday morning. After a quick stop in the school kitchen, she was out the door before anyone else was even awake.

The whole way downtown, Maeve kept thinking about the reward money that Ms. Glint was offering. A sum like that could set her up for—well, she wasn't sure exactly, but it would be a long time. She wouldn't need magic if she had money like that.

She kept turning it over and over in her mind as she walked toward the garden. It was still early enough that the fire escape was empty. She faced the fence—or at least where the fence should have been.

Maeve gulped. The garden was gone.

There was no space in between the brick tenement buildings. She didn't understand. Had Extinguishing been the first step and now the garden was truly gone? Or had the kits decided they, like everyone else she knew, were better off without her and truly sealed the garden against her? Maeve stared at the solid brick walls, feeling even more lost and lonely than she had before she found the garden.

She thought of the reward again and felt sick to her stomach. She never would have turned those kits in, no matter how much money some rich person offered.

Maeve shut her eyes against the bright glare of morning sun. But wait—she was facing a brick wall. How could that be? She blinked her eyes open and once again found the ramshackle fence in front of her.

Tears glistened in the corners of her eyes. "Thank you," she whispered to whatever magic had seen what was in her heart and decided to let her back in. She promised herself she'd never even think about the reward money ever again.

The kits were overjoyed to see her—especially since she'd brought chicken and more jerky—and no one at the school noticed when Maeve slipped back inside during the usual pre-breakfast chaos. On Wednesday, she did it again, but this time she didn't have any trouble getting into the garden.

On Saturday morning, Maeve was up at the crack of dawn and excited to spend a whole day at the garden. She stopped by the kitchen, as had already become her habit, and headed out into the morning air. The bright blue sky promised a beautiful spring day. It was a relief to leave the school and the complicated feelings that went with being there.

But the relief was short-lived. As she walked toward

the Third Avenue el, Maeve noticed that one of the brightly colored houses on Gem Row had gone ashy and gray. There was a crowd of people in front of the house, including several uniformed police officers.

"The family is away on vacation. Thank goodness no one was hurt when it Extinguished," one officer said to another.

Maeve walked faster. An Extinguishment on the same street as her school was a little too close for comfort. She hadn't sparked when she'd walked this way before, had she? No: Maybe she'd caused the garden to Extinguish like the boy said, but she didn't think she'd caused this one. It only made her more confused, though.

At the base of the stairs to the train, she spotted a familiar face.

"Extra! Exings continue to haunt the city!" Tom called, holding a folded newspaper above his head with *The Kindled Courier* written across the masthead in fancy script.

Maeve instinctively ducked behind a mailbox. She watched as a young man in a flat cap and vest bought a paper from Tom. The penny flashed copper as it passed between their fingers.

Her hand strayed to her satchel. If she wanted answers, the newspapers were as good a place to start as any. She took a deep breath and stepped out from behind the mailbox. Making an effort to keep her head held high and act natural, she headed toward the stairs.

Tom waved. "You're up early. What are you doing out and about, Maevers?"

Maeve blinked. The warmth of the nickname took her by surprise. "I'm going downtown," she mumbled. "May I buy a paper, please?"

She held up her coin.

"Got you hooked, eh? I always say, if you live in the world, you should know what's happening." To her surprise and relief, Tom didn't press for any more details. He took her penny and handed her a *Kindled Courier*.

"Thanks," Maeve muttered. Her mind was already a mile away, downtown in an empty lot full of ashes. She headed up the stairs.

"Hey, Maeve? May I offer you a word of advice?" Tom called. She turned and nodded. "I read a lot of papers so I know that some of them are more opinion than fact. *Kindled Courier*'s decent, but a few of the other newspapers have been downright nasty about your sister and kids like us learning to kindle. I know how upsetting it can be when you stumble across something like that. Let me know if you ever wanna talk about anything you read."

"Thanks," Maeve said, though she wasn't sure she'd ever take him up on it. She barely even felt comfortable going to her own sister with her worries.

Tom went back to selling papers while Maeve continued up the stairs. She paid the nickel fare and counted the rest of her change while she waited on the platform. Maeve still had a good amount left from the five dollars that Emma had given her and it should last awhile. She knew she should hope that Aria would return soon and the kits wouldn't need her to come to the garden, but she looked forward to seeing them so much. They'd had so much fun playing tag and hide-and-seek before she left on Wednesday morning, and for a full half hour, she hadn't thought about any of the worries that plagued her.

The train arrived a moment later. She claimed a seat by the window and spread the newspaper across her lap to read. Fortunately, this one was full of facts and had a full recap of the Exings. So far, twenty-four structures had Extinguished, running the gamut from landmarks to private homes. Another building had Extinguished overnight. This time it was the Lariat Library. She felt like she'd heard that name recently but couldn't place it.

The only link the police had found so far was that all of the Extinguished buildings had been designed and built by magitects. Maeve knew from her da's work and Mr. Harris's art lessons that the majority of the buildings in the city had been built with ordinary construction materials for ordinary people. Which meant that the Extinguishings were specifically happening to magical places. Maeve read through the list of sites. To her relief, there was no mention of the garden or discovery of the kits. They were still safe.

Then she remembered where she'd heard of Lariat Library and her toes curled in her boots. Figgy had sent his pigeon note to the Lariat's house dragons, looking for the kits. What a strange coincidence.

"Reading about the Exings?" A professionally dressed woman holding on to the pole in front of Maeve eyed the newspaper.

"Yes," Maeve squeaked, frightened by being noticed.

The woman smiled kindly, misinterpreting her fear. "Don't worry. It always happens at night when the buildings are empty." She smiled as if this made everything fine. The woman got off at the next stop and left Maeve feeling more confused. What was causing the Extinguishings? Had it been her magic that Extinguished the garden or something else?

She was so busy thinking that she didn't see the boy waiting for her as she approached the garden.

"You again," he said accusingly. His long legs dangled over the side of the fire escape. "Don't you know to stay away? I told you not to come back."

He frowned at Maeve and she frowned right back. The morning sunlight cut a harsh line across the brick wall behind him and Maeve had to squint in the glare.

She put her hands on her hips. "Don't *you* know it's rude to shout at people? If you want to talk to me then come down here."

He glanced at the open window behind him. "I can't. I'm not allowed to leave the apartment when my parents are at work." He shook his head in frustration. "My mameh and tateh work ten hours a day, seven days a week at a garment factory. So they're always gone and I'm always here. Alone." He said this in a rush like he'd been holding it in and waiting for someone to ask for a long time.

Maeve had been five when Da lost his job and Mam went to work in a garment factory. Then when Da was out looking for work the girls had to stay in the apartment and not make any noise so no one knew they were there alone.

In the evenings, Mam was so tired she could barely keep her eyes open while making dinner. It had been a hard time, but at least Maeve had had Izzy.

"But why do you have to stay inside? That must get very lonely," she said.

"Because of this." He held up his rag-wrapped hands. "I might spark and hurt someone. Magic is dangerous."

Maeve's breath caught. His words were like a mirror and she saw herself in them.

"Is that why you were crying the other day?"

"You weren't supposed to see that," the boy snapped. He tucked his hands behind his back. "I should go. I'm not supposed to talk to anyone." He stood and turned toward the window.

"Wait!" Maeve called after him. He stopped. The loose set of his shoulders made her think he'd wanted her to stop him.

To her surprise, she felt an equal sense of relief that he'd stopped. No one she'd talked to since she'd come back to New York understood how alone and afraid she felt. She sensed that this boy might.

But first, she had to make amends. She checked the block before she spoke, but their only audience were a couple of rats shuffling around a refuse pile across the street and a small flock of pigeons roosting on the windowsills. "I wanted to apologize. I didn't mean to destroy your garden."

He studied her. "I think I believe you. If you were a mean person, you wouldn't stop for a polite conversation like this."

"Probably not." Maeve laughed, actually *laughed*, out loud.

The boy's head reeled back and his brow furrowed. But when he realized she wasn't laughing *at* him, a shy smile spread across his face.

"How old are you?" he asked. His voice was less sharp than it had been.

"Eleven," Maeve said.

"Me too." His eyes lit up. "I'm Avi Sigal."

"Maeve O'Donnell."

He extended his rag-wrapped right hand toward her. Intuiting what he meant, Maeve held out her right hand as well, and they pantomimed shaking hands.

"Is it uncomfortable wearing those rags on your hands?" Maeve asked.

"It was at first but I'm used to it now." Avi shrugged. "Maybe you should try it instead of burning down people's gardens."

This made Maeve pause, but Avi was looking at her with amusement, not judgment. It gave her the courage to be honest. "Maybe I should. Honestly, I'm not very good at magic. I'm sorry about your garden."

"I'll be honest too. It's not my garden." Avi sat down on the fire escape. He let his feet dangle over the edge. "My uncle made it."

"Your uncle has magic?" Maeve was shocked. She'd never met a grown-up in the Tarnish who had magic before.

"He did, but he's dead now." He folded his arms. "The magic killed him and my mameh says if I'm not careful, it'll kill me too. After the early Wind last year, she pulled me out of school to keep me safe. That's when I started wearing these." He held up his rag-wrapped hands. "It'll be good when I snuff next year. Then I won't be the only one in the family with magic."

Avi said all this like he was reciting it. Perhaps he'd been alone so long, he'd already had these conversations over and over in his head. But Maeve was still stuck on the last thing he'd said.

"No one else in your family has magic?"

Avi shook his head. "My sister sparked, but she snuffed her magic. She's much older than me and lives with her husband in Baltimore."

Maeve couldn't stop herself from asking questions. "But your uncle kindled?"

It was as if a cloud passed over the sun, and Avi's face darkened. "I shouldn't have told you that. Forget I said anything. Leave me alone." Though he'd just sat down, Avi climbed to his feet suddenly, as angry as when she'd first arrived.

One of the boys at the stockyard had had a yo-yo. Talking to Avi reminded Maeve of its constant up and down. "Do you want me to leave you alone?"

Avi tilted his head, considering it. He exhaled loudly. "No. Well, maybe for a little bit." He pointed at the garden. "I saw the kittens in there. You're feeding them, aren't you? That's why you're here."

Maeve's shoulders relaxed. So he didn't know they were house dragons. "Are you going to stop me?"

Avi shrugged. "I don't see how you can make it any worse. Will you stop and talk to me on your way out again?"

"Sure," Maeve agreed. It was a toll she'd happily pay if she got to see the kits.

"If I'm inside the apartment, you can shout for me." Avi sat down on the fire escape and opened a book. "See you in a bit, Maeve."

Maeve pushed aside the board. She glanced over her shoulder, but Avi was already absorbed in reading. That had been one of the strangest, and yet one of the most comforting, conversations she'd had in a long time. To her surprise, she looked forward to talking with Avi again on her way out.

Inside the garden, the air smelled of ashes, but there was a new scent behind it. It was like the scent of the last day of winter, with the promise of spring on the horizon.

"She's here! Let's eat!" Treble shouted with joy when she rounded the bend behind the apple trees.

Being in the garden sealed out Maeve's worries as effectively as the garden silenced the noise from the street. The kits bounded around her ankles and told her everything that had happened that week, which was mostly tattling on each other's misbehavings. She listened sympathetically as Treble whined that Forte had tried to trick him into climbing into the squirrel's nest and told him he had to live there.

"I don't want to be a squirrel," Treble explained with a pout, while Maeve set out the chicken on a blanket she'd taken from the school linen cabinet.

"Then you've gotta learn to use your magic," Forte

said. Tiny puffs of steam rose from his ears as if to illustrate his point.

While they ate, Maeve shared what she'd learned about the Exings. The kits were suitably impressed.

"You were busy this week," Forte said through a mouthful of chicken. Cadenza glared at him and he closed his mouth and chewed politely.

"I wish I knew more." In fact, she had felt like she hadn't done enough. "You're sure we can't tell anyone else about you? There's a house dragon at my school named Fi—"

"No one," Cadenza insisted, and her brothers nodded in emphasis.

Maeve had anticipated this, but she was slightly disappointed. Figgy seemed to know a lot of things and might have been able to help. "In that case, I want to look into the Opera House. There has to be a clue about where your mother went."

"We're going to find Mother!" Cadenza cried, pouncing on Treble.

The tabby coughed on his chicken and swatted his sister. Forte jumped on top of them and Maeve laughed at the kits' antics as they kicked and tumbled. Without warning, Forte came bursting out of the scrum like a marmalade blur. He leaped at Maeve's shin and kicked off her to scamper away again.

"Tag! You're it!" he shouted.

Maeve was stunned for a split second by the shift in the game and her sudden inclusion, but it passed quickly. She stretched out her hands and the kits scattered, mewing with excitement. Cadenza darted away nimbly, her tail straight up in the air, while Forte raced around Maeve's heels, daring to get close. Treble tried to scramble up a tree, got about five inches, and fell back on his rump.

Maeve scooped him up and kissed between his gray ears. "Tag," she said.

"Darn." Treble pouted.

She set him back down and he lumbered after Forte, who stuck out his pink tongue, daring his brother to catch him.

Maeve laughed and scooted away as Treble gave up the chase and reached a paw for her boots instead. He dashed around a stone birdbath lying in the undergrowth and came charging for her again. The game continued for some time and everyone served a turn being "it." As they played, Maeve's heart warmed even more. She would do anything to protect these delightful little creatures. She had to keep them safe and find their mother as soon as possible.

Cadenza stopped running and stared openmouthed behind them. "Look!"

Maeve gasped. Thin lines of green grass had burst from the ashes. They looped and whirled like calligraphy written in a language she did not understand.

Treble had been halfway over a fallen branch. With a loud "whoa," he lost his balance and tumbled forward in a somersault. A trail of green grass sprouted up where he had rolled.

"How are you doing that?" Maeve asked.

"Doing what?" Then Treble saw the grass behind him.

"*Ah!*" he cried in surprise. He jumped sideways and tiny grass stalks sprouted under his paws where he landed.

"You're doing it too," Cadenza said.

Tendrils of delicate young grass curled around the toes of Maeve's boots. A trail of newly grown green led to the place where she now stood.

"It's not possible." Maeve picked up her foot and put it down, hardly daring to believe her own eyes. Her magic destroyed things. It didn't make them grow. Or could it? She thought about the prairie roses. She'd been so focused on the destruction they'd caused; she'd never stopped to think about the fact they'd grown because of her magic in the first place.

Tempted to try, Maeve dropped to her knees in the ash. She moved her hands over the ground until she *felt* something below the soil. It was like the prairie rose seeds in her sachet, but this time, she focused her magic into the soil instead of lashing out. It was hard to control it and she almost gave up, but then a green stalk rose from the earth with a yellow bud on the tip. Maeve fought the urge to push harder and instead kept her magic nice and even. Long, slightly pointed leaves rose beside the stalk, growing in moments what would usually take days or weeks. The bud opened and five white petals unfurled, a bright yellow trumpet shape in the middle.

"What is it?" Forte asked, coming over to paw at the flower.

Maeve sat back on her heels. "It's a daffodil."

"Can we eat it?" Treble asked hopefully.

"I don't think so." The heat of the enchantment had caused her cheeks to flush. She pressed her fingertips against them and felt the warmth. "It must be a fluke. I can never do magic this well in school."

"Mother says that magic works best when it's linked to a strong emotion." Cadenza sat down beside her. "How were you feeling when you did that?"

"Happy." The truth of it made the word catch in her throat. "Happier than I've been in a long time."

But a dark cloud obscured the brightness of her joy. Yes, she could grow things with her magic, but she could destroy them too. How could she know which would happen when she tried? She looked at the burnt apple tree. Maybe she could practice here. The damage had already been done and it was as safe as she could get.

Cadenza purred and rubbed her cheek against Maeve's leg. Maeve reached down and stroked her soft back.

She wondered if she could do more magic. Focusing on the pride she'd felt watching the first flower bloom, she reached for her magic again. She moved her hands over the ground until she felt the same feeling as before. It was as if she could sense something sleeping under the soil. Then she focused her magic into it and pushed. Moments later, another daffodil swayed gently in the breeze a foot away from the first.

She was doing magic. It felt so good. Tears formed in her eyes.

Out of the corner of her eye, she saw Forte trot out

of the undergrowth. Her gold bracelet dangled from his mouth. It was covered with dirt but still sparkled in the sun.

"We figured it's about time to return this to you," Cadenza explained.

Maeve took it. In her mind, it had grown to a thing of such importance, she was surprised to find it so light and fragile. "I changed my mind. Will you hold on to it for a bit longer for me, please? This way you'll know I'm coming back for you."

This way she wouldn't have to see it and feel pressured to wear it before she'd made up her mind. The kits looked surprised but agreed, and Forte returned the bracelet to its hiding place.

Then the kits struck up a cheer of "Again! Again!" and danced through the daffodils until Maeve took out one of the broken halves of her crystal.

The magic didn't work everywhere she tried. She had to search for the right spots, but by early afternoon, a small flock of daffodils lifted their yellow faces toward the sun and Maeve stopped to take a break. She dug her canteen out of her satchel and took a long drink of cool water. Between her magic and the afternoon sun, the garden was significantly warmer than when she'd arrived.

As she approached the fence at the end of the afternoon, Avi unfolded himself from the shadows on the fire escape. Had he been out there waiting for her the whole time?

"You lied," he said, and she froze.

This was it. He was going to tell her to never come back. She'd lose that wonderful feeling of having done magic.

Then a slow smile spread across Avi's face. "You *are* good at magic. I saw you fixing the garden."

"Maybe. It didn't work consistently." Maeve shifted her weight. She'd been so enraptured with making things grow that she'd forgotten he might be watching.

"I know why." Avi jutted his chin toward the garden. "There are bulbs buried underground already. It worked when your magic found one of those." He swallowed and the lump in his throat bobbed up and down. "My uncle could grow them like that. I'd forgotten until I saw you doing it today. You'll need more bulbs and seeds. Will you come back tomorrow?"

The words felt like a key, giving her permission to open the door.

"I'll get here as early as I can. You could help me. I could show you what I did and maybe you'd recall more of what your uncle taught you."

Avi's features hardened. "I can't." Without another word, he climbed through the open window behind him. The curtain swung shut, hiding him from sight.

Maeve headed toward the school feeling like she had uncovered more questions today than answers.

TEN

Magic in the Tarnish?

Maeve

On Thursday evening later that week, Maeve decided to visit the school library after dinner. She hoped to find something about the opera house and, if she was lucky, something about house dragons or magical gardens.

The main hall smelled like freshly cut wood as Maeve headed toward the library. Miss Clementine's weeklong frost enchantment had done its part to wither the prairie roses, and contractors had arrived that morning to begin clearing away the tangled mess of vines. As Maeve pushed open the door to the library, the skylight in the hall flashed with lightning. She thought about the kits in the garden. Were they scared of the storm? She wished she could go to them, but it was less than an hour until bedtime and her absence would be noticed.

She was distracted from her thoughts of the kits by the sight of Figgy Pudding, who was sitting on one of the plush library love seats. Stacks of books surrounded his seat and he muttered to himself, too absorbed in his reading to notice her. This was perfect. Maeve wouldn't bother anyone, and there was no one to question why she wanted books about house dragons and gardens.

Thunder rumbled overhead as someone came around the corner carrying a large stack of books.

"Maeve!" The delight in Emma's voice was obvious. "Do you need help finding a book?"

"Hi. I'm fine, thanks," Maeve replied quickly. She turned to the nearest shelf, hoping Emma would take the hint and leave her alone. The books on this shelf were about transportation. She ran her finger along the spines of the books, but it was hard to pretend to be completely absorbed by *Steam Power & Gems: A Burgeoning Industry* and *Magical Motors*.

"Please let me help you," Emma insisted. "Are you looking for something for class? Or some light reading? We have novels too if you like fiction."

Maeve peered around the huge room. There were hundreds of books here and she barely knew where to begin. She didn't have to tell Emma everything, just enough. "Where might I find books about magical animals?"

"I know the perfect thing." Emma shifted the books she was holding so she could pull one out from the middle of the stack. "The section about polar bear magic and the Northern Lights is fascinating."

Maeve was going to have to be more specific. "Actually,

I'm looking for something about house dragons. Do we have anything like that?"

Emma put the book back on the stack. "Figgy would know best."

"I don't want to bother him," Maeve protested, but Emma was already heading toward him.

"Excuse me, Figgy?"

Figgy was reading his book with his paws clamped to his forehead in dismay. Emma walked over to him and set the stack of books she'd been carrying on the floor beside his chair.

"Figs?" She put a hand on his back, and he jumped.

"Sorry." He smoothed his ear with his paw. "I was seeing if there was anything related to the Extinguishings in Ferguson's *Magical Calamities*, but the closest I could find was the Great Chicago Fire in 1871. An untrained girl sparked in a barn and the fire spread for four miles." He shook his head. "So dangerous."

Maeve gulped. She knew that because it had been cited against her over and over as the families returned her to the Gemstone Society when they discovered her magic. Maybe she should wrap her hands like Avi.

"It was probably an accident," Maeve said.

Figgy looked at her. "I quite agree. The danger isn't in the sparking itself, it's the fact that we live in a system that values snuffing over teaching all children how to control their magic." Maeve was still trying to absorb this statement when Figgy turned to Emma. "Did you need something?"

"Can you recommend any books about house dragon magic?" Emma asked him.

"For *humans* to read?" Figgy pressed a paw to his chest like he was scandalized by the very idea. "Hmm. We have biographies of the great house dragons of history. I particularly enjoy the story of Major Drumsticks, who guarded the White House during the Lincoln Administration."

"Um, thanks, but maybe not right now." Maeve felt bad rejecting his suggestion, but she had a mission. "Have you heard anything back about your missing cousin?"

Figgy sighed. "No word yet. The Wigglebottoms are probably very busy dealing with their Extinguished library, so I'm not surprised."

"So if they don't know where she is, how would you find her? A house dragon seems a very small thing to find in a big city." Maeve stumbled over her words.

Figgy scratched his ear with his hind paw. "Still determined to go for the reward, are you?"

"I just want to make sure they're safe, together, and happy," Maeve said honestly.

Figgy leveled his gaze at her. "Fair enough, then." He closed the book he'd been reading and pushed it away. "If I wanted to find a lost litter of house dragon kits, I'd start with reaching out to other house dragons, which I have already begun." Figgy's tail tapped the chair. "It's tedious, but not a laborious process. There's so few of us left, maybe a hundred." He flicked his ears toward Emma. "Briolette has a house dragon. Perhaps you could speak with her?"

Emma fidgeted. "She's not like you, Figgy. She keeps to herself for the most part. I tried to say hello and she stalked off."

"Patchouli Rose is shy, not aloof. Try again." Figgy chuckled.

"What else?" Maeve prompted. "Isn't there some kind of locator enchantment we could try . . . ?" Her voice faded when Figgy shook his head.

"I wish, but magic has its limits." He stilled. "Theoretically, if someone were out of other options, they could try to pinpoint the house dragon's cave."

"Cave?" Maeve echoed. "Like an actual cave?"

"Yes, carved with magic. Every house dragon has a cave hidden in the buildings they protect. It's where we store our treasures. If Aria had any inkling that something was about to happen, she might have left a clue about where she'd taken the kits. That way, only someone she trusted with the secret of her cave would be able to find the kits." He licked his paw. "It's what I would do."

Maeve swallowed. Perhaps Aria would have left a clue to her own whereabouts? "The cave would be in the opera house? The one that Extinguished?"

Figgy nodded. "Yes, though I cannot recommend you visit there, Maeve. Since no one knows what's causing the Extinguishings, we can't be certain it's safe. Plus, the loss of magic there would make the already challenging proposition of finding their cave next to impossible unless you already knew the location." His eyes flashed a warning.

"Before you ask: No. I don't know where Aria's cave is, and I wouldn't tell you even if I did. The location of our cave is a house dragon's deepest secret."

"Oh," Maeve said. That sounded complicated, hard, and scary.

Emma's eyes widened. "Wait, Figgy. Does that mean you have a cave here somewhere?"

"Yes," Figgy said simply. His ears swiveled like he was listening to something Maeve couldn't hear. "I should go. That sounded like Cook knocked a bowl off the counter." He licked his lips. "If you're absolutely determined, Maeve, there's a floor plan of the opera house in *Magical Manhattan*. Third bookshelf from the window. Though, again, I'd advise against it."

"Thank you," Maeve said.

He sauntered out the door and Maeve turned to the bookshelf. She figured she might as well take a look.

Emma stepped in front of her. "Don't even think about it, Maeve. Papa, Izzy, and I drove by the opera house on our way to dinner last weekend. The whole place is boarded up. It looks creepy." Emma shuddered.

Maeve wasn't sure what she disliked more: being told what to do by Emma or the fact they'd gone to dinner without her. Not that she would have wanted to go.

She crossed her arms. "You don't get to tell me what to do. You're not my sister."

To her surprise, Emma backed down immediately. "You're right. I'm sorry. I just want to help."

Maeve was surprised by how much she wanted Emma

to fight her back. She wanted to scare Emma off and push her away. Maybe then she'd leave Izzy and Maeve alone and they could go back to being *the O'Donnell Sisters* instead of Maeve feeling like the odd one out.

But for now, what she really needed was to get Emma away so she could grab the book that Figgy had mentioned. "Do we have any books about plants?" Maeve asked as casually as she could.

"Plants?" Emma's eyes lit up with an idea. "I'll be right back."

She hurried to the other side of the room. Maeve quickly scanned the shelf and found *Magical Manhattan*. It was a thin volume. She flipped it open to the table of contents and immediately spotted "Music and Concert Venues," but her eye was drawn down to the chapter title containing a question mark: "Magic in the Tarnish?"

When Emma returned, Maeve hid the book behind her back and tucked it into the sash of her pinafore.

Emma pointed deeper into the library. "There's not much about plants, I'm afraid. We have a field guide to Central Park and I think there are some biology texts. What are you looking for exactly? If we don't have it, I can always order something."

Maeve edged away. "I was hoping for something about gardening, but don't trouble yourself. I'll just go—"

"Gardening books. I'll do some digging. Get it?" Emma chuckled at her own joke.

"Right. See you later," Maeve mumbled, trying to figure out how fast she could walk away without turning her back to Emma. She ended up scuttling sideways like a crab, keeping her back to the bookshelves.

"Maeve?" Emma tilted her head like a concerned kitten. "I'd like us to be friends. Would that be all right with you?"

"Um," Maeve said, but what she really meant was no. This was Emma, the girl who had usurped Maeve's place in Izzy's life. She looked at Emma, trying to see what Izzy saw. Emma was friendlier, wealthier, and had magic. She fit into Izzy's new life. With a pang, Maeve wondered if Izzy would rather have Emma as a sister than her.

"I'm sorry, I overstepped. I'm only trying to help. Maeve—" Emma reached out a hand like she meant to catch her shoulder and stop her, so Maeve fled.

Maeve didn't stop until she was outside her bedroom door. She didn't want to think about Izzy or Emma anymore, so she changed into her pajamas and settled into bed to read *Magical Manhattan*.

Of the hundred or so buildings that had been made entirely with magic in New York, the book dubbed the Bezel Opera House *the most magicked place in Manhattan*. She read through several paragraphs detailing the astounding amount of magic that had gone into making the building itself as well as the sets and costumes for every production. Then she found what she'd been hoping for: a detailed floor plan of the opera house, showing the auditorium, stage, and wings. There was also a sketch of the enormous fly space above the stage, where scenery could be lifted when not in use. Of course, no house dragon cave appeared on the map.

Maeve scanned the images again. The opera house

looked huge and intimidating. She hoped that one of Figgy's contacts would come back with Aria's whereabouts soon so she could avoid having to take her dangerous magic to *the most magicked place in Manhattan.*

To distract herself from the frightening thoughts of what her magic might do there, she flipped to "Magic in the Tarnish?" The chapter began with details of what the author called *safety measures,* including snuffing buckets and the absence of kindling schools in the neighborhood. A paragraph halfway down the page caught her attention:

Of all the secret societies in New York, none is more mysterious (or perhaps more fictional) than the so-called Ember Society. It is unclear whether the name comes from the fact that embers can burn unde-tected long after a fire has gone out, or whether it's simply a nod to December and the illegal kindling of the society's members. Local legend holds that the Ember Society will reveal themselves to "wor-thy" children when the Kindling Winds blow and help them to kindle their magic. Though blamed for several small fires in the Tarnish in the early 1890s, the group has never been proven to actually exist. Nevertheless, the rumors of their magical aid continue to inspire children to needlessly risk their lives every year attempting to kindle.

Maeve's eye caught on the word *inspire.* It was such a positive word in a disapproving paragraph. She turned the page, hoping to find more, but the author dove back into a detailed history of snuffing buckets.

Maeve and Izzy had loved playing Ember Society when they were younger—secretly, of course, because that was the point. Whenever Mam caught them at it, she'd told them never to put too much stock in hope alone. They had to work hard if they wanted something in life. The girls would nod dutifully but grumble the moment they were alone. Mam didn't understand how exciting it was to think there was a secret group of people just like them and who had kept their magic. But then they'd witnessed Jimmy's snuffing and Maeve hadn't wanted to even pretend to kindle anymore.

The bedroom door opened and Antonia entered, yawning. "What are you reading?"

Maeve snapped the book shut. "Nothing," she said automatically.

Antonia's gaze followed the book as Maeve slid it under her pillow, but she didn't ask any more questions. Maeve got ready for bed in silence, thinking about Mam, and snuffing buckets, and that strange word: *inspire*. For the first time in a long time, she found herself wishing that the Ember Society was real and that there was a group of people waiting and watching to help when they were needed. It made the world feel a little safer.

She rolled over and pretended to be asleep until Antonia was snoring gently. With so much on her mind, Maeve doubted she'd be able to sleep, but somehow, she did.

ELEVEN

A Wish for Seeds

Maeve

The next morning, Miss Clementine set the students to channeling tiny bits of magic into corn kernels. The whole school smelled of delicious popcorn for several hours, long after the unkindled magic had reduced them again to kernels. Maeve sat on her hands and stared at the unpopped kernels in front of her. She didn't dare risk turning the school into a cornfield, but the kernels did give her an idea.

That Saturday, Maeve headed toward the noise of the shops and main streets of the Tarnish. Despite the early hour, the air was filled with the shouts of street hawkers selling their wares in different languages. Maeve kept her eye out for the familiar awning of Evergreen's Everything Store.

Their downstairs neighbor on Rust Street, Mr. Green, had done so well as a pushcart vendor, he'd eventually been able to open his own store. Izzy and Maeve had loved visiting because it felt like Mr. Green really did sell everything: shoes, pots and pans, dress patterns, hairbrushes and combs, glass jars of all shapes and sizes. Most important, Maeve had a distinctive memory of staring at a display of seed packets.

She passed snuffing bucket after snuffing bucket. When she turned onto the block where Evergreen's was, she saw that most of the signs were different now. Indeed, Evergreen's was now a store called East Side Carpets. Maeve stared at the block letters on the window and felt a pang of sadness that the delightful Evergreen's was gone. She wondered what had happened to Mr. Green or any of their old neighbors, for that matter. How long had it taken Jimmy Pickett to get used to not having magic like his da had said? Maeve pictured the people she knew, scattered to the wind like dandelion seeds.

Feeling more downcast than when she'd arrived, Maeve turned to go.

"Welcome to the Ember Society," a child's voice said loudly behind her.

Maeve's curiosity stopped her feet. A girl of around seven balanced on an upside-down pushcart in the gutter. She had light brown skin and large, inquisitive eyes. Her black hair was parted in the middle and tied back in two bows. There were several moldy potatoes scattered at the girl's feet. She held one aloft for her sole audience member, a tiny boy who Maeve guessed was her younger brother.

"Who desires to kindle?" the girl asked in a comically mystical voice.

The boy raised his hand. He peered over his shoulder like he expected there to be a line. Maeve chuckled as his sister handed him a moldy potato of his own.

"You need a gem." The girl spotted Maeve. "Do you want to kindle with us too?" She held up her hand so that her brother couldn't see her lips. "It isn't real kindling."

Maeve was amused and surprised to be invited. "What do I have to do?"

The girl shifted the potato to her other hand and scratched her ear. "Um. You have to touch your toes, turn around three times, and say, *Magic*. Here." She offered her potato to Maeve.

The little boy looked from the withered potato to Maeve and smiled when she took it. Together, they bent over to touch their toes and then turned in a circle three times.

"Magic," they said in near unison.

Maeve grinned at the boy and he grinned back. She whispered her name to him and he told her in a barely audible voice that his name was Nareg Kalfayan and the girl was his sister, Anoush. "She's loud," he explained.

"Welcome, fellow Embers!" Anoush spread her arms wide. "As a gift, I will now use my magic to grant you each one wish." She picked up another moldy potato.

"I wish to be taller," Nareg said.

Anoush groaned. "Magic doesn't work on people. What else do you want?" Nareg shrugged so she spun to face Maeve. "What about you?"

"I wish to find seeds," Maeve said.

"Seeds? That's not a very good wish." Anoush jumped

off the pushcart and pointed at the storefront of East Side Carpets. "They sell seeds in there. I'll show you."

A brass bell above the door jingled as they entered the shop. A few other shoppers looked up and then went back to perusing the carpets for sale. Anoush waved at the woman behind the counter. "Mamajan, this is our new friend! She did magic with us."

Maeve and Mrs. Kalfayan introduced themselves.

"It wasn't real magic," Maeve assured her.

"Thank you, but I'm not concerned. I loved playing magic when I was a child." Mrs. Kalfayan turned to her children. "But you two were supposed to be upstairs doing your homework and folding the laundry."

"It's already done. May we show her the seeds in the back, pleeeeease?" Anoush bounced with excitement.

"They're for my garden," Maeve explained. She was still thinking about what Mrs. Kalfayan had said about loving her magic. So few adults would talk about their childhood magic after they snuffed it. There had to be others who felt that way.

Mrs. Kalfayan pointed deeper into the store and spoke to Maeve. "The seeds are left over from the shop here before. I don't know if they're any good so I'll give you a discount." Her forehead creased. "Anoush, why are you carrying that old potato?"

"Thank you, Mamajan." Anoush tucked the potato behind her back and led Maeve in the direction her mother had pointed. "I know the store pretty well. Mama's been working here a lot because our father's out of work. He's a construction foreman but he doesn't have magic so it's hard to get jobs."

"My father worked in construction too," Maeve said but Anoush appeared to find this connection about as interesting as the rolled-up carpets they passed.

Anoush pointed at a spinning display of seed packets in the back of the shop. "Your wish has been granted!"

It was the same display she remembered from Evergreen's. The seed envelopes were yellowed and the hand-drawn images of vegetables on the fronts had faded. The metal rack squeaked as Anoush turned it. Maeve thought the seeds might still work, especially if she got up the nerve to nudge them with her magic, but there was another problem.

"Are there any flower seeds?" There were cucumbers, tomatoes, beans, carrots, and several other fruits and vegetables. Last weekend, Avi had described his uncle's garden as *full of flowers* and she'd been hoping to surprise him.

"These are the only seeds we have." Anoush watched Maeve peruse the display. She looked so hopeful that Maeve selected ten seed packets and paid for them.

"Can we help you plant them?" Anoush asked as they walked her to the corner to say goodbye. "I like to eat carrots and onions and squash—"

"We'd have to ask Mama," Nareg interrupted her recitation.

"Of course we would." Anoush patted him on the head.

"I should probably go—" Maeve started.

"Do you need any more supplies?" Anoush asked, holding up the potato. "I'm very good at magic."

An hour later, Maeve had been introduced to half a dozen shopkeepers within a two-block radius—as far as Anoush and Nareg were allowed to travel without special permission—and purchased a small shovel called a trowel, and a rake.

As they walked her to the corner to say goodbye, Anoush and Nareg eyed the steaming snuffing bucket warily. Maeve thought about that word again, *inspire*.

"You know, you don't have to hope to become Embers to get your magic. You could apply to the Manhattan School for Magic. That's where I go."

"I've heard about that place, but isn't it way uptown?" Anoush put an arm around Nareg's shoulders and he leaned into her. "I wouldn't want to be so far from my family."

Maeve felt like an electric shock went down her spine. What was wrong with her? She sounded like one of the ladies from the Gemstone Society, swooping in and telling the kids how to live their lives.

"I completely understand." She brushed off her skirt. "Thank you for your help today."

They said their goodbyes and she promised to come see them again soon. Maeve chuckled to herself as she walked to the garden. She wasn't sure who had more energy, those kids or the kits.

When Maeve arrived at the fire escape, she held up the seed packets for Avi.

"I can't see them," he complained.

Maeve was still bubbling with excitement, so she took a risk. "Drop the ladder, I'm coming up."

"What?" His eyes widened.

"You won't come down, so let me up."

She moved out of the way so that he could lower the fire escape's metal ladder. The iron frame groaned and the ladder hit the sidewalk with a *clang*. Maeve climbed up it, feeling like she was crossing a bridge in their friendship.

Avi waited on the fire escape above her.

"Hi," he said nervously when she reached the top. He wasn't quite as tall as he'd looked from the ground.

"Hi," she said back.

He squinted at her face. "You have a lot of freckles. I never noticed that before."

She felt her cheeks redden. "Well, you should comb your hair more often."

"It wasn't an insult. I think they're nice."

"Oh. Thanks." Maeve was surprised how happy it made her to hear that.

Avi ran a wet rag–wrapped hand over his messy hair, which made it stand up in damp spikes. "May I see those seeds now?"

Maeve handed him the packets. While he flipped through them, Maeve looked past him and saw the garden from his perspective for the first time. From there, it was easy to see that the front of the garden was free of undergrowth, trees, and bushes and would make the best spot for a vegetable garden. There were trails of new green growth through the ash where she and the kits had experimented with their magic. Bright yellow daffodils dotted the lot.

A sudden thought sent a shiver of fear down her spine. "If you can see the whole garden from up here, have your parents noticed what I've been doing?"

Avi's shoulders rose toward his ears. "They can't see the garden because they don't have magic. Tateh doesn't seem bothered by it, but sometimes I catch Mameh staring at the wall. I asked her once what it looked like to her, and she said her eye slips over it, like the buildings touch and it's not even there."

Maeve recalled how the entrance had disappeared when she had thought about turning the kits in for the reward. The thought of living next to a beautiful garden that she could never see made her sad.

"Do you think—" Avi's voice faltered. He held up the seed packets. "If this works, maybe my family could have some of this to eat?"

Maeve noticed for the first time how thin Avi was. "Are you hungry, Avi?"

Avi blushed and Maeve realized it was a rude question to ask. Of course he was hungry. Probably everyone in this neighborhood was, at one point or another.

"You can eat as much as you want, Avi. It's your garden," she assured him. "Do you want to help me plan the layout?" she asked, and he brightened considerably.

Over the next week, Maeve worked on the vegetable garden. She and the kits used sticks to mark off the rows where they would plant the seeds, and then, carefully, she tilled the soil with her new trowel. The following weekend, Maeve gathered her courage and planted the seeds.

"Carefully. Don't make a mistake," she reminded herself as she poured two pumpkin seeds from a packet into the hole.

She'd instructed the kits to stay back a safe distance. Their tails twitched with curiosity as they watched her. Maeve put a finger on each of the seeds and gripped her crystal with her other hand. She grimaced as she channeled her magic into the seeds.

Like with the prairie roses, she knew right away it'd been too much. Green vines shot from the seeds like they were coiled springs and Maeve fell backward with a cry.

The kits stared at the thick, pointed leaves. Maeve held her breath, waiting for their condemnation. She'd lost control again.

Treble opened his mouth and leaned hopefully toward the plant.

Cadenza bopped him on the head with a paw. "You don't eat the leaves, silly!"

"I can't believe you grew that so fast!" Forte cheered.

The tension left Maeve's shoulders and she laughed. The kits looked at her in surprise but it only made her laugh harder. She'd made a mistake, but no one had gotten hurt—better yet, no one had even minded! This was the true beauty of the garden. Practicing her magic here felt safe and not at all dangerous.

When she planted the tomatoes, she tried harder to rein it in and felt the tingle of using just the right amount of magic. The fuzzy green stalks grew unnaturally fast as she concentrated, but never got out of control. She was surprised by how *right* it felt.

Maeve sat back on her heels and admired the plants for several heartbeats. Then she got to work. After all, there was a lot to do.

As the vegetable garden grew, Avi's appearance also changed. One day, Maeve arrived to find he'd trimmed and brushed his hair. The next, he'd put on clean clothes. The following weekend, she could tell he'd tried to iron— the back of his shirt had a triangular mark burned into it. She smiled about it the whole afternoon as she checked on the new growth in her vegetable patch and began reviving some of the older plants with her magic. Maybe people, like gardens, needed tending. Someone to care and to show up for them, day after day.

That afternoon, Avi lowered the ladder and she climbed up to sit with him as had become their custom at the end of the day. The sky was a brilliant blue dotted with clouds. Maeve watched them drift over the roof of the tenement across the street as she and Avi let their legs dangle over the end of the fire escape.

"I've been thinking—and I have a lot of time to think during the week when you're not here." Avi's cheeks flushed. "I might have been wrong. I don't think you caused the garden to Extinguish."

Maeve took a deep breath. "Oh?" she asked casually. "Why's that?"

"*That's* what your magic did to the garden." Avi pointed to the increasingly large green patches and the new growth in the vegetable garden. "I see how hard you work at it and how long it takes. Don't you think to burn the entire place would take even more work?"

Maeve had begun to suspect the same thing, but hearing Avi say it loosened a knot in her gut. "I agree. It'd take a lot of magic."

"Probably more than we've got between the two of us." Avi shrugged.

Maeve swung her feet alongside his. "And how much do you think that is?"

"You? A lot. Me?" He held up his rag-wrapped hands.

"I could help you learn to use your magic," Maeve offered cautiously.

"I know, but I shouldn't." Avi pulled his legs up and hugged them. His voice sounded sad. "I mean, I can't."

Talking to Avi usually felt easy. He didn't ask a lot of questions about her past. Avi told about the people and things he saw from his fire escape perch and they mostly talked about life in the neighborhood or made plans for the garden. At every mention of magic, he fled. Today was no different.

"You'd better go. It's getting late." Avi stood up abruptly and reached for the rusty crank that raised and lowered the fire escape ladder.

It wasn't really that late but Maeve said goodbye anyway. She stopped on the corner and looked back. Avi was staring at the garden with his rag-wrapped hands hanging loosely at his sides.

She wished he could believe in himself as much as he believed in her. The thought warmed her the whole way back to the train. Avi believed in her. He thought her magic was helping the garden, not hurting it.

As she stepped on board the crowded train car, she had another thought: If she hadn't Extinguished the garden, then who had? Did that mean someone else knew about it?

The questions chilled her to the bone and haunted her thoughts all the way home.

TWELVE

Glint Kindling Academy

Izzy

The notice appeared in all the magical newspapers on June 3. Izzy nearly choked on her omelet when she read it at breakfast.

> The Board of Magical Education, led by Katherine Nimby, Acting Commissioner, will be hosting a public forum about the new schools opened under the Isabelle O'Donnell License, on Tuesday, June 4, at 7:00 p.m.
>
> The meeting will be hosted by the Glint Kindling Academy. Admission by selected RSVP only.

She brought the paper to the headmistress's attention right away.

"I wasn't sure you'd want to go. It could get vicious, Izzy," Miss Clementine warned.

"Of course I want to go. It has my name on it." Izzy took a seat across from Miss Clementine, who was behind her sturdy desk. "Why do people have to respond if it's a public forum? And what does 'selected RSVP' mean?"

Miss Clementine sighed. "Crowd control, I'm afraid. Anyone can reply, but the Board selects who actually gets in. They do that when they predict a meeting could get out of hand."

Izzy flopped back in her chair and looked around the room while Miss Clementine reread the notice.

Izzy loved the headmistress's office. The rug was a deep plum color and the bookcases flanking the fireplace were carved from warm mahogany. On the mantel, a brass clock had hands that not only showed the time but also pointed to where the busy Miss Clementine was expected to be. *Classroom, Dining Room, Sound Asleep* were a few of the options. Right now the hand pointed to *Endless Meetings*.

Miss Clementine set the newspaper down on the desk between them. "I'll respond for us now. Why don't we ask the Harrises to join us?"

Izzy thought about it. "I'll ask Maeve too."

It would be good to have the Harrises' support. And maybe this could be a bonding experience for Maeve and Emma and Mr. Harris. Izzy had told the Harrises that Maeve needed to get to know them better before accepting their offer, and they'd been as sympathetic and understanding as she'd expected. Every morning at breakfast, Izzy hoped to see the flash of diamonds on Maeve's wrist, indicating her sister might be warming to the idea. So far, the bracelet remained squirreled away in Maeve's room somewhere.

Patience was not something that Izzy possessed in great volumes, but she was doing her best to give Maeve the time she needed and not push her.

Miss Clementine picked up her pen. "Now, I believe you have work to do before our lesson this afternoon. How did your searing practice go this weekend?"

"Great," Izzy lied, and edged toward the door.

Miss Clementine saw right through her. "Izzy, you'll need to start your school applications soon and none of them will consider you if you can't sear. Do not let this meeting distract you. Focus on your magic."

Izzy grumbled as she headed to her room, but she knew Miss Clementine was right. When she reached her bedroom, she flopped into the desk chair and flipped open her textbook.

"Ready or not, sear I come," Izzy said. She wished someone was around to hear her joke.

She spent the rest of the morning shrinking buckets into teacups, but try as she might, she couldn't sear the enchantment. Learning magic had been fun when Emma was around, but this just felt like *work*. Magic had always come naturally to her and Izzy was frustrated by this difficulty now. She wondered what Emma and Frances were doing at school that day. What would it be like to go to a real school?

Izzy didn't get a chance to ask Maeve about the Board meeting until right before breakfast the next morning.

"It'd be great if you'd come with me. We could represent the school together," Izzy offered. The skylight above them in the hall was a dazzling blue with not a cloud in sight.

Maeve's shoulders caved in. "Mrs. Nimby will be there, right? Sorry, Izzy, but no thanks." Her face paled as she spotted something over Izzy's shoulder. "I've gotta go," she said, and ducked into the dining room.

Izzy turned to see what had scared off her sister and found Emma coming up the hall behind her with a confused expression on her face.

"Good morning. What are you doing here?" Izzy asked.

"Papa has a meeting with Miss Clementine and I tagged along for breakfast." Emma looked in the direction that Maeve had gone. "Did Maeve have mud on her boots?"

Izzy shrugged. "How could she have gotten mud on her boots? She just came downstairs to breakfast. Speaking of which, let's go eat."

Though she tried to focus on her lessons, Izzy had worried herself into a state of agitation long before they pulled up to Glint Kindling Academy in Mr. Harris's shiny car. A crowd had gathered outside the unembellished brick school building. Izzy pulled her hat down farther on her head, worried she might be recognized if these people were against the license. But the crowd wasn't concerned with her.

"What do you mean we're not allowed in?" a man in a flat cap demanded of the attendant guarding the front door.

"I'm sorry, sir, but the meeting is full," the attendant said while clutching his clipboard. He looked relieved when he saw Mr. Harris. "Your name, sir?"

Mr. Harris gave the names of the attendees from MSM

and the attendant ticked them off his list. "Go right in," he said with a bow of his head.

The people gathered around the door began to shout.

"It's a public meeting—you can't keep us out!" someone hollered.

"If the meeting is full, how come they can go in but we can't?" someone else demanded, but Izzy didn't hear the answer because the door slammed behind them.

Emma looked at Izzy. "Are you all right? You're unusually quiet."

"I'll be fine," Izzy said, but her squeaky voice betrayed her uncertainty. Maybe it was better that Maeve hadn't come after all.

Unlike the light-filled interior of their own school, the front hall of Glint Kindling Academy was wood-paneled and boring. There was a staircase along the wall to her left leading to a darkened second floor. Izzy craned her neck and saw several students peering between the rungs of the banister. She waved and they ducked out of sight.

They followed the sound of conversation—and, oddly for a meeting, a piano playing—down a long hallway, past several closed doors. At the end of the hall, they entered a wood-paneled room that had been set up with rows of chairs facing a long table. The room was packed with well-dressed adults and a handful of equally well-dressed kids. Everyone was carrying glasses of punch and nibbling on cookies while a grand piano played a lively tune in the corner. Gas sconces on the wall cast everyone and everything in a sickly yellowish tinge.

"Well, I've never been to a Board meeting with entertainment and refreshments before. Mr. Rote must be aiming to impress," Miss Clementine said.

Izzy did a double take. "That piano is playing itself."

Indeed, the keys pressed down as if by invisible hands, but the bench was empty.

"That's a complicated bit of magic. Someone is definitely showing off," Miss Clementine said.

"Well, it isn't me," Mr. Rote said drolly. They turned to find Glint Kindling Academy's headmaster standing behind them with Ms. Glint.

Ms. Glint swatted him on the arm. "Don't tattle on my musical talents or I'll tell them about your skill with ice sculptures."

Mr. Rote's eyes widened with discomfort. Izzy and Emma exchanged a look.

Fortunately, Mr. Harris was a skilled player at the politeness game. "It's always fun to discover a hidden talent. Lovely to see you both again."

"Mr. Harris, I'm so glad you were able to get in!" Ms. Glint clasped her hands together. "My photographer is here tonight. May we please get a picture of the two of us? The gallery opening's only two weeks away and I'd love to have the photo for the promotional materials."

"Absolutely," Mr. Harris agreed, and he let Ms. Glint lead him across the room to where a man with a large handlebar mustache was waiting next to a huge camera on a tripod.

Mr. Rote grimaced, clearly not happy to have been left alone with the MSM contingent.

Miss Clementine shifted her weight. "Where are your students? I expected some of them to be here with their families since you're hosting."

"Upstairs studying. They're very well trained." Mr. Rote cast his gaze toward the ceiling. "If you'll excuse me, I must take my seat. I believe we're about to begin."

"*Well trained*?" Emma whispered so that only Izzy could hear.

Izzy shuddered. She didn't think she'd be calling Glint Kindling Academy their rival school anymore. There was a playfulness implied in a rivalry, and Mr. Rote was cold and not at all playful.

Forgoing the refreshments, they chose seats at the end of a row so that Mr. Harris's chair would fit next to them. Miss Clementine and Emma sat on either side of Izzy.

Emma pulled two hairpins out of her hair. With a flash of her ruby ring, the pins turned into a pen and pencil. Izzy stared at them.

Emma shrugged. "What? I thought it'd be helpful if we took notes."

"Did you sear that enchantment?" Izzy felt a lump in her throat. It hadn't seemed to take Emma any effort.

"I did!" Emma grinned. "I'm really getting the hang of it."

A door at the front of the room opened, sparing Izzy from having to respond. The six members of the Board of

Magical Education filed in and took seats at the table at the front of the room. Izzy recognized Mrs. Nimby and Ms. Glint, as well as the two men from the tour. There was another man and woman, both younger and professionally dressed. A hush fell over the crowd and there was a bit of a scrum as everyone attempted to fill the chairs.

Izzy cast a subtle glance around the room. With a jolt, she suddenly understood what Miss Clementine had meant when she said that "selected RSVP" meant crowd control. Only a small handful of people in the room looked to be the working-class, magicless parents of Glint Kindling Academy and MSM students. The crowd gathered in the room was mostly well-dressed, well-off, and well-magicked.

"This meeting of the Board of Magical Education will come to order," Mrs. Nimby said, smacking a wooden gavel against the table. "Will the secretary please read last month's minutes?"

One of the bow-tied men droned on about last month's meeting, which had apparently been about the budget. A girl two rows in front of Izzy kept fidgeting and whispering with the girl next to her. They turned to look at her and Izzy almost groaned out loud when she recognized Pearl Nimby and Beatrice Scorn, a brown-haired snobby girl who had been at Miss Posterity's last year. Izzy ignored them and pretended to be absorbed in last month's meeting minutes.

"Thank you, Mr. Secretary," Mrs. Nimby said when he finished reading. She folded her hands on the table. "Now, let's move on to the matter at hand and why I suspect you're all here. The schools that have opened under the Isabelle O'Donnell License and the recent expansion of magical education."

Izzy slid a little lower in her chair as heads turned in her direction. Emma squeezed Izzy's arm reassuringly.

Mrs. Nimby cleared her throat. "As many of you know, I have been very open-minded and tried to approach the recent expansion of magical education with optimism"—Emma snorted with disbelief at that—"but on a recent visit to the Manhattan School for Magic, I witnessed firsthand the dangers of allowing just anyone to kindle. I, for one, feel lucky to have escaped with my life when I was viciously attacked by a student with rogue magic."

Izzy leaned forward in her chair and stared in shock. Mrs. Nimby was telling lies about Maeve in front of everyone. It felt different than when she had read it in the paper, and she didn't know how to handle it in person.

"I'm prepared to give the mayor the benefit of the doubt that he did not fully comprehend the consequences of passing the O'Donnell License. After all, had any of us even heard of an Extinguishment before these schools opened?"

There was a ripple through the crowd as people conferred with their neighbors.

"The mayor's a criminal and should be locked up!" a man from the back of the room shouted.

"These schools are stealing our magic!" another voice chimed in. Others clapped in agreement.

That wasn't how magic worked! Izzy fumed. Miss Clementine put a firm hand out in front of Izzy. "Steady," she whispered. "Cooler heads will prevail."

Izzy wasn't sure what *prevail* meant, but she trusted Miss Clementine. She leaned back in her chair.

Mrs. Nimby held up her hands for quiet. She'd arranged her face in a professional neutral expression but her eyes gleamed in triumph. "If the motion passes tonight, this Board will submit a list of demands to the mayor tomorrow morning. These are amendments to the current O'Donnell License, adding a test of worthiness that any potential kindling student must undergo before receiving their permit. Setting rigorous standards will ensure only the truly worthy can kindle."

More than half of the room jumped to their feet to applaud. Mrs. Nimby bowed her head and pressed a hand to her heart, accepting their praise.

There was a *pop* and a hiss as the camera in the back of the room flashed.

"This isn't a public forum. It's a performance," Miss Clementine grumbled under her breath.

Izzy swallowed hard and looked around the room to gauge how many people were on their side. Ms. Glint and one of the men on the Board had their arms crossed with their eyebrows raised skeptically. To Izzy's surprise, Mr. Rote wore the deepest frown in the room. Then again, he probably didn't like the Board meddling with his students either. Beatrice Scorn had also stayed in her chair, but Izzy knew her to be pretty lazy.

"Now let's open the floor to public comment," Mrs. Nimby said.

A dozen hands flew into the air. Mrs. Nimby called on

people in turn, and Izzy listened as, over and over, people reiterated the claims that the Extinguishings were a result of allowing more people to use magic. Next to her, Emma angrily shredded her notepaper into tiny pieces.

"I don't understand," Izzy whispered. "Magic can't be stolen. How can they all blame us?"

"They can because they want to believe it. They're scared of the Extinguishings and feel threatened by more people having magic." Emma gave the paper one final rip. "It's easier for them to blame us than for them to admit that the system they've been benefiting from for so long is wrong."

Izzy still couldn't understand how people could ignore facts in favor of their own prejudices.

Emma nudged her. "You should say something, Izzy."

"I know," Izzy said, but didn't move to raise her hand. She wanted to scream at all of them, but she had no idea what to say. Emma was the one who always found the right words and Izzy was, well, Izzy was good at magic. Or at least, she used to be. But then the mayor named the license after her and she felt like she had to be something more than what she was. Something better and more polished. A diamond, already out of the rough.

Two rows ahead of Izzy, a different hand rose in the air. It trembled slightly until Mrs. Nimby called on its owner.

Beatrice Scorn stood up. *Oh no.* Izzy groaned silently.

"I was at Miss Posterity's with Izzy O'Donnell. She helped me kindle," Beatrice said. "Izzy wouldn't steal magic. In fact,

I've never seen anyone work harder to earn it. Maybe we should give them all a chance."

Beatrice sat down. Pearl Nimby leaned away from her like she had something contagious.

"Well, that was unexpected," Izzy mumbled.

Emma nodded, her mouth agape.

For the first time since the meeting had begun, Izzy felt a flicker of hope. If Beatrice Scorn could change, perhaps there was hope they'd be able to get the others to see sense.

"Is it time to *prevail* yet?" Izzy whispered to Miss Clementine.

"I certainly hope so," Miss Clementine said, and raised her hand. When Mrs. Nimby called on her—with obvious reluctance—Miss Clementine stood. "I assume that if this so-called Worthiness Test is instated, students at all kindling schools will need to take it?"

The crowd erupted.

After Mrs. Nimby calmed everyone down, she assured them that the Worthiness Test would only apply to students at schools that had opened under the Isabelle O'Donnell License. As soon as Izzy heard that, she knew their side was in trouble.

The motion to submit the Worthiness Test to the mayor passed the Board by a vote of four to two. Ms. Glint and one of the men, who voted against it, left quickly, while the other four were ushered out by a round of applause from the crowd. The piano began to play again as the meeting took on the atmosphere of a party.

"I cannot believe Mr. Rote didn't speak up," Miss

Clementine vented as they stood. "I hope Mayor Slight sees sense, at least."

"We need to talk this through with Frances," Emma said to Izzy. "Come to Briolette and have lunch with us."

"Maybe," Izzy said. She wasn't sure she wanted to go anywhere right now. Not with the looks people were giving her as the meeting dispersed. For the first time, she heard Beatrice's words differently. "They don't think *I'm* stealing magic, do they?"

"I don't know," Emma said honestly. "But I'm worried that people are looking for someone to blame."

Izzy felt like she was standing on a bridge between two different lives, the magicless one before her kindling and the magical one after, but she couldn't fully cross over to either side and the gulf under her kept getting wider and wider. When she'd set out to kindle, all she'd wanted was her magic. Now she didn't know where she belonged.

"Izzy, you've gone green. Are you sick?" Emma asked.

Izzy mumbled something about dinner not agreeing with her, and a few minutes later they were safely in Mr. Harris's car and headed back to the school. But the gnawing in the pit of Izzy's stomach didn't let up. She let Emma play nurse and tuck her into bed. Figgy draped himself over her feet like a hot-water bottle.

In Izzy's dreams, Da's fiddle fought against a grand piano. She woke before she found out who won.

THIRTEEN

Pine Cones and Punishments

Maeve

On Friday morning, Maeve entered the classroom and took her seat. It had already been a rough morning. Cook had almost caught her slipping in the back door before breakfast and then Izzy had been in a gloomy mood while they ate. She'd been that way since the Board of Magical Education meeting earlier that week.

Most of the students had yet to trickle into the classroom, so Maeve stared at the front of the room and let her thoughts drift downtown. She had asked the kits about the location of their cave that morning and it had not gone well.

"We're not allowed to tell you that," Forte had said, bristling. "Mother was very clear that only our family can know the location of our cave."

Maeve was disappointed, though Figgy had said as much. "I'm just trying to find your mother. I'm not interested in any treasure in your cave," she tried to reassure them.

Treble drew back. "You know about our treasures?"

Maeve knew immediately that she'd said the wrong thing. "I didn't mean—"

"We'll need to discuss it among ourselves." Cadenza's tail swished in agitation as she exchanged a look with her brothers.

The kits hadn't wanted to play after that. Maeve left quickly, mentally kicking herself for bringing up the treasure. She'd only made things harder, and she was already running out of options to find their mother. Hopefully, Figgy would get a lead from one of his contacts, but every time Maeve had asked, he'd said no one had any news. Aria had been missing for just over a month now, and while the kits were no longer hungry, she knew they were worried. Frankly, she was worried. She still hadn't figured out who or what had caused the garden, the opera house, or any of the other locations to Extinguish. She didn't think it had anything to do with the students at the school, though Izzy had told her people at the Board meeting were blaming them. Maeve wished she knew more about magic so she could understand all of this.

Giggling interrupted Maeve's thoughts. Minnie, Ida, and Antonia were clustered in the back of the classroom. They were playing some game with a piece of paper folded into a diamond shape that covered Minnie's fingertips. There were numbers on the outside and when Minnie moved her fingers, the folded paper displayed an entirely different set of numbers.

"Pick a number with your magic and it tells you what you need to know." Minnie held out the paper to Ida.

Ida pointed at the number *14* and magic flashed through her crystal. Minnie unfolded the paper under the *14* and words appeared on the formerly blank paper.

"'You have a secret admirer,'" Ida read out loud, and the girls squealed with excitement.

It tells you what you need to know. Maeve didn't understand how it worked, but maybe it would give her a hint as to how to find Aria.

"May I try, please?" she asked.

Ida, Minnie, and Antonia regarded her nervously.

"You have to do magic to use it," Ida said.

Maeve stood up. "I know."

"Let her try," Antonia urged. She smiled at Maeve encouragingly.

"Be careful. It only takes a tiny bit of magic," Minnie cautioned. She held out the paper fortune-teller as far away as her arms could reach.

Maeve read the numbers: *14, 8, 41, 2.* She pulled her half crystal from her pocket and the other girls winced. Maeve imagined that she was in the garden. A tingle of magic warmed her skin like sunlight as she pointed at the number *2.* For *two* sisters who didn't need a third.

The ink on the paper swirled like she'd dropped water onto it and words appeared in Minnie's bubbly handwriting. Maeve felt a small thrill travel from her head to her toes. The other girls' eyes widened, clearly as shocked as she was.

"'Your friends will be right by your side when you need

them,'" Minnie read, and Ida and Antonia *awwed* in unison.

"I bet it means your sister," Antonia suggested.

Maeve couldn't stop grinning. Her magic had worked in the classroom! And in front of other people! It almost made up for the disappointment that the message didn't contain any clues that would lead her to Aria. She didn't know what to think about the message itself. Even after weeks, her fingers longed to rub her missing prairie rose sachet.

Miss Lawrence entered the classroom carrying a basket of pine cones to practice changing into pincushions for their Everyday Enchantments class.

"Maeve, Miss Clementine asked me to give this to you." Miss Lawrence held out a folded note.

Maeve took it and opened it. The headmistress's note informed Maeve that the contractors had finished clearing the roses and damaged plaster from the classroom and Mr. Harris had found time in his schedule to work on the repairs tomorrow. Maeve would be serving out her detention assisting him. Truthfully, she had almost forgotten she was supposed to have detention. She didn't like the prospect of losing a Saturday at the garden and wasn't sure her unkindled magic could help a magitect, but she wasn't in a position to say no.

"Want to pick a number, Miss Lawrence?" Minnie offered, holding the paper fortune-teller up.

With a wry smile, Miss Lawrence picked the number 32 and learned she was going to have a good hair day the next day. "That's a fun bit of magic, Minnie. We should probably put it away before the headmistress spots it, though," the teacher said with a wink.

Minnie tucked the fortune-teller into her desk while Maeve, Ida, and Antonia drifted toward their seats to start class.

"Well done, Maeve," Antonia said before she sat down.

Even the threat of tomorrow's detention couldn't dampen Maeve's smile. She'd done magic in the classroom! She even managed to turn her pine cone into a pincushion for a brief moment, though it still smelled wonderfully of pine. Miss Clementine was busy with another student, but Antonia and Ida saw and grinned back at her.

The next morning, Maeve headed downstairs to meet Mr. Harris and serve out her punishment. As she reached the bottom of the stairs, Figgy trotted past her with his tail held high.

Maeve stopped. She wasn't sure how to address him. "Um, excuse me, Mr. Pudding?"

Figgy preened at the formality. "How may I help you, Miss O'Donnell?"

"I was wondering if you'd heard anything else about the missing house dragons." Maeve tried not to fidget and show how nervous it made her to ask.

Figgy's ears drooped. "Sadly, no. I've heard back from almost all of my contacts and no one has heard from Aria or her kits." He noticed the disappointment on her face. "It's too soon to despair, though. I am still trying to get in touch with the Wigglebottoms. My letter may not have reached them before their home Extinguished, and I don't know where they're currently staying."

Maeve thanked him and they continued on their separate ways.

This was as she'd feared. They couldn't keep waiting for answers, and the frightening prospect of venturing into the Extinguished Bezel Opera House was becoming more of a reality. She still had *Magical Manhattan* tucked under her mattress upstairs. Maybe there was something in the floor plan that she'd missed. Or maybe there was a way to earn the kits' trust so they'd tell her about their cave.

She found Mr. Harris in the empty classroom. He was parked in the middle of the room and was peering upward, studying the plaster on the ceiling.

At the sound of her footsteps, he spun to face her and smiled. "Thanks for joining me here today."

"Miss Clementine said I had to." Maeve eyed the door.

"All the same, I'm glad you're here. Izzy tells me that your father worked in construction?"

This was unexpected. Maeve shifted. "He did."

"I'd like your opinion on this. Would you come here, please?"

It amused Maeve that at the word *here* he pointed not to the floor but to the ceiling above them. She almost said that she didn't know much about construction, as she'd been only six when her da died, but she decided that she didn't want to talk about her family with any of the Harrises.

She looked up to see where the cracked plaster had been cleared away, leaving the ceiling beams exposed like a skeleton.

"You see how these beams have been damaged?" Mr. Harris asked, pointing to two thick wooden boards running across the ceiling.

Maeve flushed. "I'm so sorry. I didn't mean to damage—"

"I'm not blaming you. We both know that what happened was an accident. If it's anyone's fault, it's mine for not making time for this sooner. I was distracted by my work at the gallery when I should have been making sure these beams got the attention that they deserve."

There was something soothing about his voice that reminded her of Da. Maeve studied Mr. Harris. While Da had a big red beard the same color as his daughters' hair, Mr. Harris was clean-shaven. This close, she saw the thin scars on Mr. Harris's cheeks and chin from where he'd been injured in the earthquake. It hit her like a punch in the gut when she realized she couldn't picture the tiny details of Da's face.

"So, here's my challenge." Mr. Harris shifted his weight and pointed again at the beams. "These are strong beams, but they need a little help. I'm contemplating using a brace right there in the middle." He gestured with his hands as he spoke. "Or I could put a crossbeam between them, but I worry that as the building shifts, it might drive them farther apart."

"Like a wedge," Maeve said.

"Exactly." Mr. Harris stroked his chin. "So my dilemma is how to best support those two beams."

Maeve suddenly understood that this conversation might not actually be about beams. "Why ask me? You're the magitect."

"True, but I would like your opinion." Mr. Harris folded his hands in his lap. He was proper and fancy, and nothing like her da.

"You should leave the beams alone." She took a step backward.

Mr. Harris frowned. "But what if the ceiling caves in?"

She backed up another step. "But what if it doesn't?"

"Maeve—" Mr. Harris started, and then shut his mouth like he'd thought better of what he was about to say. "Perhaps you're right. I'll have to think on it more and consider every option. In the meantime, I'm not very good at pushing a broom and I need help sweeping up this dust that the workmen left behind so we can have a clean workspace. Would you mind, please?" He pointed at a pencil on Miss Clementine's desk and it became a broom with a flash of his watch.

Something had changed in his manner. If Maeve had been more sympathetic to it, she might have recognized it as disappointment.

She kept her head down and did as he asked, helping him tidy and move things while he worked for the two hours. They didn't speak much, but by the time they were done, Mr. Harris had used his magic to sculpt new plaster so that it was impossible to tell the ceiling had ever been damaged.

When she left, he thanked her and she nodded in reply. As she shut the door behind herself, she wondered what he'd chosen to do about the beams.

FOURTEEN
Forever and Ever

Maeve

On Sunday, Maeve was up and out of the house before breakfast again. She stopped in the kitchen to grab some more leftover chicken for the kits and bread and cheese to share with Avi. When she opened the pantry, she was delighted to discover that Cook had made salmon jerky this week. The kits would be thrilled! Her trusty satchel bumped heavily against the skirt of her brown dress as she walked east to Third Avenue and boarded the downtown train.

As she was walking from the station to the garden, someone called her name. Maeve looked up to see Anoush and Nareg crossing the street toward her.

"How are the seeds?" Anoush asked.

"Still growing." Maeve gave the same answer she had when she'd gone to see them last week. "I can't stop today, but I'll see you soon."

They waved her goodbye as she continued on her way.

As usual, Avi was waiting for her on the fire escape when she arrived. He looked up from his book and called down to her. "I waited for you yesterday. Why didn't you come?"

"I had detention," Maeve said.

"You do have a certain disregard for rules." He flipped the page in his book and scoffed, "*Detention*," under his breath.

Maeve grumbled as she pushed aside the board. In her mind, Avi was too much of a rule-follower for his own good. She'd given up trying to get him to talk about magic and, though he loved to talk about the garden, she was starting to realize that he might never come down or set foot inside it.

The garden was still and quiet when she entered. Where were the kits? They always came running at the first squeak of the board. A gnawing worry started in Maeve's belly.

"Hello?" she called out to the back of the garden as she hurried in that direction. The vegetable patch on her right and the old-and-new growth of the garden deeper in were strangely quiet and still.

Cadenza and Forte came bounding through the undergrowth, both shouting, "Treble needs help!"

They led Maeve to the base of one of the gnarled apple trees. A frightened *mew* came from high above them. Maeve peered up to see the tiny gray kitten clinging to a leafless branch high overhead. He was a hand's distance away from the tangled mess of the squirrels' nest but clearly couldn't get any closer.

"He's stuck," Cadenza explained. She called up to him, "Maeve is here."

"No one can help me. Forte's right. I have to accept my squirrel fate," Treble said dramatically.

Maeve and Cadenza frowned at Forte, who ducked his head. "I was only teasing him."

The lowest branch was at Maeve's shoulder height. If she could get to it, the tree would be easy to climb. She spotted the stone birdbath lying on its side in the undergrowth a few feet away and hurried toward it.

The birdbath was harder to move than she anticipated. Treble's sad little mews had increased in pitch and volume by the time she had rolled it over under the apple tree.

Carefully, she climbed on top of the basin and hoisted herself up into the tree. The branches bobbed under her weight but held. She'd climbed plenty of trees in Omaha, but never dead ones like this. The higher she got, the drier and more fragile the branches felt beneath her hands and feet.

Treble twisted around to watch her climb and lost his balance. He clung to the branch with his front claw, his back legs scrambling in the air. "Help!" he cried.

"Hold on!" Maeve reached out a hand, but he was still a few inches out of reach. The blisters on her palms ached and the branches shook threateningly, but she had to climb. One more push. One more reach.

Treble lost his grip with a terrified *mrrrow*. Maeve leaned as far as she could and caught his soft furry body. She clutched him close to her chest and his tiny heart hammered next to her own.

"Treble! What were you thinking?"

"I don't want to be a squirrel." Treble sobbed. "I'm

ever so high up and ever so hungry. But Forte says I can't do magic—"

"You have to keep trying if you want it," Maeve said.

Treble shook his head. "I'm not a very good house dragon. I don't even like opera. I just like to eat."

"The house dragon at my school likes food a lot too," Maeve started to say, but she was interrupted by chattering from the nest a foot above them.

An angry squirrel stuck his head out and shook a tiny fist at them.

Treble narrowed his eyes. "How rude."

"Hang on. We're going to climb back down." She put her foot on the branch below.

There was a loud *crack* and her foot slipped. Frantic, Maeve grabbed for a branch but her fingers only scraped the rough bark. Then she was falling.

Maeve screamed. The branches whipped at her face and smacked her ribs. She felt Treble's claws tear through her dress and then she lost her grip on him. The ground got nearer and nearer. She cried out as her hip and shoulder banged the earth with a painful *thump*, followed by the side of her head.

Maeve rolled onto her back, gasping. She'd missed landing on the birdbath by mere inches. Her side had taken the brunt of the fall, but nothing felt broken. She was alive. Aching, but alive.

"Are you all right?" Treble balanced on the lowest branch of the tree. He must have grabbed hold as they fell.

"I think so," she said.

"Maeve!" Avi shouted.

She blinked. That couldn't be right. She couldn't hear Avi from inside the garden. She must have hit her head harder than she thought.

There was a blur of movement in her peripheral vision and then Avi dropped to his knees next to her. "I saw you fall. Are you hurt?"

Why was it so bright? The vivid green of the garden hurt her eyes.

Green?

Maeve sat up and gasped. There were no ashes in sight. Everywhere was green, from the grass to the freshly sprouted leaves billowing in the apple tree above her. Splashes of color—pinks and reds and purples—had spread down the vines on the wall as the morning glories and trumpet flowers opened their newborn faces to the sun. The garden had burst into bloom like magic. No, it wasn't *like* magic. It *was* magic.

Avi beheld the garden with wonder. "This is what it was like when my uncle was alive. How did you do it?"

Maeve rubbed her forehead. "I didn't."

"*Ahhh!*" With a scream, Treble fell out of the tree. Avi dove forward and caught him neatly in his hands.

Treble nuzzled the heel of Avi's hand. "Thank you, fire escape boy."

"The kitten talked!" Avi set Treble down in the grass, where the kit promptly started giving himself a bath.

"He's a house dragon—" Maeve started to explain, but then she gasped. "Avi! Your hands!"

The skin of his fingers was as pale and wrinkled as if

he'd just come out of a long bath. He stared at his hands in horror. "My rags! They must have fallen off when I was running. I have to find them before I start sparking."

He took two steps toward the front of the garden and then his mouth dropped open.

"What? What is it?" Maeve pushed herself up to her knees and then used the trunk of the tree to help herself to her feet. Treble paused grooming with his tongue stuck out.

"I—I ran through your vegetable patch," Avi stammered.

Maeve turned slowly, expecting to see her hard work trampled. Instead, she found a garden at its peak. Purple eggplants and yellow squash clung to the sprawling vines. Red chard and green lettuce sprouted like leafy fountains. All of it was ready to harvest and there was more than enough to feed a dozen families.

"Oh," she said in wonder and understanding. "Avi, this is *your* magic."

"Me? Magic? Ah!" Avi shouted in alarm. He held up his hands to show her the green sparks that crackled between his fingertips. For a moment, he appeared ready to panic, but then his thick eyebrows creased together. "It doesn't hurt?"

Maeve shook her head.

"It feels . . . good. It's been so long since I didn't try to fight it." Avi looked from the green sparks in his hands to the green of the garden.

"Maeve?" Cadenza whispered from the undergrowth. "Is it safe to come out?"

"Who said that?" Avi jumped.

Cadenza and Forte crept forward, looking at Avi like they couldn't quite believe their eyes.

Avi crouched down and petted Forte, who preened under his attention. "What are house dragons doing in our garden?"

Our garden. The words felt as warm and bright as the sun on Maeve's face. "I think we have a lot of explaining to do," Maeve said.

"Can we pleeease do it over lunch?" Treble begged.

They settled in to share the small feast that Maeve had packed. The apple trees swayed overhead, and two pigeons landed on a branch. They cooed until Maeve tossed some crumbs of bread into the grass for them to eat.

Cadenza clicked at the pigeons and scowled when they ignored her. "I'll get it right someday," she muttered.

When the food had been distributed, Maeve cleared her throat.

"It's time to talk about magic, Avi. How did your uncle learn to kindle?" she asked.

Avi fidgeted with the cuff of his sleeve. "He never told me, exactly. Someone helped him. It was a secret. He wanted me to kindle too but then he died and—"

"Wait, what?" Forte's ears flattened in confusion. "How?"

"Stories work best when you start at the beginning," Treble suggested.

Haltingly, Avi began. The story was rambling, like he'd never thought he'd actually be telling it and so had never thought it through. They listened in attentive silence as Avi told them how his mother's brother, Benjamin, had come over from Russia with his father, one of Avi's grandfathers, when Benjamin was a kid. When Avi's mother and grandmother joined them two years later, his mother had snuffed her magic and had no idea her brother had kindled. Benjamin successfully hid his magic from their family for ten years.

Maeve felt like she couldn't breathe when she heard this. It had been hard enough to hide her sparkings while she'd been in Omaha. She couldn't imagine hiding kindled magic for a full decade.

"How did your family find out he had magic?" she asked.

"I started sparking. Uncle Benjamin was so proud. He was staying with us then. He was always moving jobs and apartments. Mameh used to think he was lazy, but then we realized it was to hide his magic." Avi stared at his unwrapped hands. "He wanted to teach me to kindle. We'd come into the garden and play Ember Society. He always came up with the best details to make it feel real."

"Like what?" Treble's tail swished with excitement.

"Well, he used to say that the Ember Society's secret meeting house was even more invisible than the garden. You had to believe it was there before you could see it." Avi's eyes shone with memories. "Uncle Benjamin always played the kid who was trying to kindle and let me rescue him. He made me feel so strong."

Maeve sat back on her heels. A gentle breeze blew through the garden, filling it with the scent of summer flowers. Avi's uncle sounded wonderful, but she had already guessed he was after getting to know his garden. It was amazing to think he'd learned to kindle and built the garden on his own. He was truly an inspiration.

Maeve's eyes snapped open. There was that word again, *inspire,* that she'd read in the passage about the Ember Society. An idea seized her mind and wouldn't let go. All the pieces fit: Avi said how his uncle Benjamin learned to kindle was a secret. He'd wanted Avi to kindle too one day. He knew interesting details about the Ember Society because *he was one of them.*

All except for one giant piece: The Ember Society wasn't real.

Then again, she never would have thought an invisible garden in the middle of the Tarnish could be real either. Her heart beat rapidly in her chest at the thought that maybe, just maybe, the Ember Society was real, and Avi's uncle and the garden were connected to it. The idea made her insides feel like she'd taken a sip of something bubbly, but she didn't want to interrupt Avi's story and kept the thought to herself for now.

"So why did your uncle stop coming to the garden?" Forte asked. "I've never seen him here."

"He died." Avi cast his gaze down. "It's my fault. Mameh didn't want me to live how he did, always having to move from place to place and hide his magic. The two of them had a big fight about it." He turned to Maeve. "You've lived in the tenements. You know how thin the walls are. One of our neighbors reported him to the Registry. We never found out who it was, but the Registry showed up the next afternoon and arrested him." Avi's voice got very small and no one moved. They were too wrapped up in his story. "He was gone for a year. Then one day we found him sleeping on our doorstep in the snow. He was so sick . . . Mameh says it was the magic that killed him."

They sat quietly, each lost in their own thoughts. His words stirred something deep within Maeve's soul. She thought about what Figgy had said in the library.

"I think you've got it backward," Maeve said gently. "The danger isn't in the magic, it's in a system that values making sure kids snuff their magic over teaching them how to control it. It wasn't the magic itself, it was the unfair laws that made his magic illegal. He was worthy of magic and so are you, Avi."

Avi was quiet, but Maeve could tell he was having a serious inner conversation. She was so busy watching his face that it took a moment for her to notice what was happening.

"Avi," she gasped. "Look what you're doing!"

Without realizing it, he had pressed his hands to the ground. Green sparks rolled from his fingers down into the soil and the garden was responding around him. Above their heads, white blossoms burst into bloom and swelled into apples. They would have taken months to grow normally, but within a matter of minutes, they were ripe and ready to eat.

"It's just like he showed me," Avi whispered. "I always wanted to be like him."

Maeve stood up and picked an apple. She held it out to

Avi and he took it and weighed it in his palm. For a moment, she thought he was going to toss it away and run back to his fire escape, but then he raised the apple and took a bite.

Juice dribbled down his chin and he closed his eyes. "You're right. It wasn't the magic that killed him. He wanted me to kindle too."

Another wonderful idea grew in Maeve's mind.

"What if you could?" she asked in a rush. "I could teach you what I'm learning at school. We could practice doing magic together until we know we can do it safely. Think of what your magic already did. We could kindle together and fix the garden." Maeve ran to her satchel and pulled out one half of her broken crystal. She offered it to him. "It's yours if you want it."

Avi looked toward the fire escape. "I love Mameh too much to go against her wishes, but if I could show her that it was safe, I might be able to change her mind."

Maeve's pulse picked up at the hope in his voice. "The garden will keep us safe."

Avi took the crystal in his hand and stepped into the sunlight. Slowly, he spun in a circle, drinking it in like a boy who had been too long parched with thirst and didn't know it. "I never thought it would be possible." His words were a whisper, a thanks, and a prayer. "We'll keep it a secret. No one can know until we're ready."

"We'll help too!" Cadenza announced on behalf of her siblings. Forte and Treble bounced around in circles. "We'll be magic together!"

Ignoring the ache in her side, Maeve threw her arms in the air. "I am magic and you are magic and the garden is magic!"

"I am magic!" Avi spread his arms wide. A flush of happiness blossomed across his cheeks and his smile was as bright as the sun. He twirled, shouting at the top of his lungs. "I'm going to kindle and magic will be mine forever and ever!"

Maeve whooped with joy and Avi grabbed her hands. Golden sparks rained from their fingertips, enriching the soil as they spun around and around. Long dormant roses and azaleas drank in the magic and unfurled their leaves and flowers. For the first time in as long as she could remember, Maeve welcomed the magic and didn't feel even a pinprick of fear.

She threw her head back and laughed as the garden flashed by in a blur of green and white and pink and red until the colors seeped into her heart and she knew she could re-create them with magic if she tried. As they spun, daisies sprouted around them in the grass, turning their yellow and white blooms to the sun as the garden celebrated with them.

FIFTEEN

Briolette

Izzy

Emma kept bugging her about the idea, so Izzy finally agreed to join her and Frances for lunch at Briolette on Friday a week later. She wasn't looking forward to recapping the Board meeting with Frances but, truthfully, she was excited to see the school.

Despite the rain, Izzy rode a series of streetcars downtown to the Gramercy Park neighborhood. She passed several sites that had Extinguished, looking like bad teeth in the city's smile. To distract herself, Izzy imagined strolling the halls of Briolette with her head held high, while behind her, the headmistress and teachers followed, begging her to attend now that they saw how classy and magical she truly was. She was so busy dreaming that she almost missed her stop.

Briolette was a huge stone building that dominated the entire block between Twenty-First and Twenty-Second

Streets. It was covered in gothic architecture features that Izzy couldn't identify but was sure Emma would know, like the pointed tops on the tall, narrow windows and brightly colored stained glass. The combined effect of the stone and colored glass brought to mind the word *established*.

"You're here!" Emma wore the green dress uniform of Briolette, belted at the waist. Her gold Briolette pin sparkled on her chest as she stood in the doorway and beckoned Izzy inside.

The main entrance hall was cavernous with an enormous gold chandelier. Emma took Izzy's umbrella and put it in a gold umbrella stand. "How are things at the school?"

Izzy shrugged. "Not bad. Figgy's got everyone walking around with books on their heads to practice good posture."

"I wonder how long it will take them to figure out they can stick the books to their head with magic." Emma winked. "Come on, the dining hall is this way."

Emma launched into tour-guide mode as they walked. "This is Headmistress Hall," she said as she swept her hand side to side to indicate the portraits lining the walls. Each depicted a woman with gray hair and a stern expression. Below each portrait, a golden plaque listed the name of the headmistress and the dates she'd run the school. The farther Izzy walked, the more old-fashioned the headmistresses' dresses and hairstyles got. This school was *old*.

Emma led her past an open set of double doors. "That's the Gold Ballroom."

"Your school has a *ballroom*?" Izzy said, eyeing the

sign above the door that said the interior had been a gift from the class of 1876. Inside, someone was playing the piano. Izzy peeked through the doors and gasped. The ballroom was like a flamboyant hatbox, decorated in white and gold stripes. To her even greater surprise, Beatrice Scorn was alone at the grand piano. Beatrice's eyebrows were knit in concentration as she stared at the sheet music in front of her. Izzy thought about what Beatrice had said at the meeting the other night. She hesitated in the doorway, torn between thanking Beatrice and continuing on unseen.

"Are you coming?" Emma called, and Izzy hurried after her. Down the hall, they entered a dining room that was at least four times the size of the one at the Manhattan School for Magic. Fifty or so well-cared-for, happy girls sat at round tables that dotted the room.

Every table appeared to be occupied and Izzy was wondering how they were going to find a seat when she spotted Frances Slight's long black hair and pale face. Their friend waved them over to the table nearest the windows on the far side of the room.

Emma greeted some of the other girls as they wove through the tables toward Frances. They smiled at her and peered curiously at Izzy. She didn't miss the way they whispered as soon as she passed.

"Finally! I'm starving," Frances said when they reached her. She stood up and hugged Izzy.

"Good to see you too," Izzy teased as they sat down.

Frances's amber bracelet flashed with magic and lit the

candle in the center of the table. "They'll be by to take our order in a minute," she explained to Izzy. "Speaking of starving, how's Figgy?"

Emma snorted with laughter. "I told Frances what Mrs. Nimby said on the tour."

Izzy sat up straight. She couldn't believe she'd forgotten. "Wait. Pearl Nimby goes here, doesn't she?"

Frances jerked her head toward the opposite wall. "She usually sits way over there with Beatrice. Don't worry."

Indeed, Izzy spotted a very familiar nose in the air at a table on the opposite side of the room. The girls sitting around Pearl had an air of polish to them that spoke of money.

"Well, I heard that Pearl and Beatrice aren't friends anymore." Emma began recapping the Board meeting for Frances. Izzy slouched in her chair, feeling suddenly uncomfortable about being there, uncomfortable about what had happened at the Board meeting, and uncomfortable in general because the chair was really hard. She knew Figgy had been wrong when he called her a leader. All she wanted to do was crawl under the table, or somehow enchant a trapdoor to appear under her feet so she could escape.

It took Izzy a moment to realize Emma was speaking to her. "What?"

"I said we should find Patchouli Rose while you're here and ask her about Figgy's missing cousin."

Right. Patchouli Rose was the Briolette house dragon. "Sure," Izzy agreed, but she was distracted when everyone at Pearl Nimby's table burst into laughter.

"Patchouli's been extra shy lately. I haven't seen her all week," Frances said.

"Is something burning?" Emma sniffed. "It smells like smoke."

"I hope it isn't lunch." Frances twisted around in her chair.

Emma had grown very still and pale. "Something's wrong," she said, and the fear in her voice pulled Izzy out of her thoughts.

Izzy glanced across the room toward Pearl's table, but her eyes went right past it to the line of red char creeping down the wall. It moved steadily toward the floor, leaving gray peeling wallpaper in its wake.

"Look at the wall!" Izzy gasped.

"*What in the stones?*" Emma cursed behind her.

The conversation in the dining hall died as the line of char expanded and more girls noticed. Izzy could hear a sizzling sound, like an egg hitting a hot pan.

"The school is on fire!" someone shouted, but Izzy knew it was worse than that.

When Miss Posterity's had burned down, there had been flames. Here there was only that ominous red line. What it left behind appeared to have been burned long ago. Izzy had never seen anything like it, but she recognized what was happening.

"It's Extinguishing. Everyone has to get out," Izzy said in a loud, confident voice that she hadn't known she possessed.

Students jumped to their feet, knocking over chairs in

their haste to flee. Izzy and her friends followed into the hallway. Most of the girls headed toward a door at the end of the hall, through which Izzy could see gray daylight.

"Come on." Emma tugged her by the arm toward the door.

Izzy glanced over her shoulder at Headmistress Hall and saw the line of char spreading down it. Her gaze caught on the double doors of the ballroom. Beatrice was in there, alone, and the Extinguishing was headed straight toward her. Izzy changed direction.

Izzy was halfway down the hall when she smelled the smoke. It wasn't the hot smoke of a fresh burn, but the cold, sneeze-inducing scent of a dirty fireplace. She ran through the doors of the ballroom and crashed into Beatrice, who was tugging the glossy black grand piano behind her. It was on wheels, but it was immediately clear this was a futile and slow-moving endeavor.

"Watch where you're going!" Beatrice's eyes widened when she saw who she'd run into.

"Izzy? How do you always turn up when my school is on fire?"

"Just lucky, I guess. Let's go." Izzy pointed at the door at the end of the hall.

Beatrice tugged her piano toward the hall again. Emma and Frances caught up to Izzy, their chests heaving. "It's spreading faster." Emma panted.

"Priorities, Beatrice!" Izzy hollered, already turning toward the hallway. "Just leave it!"

Fortunately, Emma was a quick thinker and could sear enchantments. With a flash of Emma's ring, the piano shrank to pocket-size. She picked it up and handed it to Beatrice. "Here. Now, let's go!"

They headed toward the exit at the end of the hall. Izzy had only gone a few steps when two red lines of char collided above them on the ceiling.

"Look out!" Frances shouted, and they dove out of the way. A mound of plaster and blackened boards fell, blocking their exit.

"Back the other way. Hurry!" Emma managed between coughs.

The piano clanged discordantly in Beatrice's hands as the four of them ran toward the front of the school. The thin red line of char pursued them as they raced down the hall as fast as their feet could carry them. They ducked as the gaslight wall sconces burst, spraying shattered glass.

"If we live through this, someone is going to explain what's happening," Beatrice shouted.

"Deal," Izzy shouted back.

They ran down the hallway, past the portraits of the Briolette headmistresses. Beatrice turned toward the front hall, but Izzy grabbed her arm and pulled her away just in time as the chandelier fell from the ceiling and crashed onto the tile. Stripped of magic, it became a twisted hulk of rusted metal.

"*Great gems*," Beatrice cursed, staring at the spot in the floor where she would have been.

"This way." Frances led them around the chandelier, casting glances at the ceiling as they went. The thick red line of char pursued them all the way out the door.

Rain pelted their faces as they raced out to the sidewalk. The building behind them had lost its luster. The magically stained glass windows were colorless, and the stone facade had turned dull and gray. Steam rose from where the rain hit the roof. Izzy leaned forward and rested her hands on her knees to catch her breath. They'd made it. They were safe—or so she thought.

"What is *she* doing here?" Pearl Nimby's indignant cry made Izzy's head jerk up.

A group of students were clustered together on the sidewalk across the street. Several were crying as they huddled under umbrellas and stared at the sizzling exterior of their school.

Pearl Nimby and her mother were at the front of the group. The daughter pointed at them.

"That's Izzy O'Donnell! Mother warned us about her!" Pearl shouted, loud enough for everyone on the block to hear.

Izzy saw the way the students and teachers clustered tighter together, as if trying to shield themselves against her.

"Oh no," Emma whispered.

Mrs. Nimby's face went red with fury as she looked between Izzy and the smoking ruins of Briolette. "She's stolen our magic!"

SIXTEEN

A Circle of Snuffing Buckets

Izzy

By the next morning, all of Manhattan magical society knew that Izzy O'Donnell had been at Briolette when it Extinguished.

Izzy awoke in the spare bed in Emma's room at the Harrises' apartment. Mr. Harris had been at work on the gallery when he heard about the calamity at Briolette. He'd sped uptown in his motorcar and arrived to find Emma in tears and a crowd of policemen and reporters trying to get Izzy to confess to the crime of Extinguishing Briolette. Mr. Harris whisked the girls away to the safety and quiet of the Harrises' apartment and sent a telegram to Miss Clementine to let them know they'd be staying there. Izzy had asked him to include a note to Maeve. There were so many things she wished she could say to her sister, but she couldn't find the words. In the end, her message said she'd be fine and told Maeve not to worry.

Izzy sat up in bed. She twisted her diamond bracelet around on her wrist. Would the Harrises still want her? What would Maeve think when she heard her sister stood accused of Extinguishing Briolette? The only answer was the rumble of Izzy's empty stomach. She got out of bed and headed down the hall, to where she could hear Emma and Mr. Harris having breakfast.

The Harrises lived in a luxury apartment building on Seventy-Second and Central Park West known as the Dakota. Emma had said something about the exterior being inspired by German Renaissance design, but Izzy just cared that it was huge and luxurious inside. Izzy had always admired how Mr. Harris had decorated it with furniture he'd acquired in his travels, but that morning, Izzy's thoughts kept traveling back to her family's apartment in the Tarnish. It had been small and in terrible shape with sparse and worn-out furniture, but there was always someone she loved close at hand whenever she needed a hug.

Izzy had just settled in with a plate of toast and eggs when there was a loud knock on the apartment front door. Emma left the breakfast table and returned with pink cheeks and Tom in tow.

"You'd better see this, Iz." Tom tossed a newspaper on the table, barely missing Izzy's toast.

"What's this?" Mr. Harris asked, leaning toward them, but the huge headline across the paper answered the question better than any of them could have.

"MAYOR SLIGHT'S MISTAKE," it read, with a photograph of Izzy in front of the Extinguished exterior of Briolette.

Izzy didn't say a word as she read the article. It was full of quotes from Pearl and Mrs. Nimby, not only about Briolette but also about Maeve and the prairie rose incident, which they somehow made sound like Izzy's fault too. The article painted Izzy as a thief, an unworthy girl stealing magic from its rightful users. There was a quote from Pearl Nimby speculating that Izzy was Extinguishing the magic out of famous buildings to use for herself.

"She knows that's not how magic works," Emma fumed.

Izzy picked up the paper and finished the article out loud for everyone to hear. "'Who knows what magical site O'Donnell will target next? The Park Avenue Armory? The Metropolitan Museum of Art? None of our magical buildings are safe. Izzy O'Donnell is a dangerous criminal who kindled illegally. She should be locked up and the Manhattan School shut down immediately.'" Izzy's shoulders slumped.

"It's one paper." Emma gave her arm a gentle squeeze.

Tom coughed. "Actually, they're all like that."

"I'll telegram my lawyers and have them issue a cease and desist." Mr. Harris pushed his chair away from the table like he meant to do it immediately.

"We need to go see Miss Clementine," Emma said decisively. "She'll know what to do."

Izzy had no idea how the headmistress could help, but going to her would take her one step closer to Maeve, so she agreed.

"I wish I could come with you, but the gallery opens on Thursday and I have so much left to do. I can have my driver drop you off on the way," Mr. Harris said. His brow was creased with worry. Emma patted his hand and assured him that they'd be fine, but a ride would certainly help.

Tom looked from Emma to Izzy. "I should get back to selling papers, but I can spare a few minutes to come with you. I read the other articles, so maybe I can help."

"Great. You can fill us in on the other terrible things they're saying about me." Izzy pushed her plate away. "Let's go. I can't eat anyway."

It was a tight fit in the motorcar with the four of them, the chauffeur, and Mr. Harris's chair, but Izzy took comfort from their closeness. When they pulled up in front of the school, Emma peered out the window and gasped.

"Keep driving," she said quickly to the chauffeur and pressed herself flat against the seat.

"What is it?" Izzy asked, but the sound of angry voices outside answered her question.

"Reporters." Tom nodded like he'd expected it.

"We'll go to the kitchen entrance. Most magical people wouldn't think to use a servant's entrance," Emma announced, and fortunately, she proved to be right.

They arrived as Cook and three of the students were cleaning up from breakfast. Cook immediately rushed to Izzy and smooshed her into a hug. When she let go, Izzy said hello to the students and then headed to Miss Clementine's office with Emma and Tom.

They found the headmistress surrounded by a pile of newspapers and Figgy Pudding, who looked like he hadn't slept a wink.

Miss Clementine gave the three of them a hug and Izzy thought she might have had more hugs this morning than she'd had in the past few months combined. But none of them had been the hug she was craving.

"Is it as bad out there as it seems from in here?" Miss Clementine asked.

"Worse, probably." Izzy sat down on the hearth and stroked Figgy's back.

He put his chin on her knee and gazed at her with big yellow eyes. "I'm glad you're all right, Isabelle."

Tom shoved his hands in his pockets and his shoulders rose toward his ears. "The whole city's abuzz about what happened at Briolette, and from what Em's told me, most of them are getting it wrong. There's a lot of anger being directed at MSM." The corner of his mouth quirked up. "Good day for selling papers, though." He ducked his head to avoid Emma's frown. "Sorry, but it's true."

Emma finished flipping through the papers. "Maybe we should talk to the reporters. We could tell them what happened and—"

Miss Clementine cut her off with a wave of her hand. "Absolutely not. You will leave those vultures to me." She turned to Tom. "No offense."

He shrugged. "It's warranted in this situation."

Miss Clementine grimaced at the newspapers. "We'll let you get back to work now, Tom. And Tom?" Miss Clementine called, as he paused on his way to the door. "Perhaps it's best if you use the back door for now, not only to avoid the reporters."

Izzy was about to ask what she meant, but Tom nodded like he understood and left. "Why else should he use the back door?" she asked again after the door closed behind him.

Miss Clementine folded her hands on her desk. "I anticipate there will be more threats to the school or our students. Figgy and I have been busy taking precautions this morning."

Izzy's brain caught on the word *threats*, but Emma heard something else.

"*More* threats? What was the first one?" she demanded.

Miss Clementine hesitated before she spoke. "I tell you this not to alarm you, but to impress upon you the severity of the situation." She reached into her desk drawer and pulled out two round garden stones. "Someone threw these through the drawing room window this morning."

The world felt fuzzy as Izzy stared at the stones. Someone had thrown rocks through the window of a children's school. It shifted the way she understood the world, and she knew she would never view it the same way again. She stared at the stones, unable to find her voice.

Figgy's whiskers bristled with indignation. "This is pure cowardice, I tell you."

"I've contacted the police. They're investigating." Miss Clementine's lips pressed in a dissatisfied way that implied she thought it was not nearly enough.

The door to Miss Clementine's study opened and Izzy finally saw the person she most wanted to hug. Maeve had dark circles under her eyes and her hair was a tangled mess, but Izzy had never been happier to see her sister.

"Izzy? I was so worried about you." Maeve's voice caught.

It was everything Izzy needed.

"Maeve!" Izzy cried, spreading her arms wide and rushing to engulf her sister.

Maeve let out a surprised *oof*, but then flung her arms around Izzy as well. "They're saying terrible things, but I know they're lies."

Izzy pulled back to see her. She hadn't even known that was her worst fear, that Maeve would believe the terrible things they said about her, until she heard from her sister's lips that it wasn't the case. A terrible knot of worry in her gut relaxed. She sank down into the nearest chair, exhausted, but she kept hold of Maeve's hand. "What are we going to do?"

"Don't worry about those people." Maeve sat down next to her and squeezed Izzy's hand. Her sleeve had slid up, revealing a bare wrist, but Izzy barely thought about the bracelet's absence. She was just glad that Maeve was there. "We don't need anybody else. We can take care of each other."

Emma coughed awkwardly and sat on the chair opposite them. To do so, she moved a flame-shaped pillow out of her way. Above a teardrop flame embroidered in yellow, red, and blue, the stitching read *When things get dark, we must shine brighter.*

"Is this new?" Emma asked.

Miss Clementine blushed. "Yes, it was a gift from your father. Apparently, he liked my phrasing." She cleared her throat. "I suppose I was right, though. For now, we stay inside, take what precautions we can, and carry on, agreed?" Miss Clementine sat behind her desk. "Izzy and Maeve, that means you're to head to your studies. Emma, don't you need to get to school?"

Emma coughed. "It's Saturday, Miss Clementine."

"Oh. Right." The headmistress sat down at her desk and massaged her temples.

"I thought I could stay with Izzy—" Emma began.

"You don't have to. She's my sister," Maeve cut her off.

"Well, she's my friend," Emma countered.

Izzy looked between them. "We could all stay together?"

Miss Clementine didn't seem to notice the tension. "Emma, you're welcome to remain here. Perhaps you could help Izzy with her searing homework." She arranged the newspapers into a pile. "Please let me know if you decide to go back to your family's apartment at any point. To be safe, no one is to leave the school without my permission until further notice."

Maeve's hand went slack in Izzy's. "But . . ."

Izzy was surprised. "Do you have somewhere you need to go?"

For a moment, it seemed like Maeve was going to say something, but then a dark cloud passed over her face and she shook her head. "Nothing. It's nothing."

"Promise me you won't go looking for any more trouble," Miss Clementine said.

The three girls exchanged a glance. "We promise," they said.

There was no need to go looking for trouble, however, because trouble was already coming for them. The next morning, Miss Clementine's prediction of more threats came true.

All day, well-dressed protesters marched up and down in front of the school gate. They carried signs that read NIMBY WAS RIGHT, STOP THE MAGIC THIEF, and HANDS OFF MY MAGIC, and didn't leave the sidewalk until dusk. Izzy tried to follow Miss Clementine's admonishment to shine brightly, but it was hard to read the instructions for searing muffins into earmuffs when someone outside kept shouting, "Keep what's left of magic in the right hands" to enthusiastic applause—which only made her want those earmuffs even more.

It grew worse from there. On Monday morning, the school woke to find the entire building encircled by snuffing buckets. An eerie mist rose from the magically warmed water. It fogged up the windows of the school. The buckets had one benefit, which was that they drove away the reporters and protesters. Even kindled adults found them creepy.

Mr. Harris picked up Emma to help him with a few final touches for the gallery. Whenever Izzy saw her sister, Maeve was staring out a window or wandering the halls with a lost expression on her face. It only made Izzy feel worse. Maeve was clearly upset and worried by this whole situation. Izzy had never meant to cause her sister pain.

That afternoon, Zuzanna's parents arrived to take her home. They had read the stories about Izzy and didn't want to be connected to the school anymore. "We've applied to Glint Academy, where she'll be safe," her mother explained as she marched her daughter out of the school. Zuzanna's roommate, Felicity, cried in the foyer until Cook invited her into the kitchen for a restorative cup of tea.

"What did Zuzanna's mother mean about Glint Academy being safe?" Izzy asked Miss Clementine later that evening when she found the headmistress alone in her office.

Miss Clementine massaged her temples with her fingers. "Apparently, Glint Academy sent letters to the parents of our students, urging them to consider transferring. Mrs. Sabetti alerted me after she received one about Antonia."

Under normal circumstances, Izzy might have been furious, but now she felt even more gutted. "Aren't people trying to shut down Glint Academy too?" she asked, but she already guessed the answer and wasn't surprised when Miss Clementine shook her head. "It's because of me, isn't it?"

"It's possible, but truthfully, I don't know what it is," Miss Clementine said. "I'm sorry, Izzy."

At that point, Izzy went up to her room and pulled the covers over her head. She felt like she was watching everything she'd built unravel like an unseared enchantment.

Claws tapped across the floorboards and then something soft but heavy draped itself across her shins. "This is not the time for sulking, Isabelle."

"I don't see what else there is to do." The covers muffled Izzy's reply. Claws pricked her skin and she squawked in protest.

"I have an idea," Figgy said.

Izzy pushed the covers down and pried Figgy's paws from her blanket. "About how best to annoy me?"

"Stop thinking about yourself for a few moments." Figgy's tail tapped the covers with impatience. "It's about the Extinguishings. There's something very curious in a book I'm reading called *Magical Pests and Pestilence*—yes, I've made it to the home maintenance section out of sheer desperation. But there's something about the magic that makes me think of mice."

"Figgy, we don't have any mice here." Izzy started to lean back and pull the covers over her head again.

"Precisely." Figgy tapped his tail with agitation. "House dragons are charged with preventing mice from eating the magic out of the buildings that we protect. Our powers have evolved specifically for it. This feels like mice, but also distinctly not. I'd almost say it was—"

Izzy wasn't in the mood to listen to him pontificating. "No one knows what's happening, Figgy. I wish we did. Then we could prove it's not me." Izzy draped an arm over her eyes. She couldn't imagine the Nimbys taking back their words or the papers retracting the articles. "Not that it would help. They're never going to accept me, are they? I'll never fit in."

Figgy nudged her arm with his nose. "I'm not sure which *they* you're referring to," Figgy said. "But in case you hadn't noticed, there's a whole house full of people downstairs that care about you. Get up, Isabelle, and learn to use your voice."

Izzy felt his weight leave the bed and the soft *thump* of his paws hitting the floor. She sat up. "What's that supposed to mean?" She looked around the room. "Figgy? Where'd you go?" But the only answer was the tap of Figgy's nails on the floorboards as he hurried back to the library.

SEVENTEEN

An Unexpected Ally

Maeve

On Monday evening, Miss Clementine and Figgy put anti-break-in enchantments on the school's windows and doors. They would open only with Miss Clementine's permission or in the case of an emergency.

Maeve roamed the school like a sheep in a too-small pen. The kits and Avi had been expecting her this weekend and would surely be worried by now. The thought of the kits feeling abandoned all over again weighed heavily on her heart. She'd promised to teach Avi magic and then she'd disappeared. She had to get down to the garden.

Maeve was pacing past the kitchen door when she heard a loud "Psst. Come here."

She was confused to find Cook gesturing at her from inside the kitchen. Maeve had never really spoken to her outside of her kitchen rotation.

Curious, Maeve went into the kitchen. Even curiouser, Cook shut the door behind her. She put her hands on her hips and faced Maeve.

"I can't stand watching you pace the halls anymore. If you want my help, you're going to have to tell me who you've been feeding."

Maeve froze. She felt like she was standing in the rear pen again, trapped and waiting for the bull to charge.

Cook sat down on one of the tall stools next to the counter. "You think I didn't notice food going missing from the kitchen every weekend, not to mention my entire store of jerky? For a while, I thought I was being absentminded or misplacing it. Then I hid down here last week to see what was happening. Imagine my surprise."

"Um," Maeve said, and eyed the door, wondering if she could make a break for it.

Cook pointed at the stool next to her. "If you leave, I'm going straight to Miss Clementine. Sit."

Maeve sat down. There was a steaming pot of tea waiting on the counter.

Cook poured the tea and handed her a cup. "Now, tell me what's been going on."

Maeve stared into her cup and said nothing.

"I'm pretty good at keeping secrets, you know," Cook said. "I knew your sister and Emma were running around trying to get their magic last year and I never said a word." She inclined her head toward the back of the kitchen. "I also have the only door in the school that doesn't require Miss Clementine's permission to open, though it still needs mine."

Maeve recognized the offer in her words. She also recognized that she was out of options. Still she hesitated. "I can't tell you. I have to do this on my own. I want to be brave like Izzy."

Cook sipped her tea and set it back down. "You know," she said, "sometimes the bravest thing to do is to ask for help."

Maeve stared at her. She'd never thought about it that way before. Maybe being brave didn't necessarily mean doing things on her own. Maybe it meant facing her fears in whatever form they took.

"I'm trying to find a missing house dragon," Maeve admitted. "The one from the opera house. I need to leave the school to locate her."

Cook leaned in. "And why do you need to steal my chicken and jerky to do that?"

"I'm sorry." Maeve was embarrassed. She'd felt so right about helping the kits, she hadn't stopped to think that she was stealing.

Cook took off her spectacles and wiped them on her apron. "It seems that we have two options here. You tell me the whole truth, or I tell Miss Clementine. It's your choice."

The pressure of the secret had been building up inside Maeve for weeks now. She opened her mouth and the story came shooting out like a cork from a bottle. By the time Maeve finished, her untouched cup of tea had gone cold. "So you see why I have to help them," she said.

Cook rested her elbow on the counter and studied Maeve like she was seeing her for the first time. "You haven't told anyone else? Not even your sister?"

Maeve shook her head.

"That is a very heavy burden to carry alone." Cook stood and walked over to the icebox. "What can I send them? Do they like pork chops?"

Maeve nearly fell off her stool. "You're not going to tell on me?"

Cook opened the door of the icebox and peered in. "I gave you a choice and I'll honor it, though I think you should tell the headmistress yourself." She pulled out a bowl covered by a towel. "I think you should tell your sister too."

"She's got enough to worry about." Maeve swirled the tea in her cup and took a sip, letting the bitter taste wash over her tongue.

Cook snorted. "You O'Donnells are two of the stubbornest girls I've ever met, and thank goodness for that. The world needs stubborn dreamers to get things done." She shut the door of the icebox. "I'll tie everything up in a red kerchief for you to take tomorrow. Use the back door and return before lunch or I won't be able to cover for you."

Maeve leaped up. She'd expected punishment, not permission, and she certainly hadn't expected Cook to look out for her. "Thank you, thank you, thank you." Before she knew what she was doing, she threw her arms around Cook's waist and hugged her. The scratch of Cook's cotton apron on her cheek reminded her of hugging Mam.

Cook patted her back. "Thanks, dearie. Now, run along. I've got work to do."

Maeve left the kitchen with a lightness in her step. It felt good to have an ally, albeit an unexpected one. She started up the steps to her room. Tomorrow might be her only chance to leave the school for a while. She'd have to make the most of it.

The next morning, long before anyone else was awake, Maeve tiptoed out of her bedroom. She nearly tripped over a rectangular package wrapped in brown paper lying in front of the door with *Maeve* scrawled in unfamiliar handwriting. Inside, she found a beautiful, brand-new illustrated guide to home gardening. When she opened the cover, a note on cream-colored stationery fell out.

Maeve, I hope this helps. Please return it to the library when you're done so that others may use it too.—Emma

Maeve smiled. She'd forgotten about Emma's promise to locate a book for her, but apparently, Emma hadn't. Then she realized she was smiling about something Emma had done and shut the book. It was still useful, though, so she put it in her satchel alongside *Magical Manhattan* and headed downstairs.

In the kitchen she found the pork chops in the icebox. They were tied in a red handkerchief, as Cook had said they'd be. Cook came in as Maeve headed for the door. "Back before lunch, remember? Don't make me regret this." She tossed Maeve a gray shawl. "And cover that recognizable hair of yours."

Maeve wrapped the shawl around her head as she went out the door. It smelled like freshly baked bread.

When she arrived at the garden, Treble ran toward Maeve so fast he crashed into her shins. "We thought you'd gone away forever!"

Cadenza and Forte rubbed around Maeve's ankles and purred while little puffs of steam rose from their ears.

Maeve gave them each a kiss on the forehead. "I missed you so much, but I wasn't allowed to leave the school. You must be so hungry."

The kits shook their heads. "Avi took care of us," Treble said.

Avi stood up and brushed off his hands. Maeve hadn't noticed him next to a small mountain of bean sprouts. A half-built trellis lay at his feet. "I thought maybe the Registry had got you for trying to help me."

"I didn't mean to make you worry." Maeve pulled the pork chops and the books out of her satchel while she told them about the snuffing buckets and threats. "This might be the last time I can get out for a while," she finished.

It was as if the sun had shifted behind a cloud and everything darkened.

"First Mother leaves, then you." Treble looked away.

"I'll come back as soon as I can," Maeve promised, but the kits didn't appear convinced. She wished there was a way to show them that she truly meant it. "Let's have some fun while I'm still here." She turned to Avi and grinned. "Want to do some magic?"

Avi shuffled his foot against the grass. "I tried a little bit while you were gone." He indicated the huge tangle of bean sprouts he'd been working on. "I'm sorry it's such a mess. I won't do it again."

Maeve bent down to inspect the green shoots. Little white flowers promised many beans to come soon. She used to think making mistakes was dangerous, but the garden had helped her understand that mistakes sometimes brought wonderful things. Finding the garden in and of itself had been a mistake that she felt lucky to have made, and if she hadn't made the mistake with the prairie roses, she might never have discovered how to make the garden grow.

"Avi, this is amazing! Maybe you went a little overboard, but you'll get better at it if you keep trying." Maeve stood up. "Come on, let's do some more."

Avi hung back as Maeve knelt next to the carrots. She touched their leafy green tops with one hand and gripped her half crystal with the other. The carrots grew until orange tops poked up from the soil. Her enthusiasm was too contagious for Avi to resist. He started on the other end of the row of vegetables and worked toward her. They laughed and whooped whenever one of them used a little too much magic and the plants erupted.

When they were done, they sat down on the green grass to admire their bounty.

"What are we going to do with this many vegetables?" Avi hugged his knees to his chest.

"Look what we found!" Treble trotted up behind them.

Maeve twisted around to see Forte with a corner of *Magical Manhattan* gripped in his teeth. He dragged it across the ground toward her. It was open to her bookmark.

Avi craned his neck to read the label on the map. "The Bezel Opera House?"

"It's a map of our home!" Forte announced when he released the book.

Avi gasped. "Why didn't any of you mention this before? Uncle Benjamin worked at the Opera House as a stagehand for a couple of years. He said it was the best job he ever had."

Everyone stilled as his words sank in.

"He must have told Mother about the garden. He's how she knew it was here," Cadenza guessed.

Avi sat down and the kits piled into his lap. "He only told his closest friends about the garden. She must have been one of them."

Treble put a paw on his knee. "We can be friends too."

"I'd like that. I don't have many friends." Avi ran a hand down Treble's back and the kit purred.

Maeve sat back on her heels. This was the missing piece of the puzzle. If Aria had brought her kits to her old friend's garden, she must have known something bad was about to happen. Maeve had to hope that Figgy was right about Aria leaving a clue in their cave. But that meant she'd have to go inside the Extinguished Opera House like she'd been dreading for so long.

"It has to be today. I may not be able to leave the school again for a while." Maeve didn't realize she'd spoken out loud until she saw her friends staring at her.

"You're leaving, aren't you?" Treble asked. His ears drooped.

"I have to—" Maeve started.

"You probably want your sparkly bracelet back now, don't you?" Forte hung his head low.

Maeve had almost forgotten that they still had it. She saw her opportunity to prove her commitment to them. "Why don't you hold on to it until I get back?"

The kits' ears flicked back and forth in surprise and delight.

"If you insist," Cadenza said.

"Until you're back," Forte agreed.

"Which will be soon," Treble added. Maeve thought he was going to say something about food, but he surprised her. "Otherwise, we'll miss you too much."

Maeve gave them each another kiss between the ears and they purred. Then she worked up her courage. "I'm going to the opera house now. I'm not even sure I'll be able to get inside, but this may be my last opportunity to look for your mother for a while. I know you don't want to tell me where your cave is—"

Cadenza held up a paw, cutting her off. "Maeve, you've been showing up for us day after day for two months now. You've kept every promise. We've discussed it and, with Mother gone, you're the closest thing we have to family right now."

"We trust you," Forte added.

Treble nuzzled her shin. "We love you. And we know you'll respect our treasure."

"You think of me as family?" Maeve swallowed the lump in her throat. "I love you all too."

Perhaps because Maeve had been shuttled around so much in Omaha, she'd never thought she'd find that kind of love outside of her blood family. Just like magic, she hadn't thought she was worthy of it. She had thought she was better off alone, but having her friends by her side made her feel braver and better.

Cadenza lifted up on her hind paws. "Pick me up and I'll whisker the location of our cave."

Maeve thought the kit had meant *whisper*, so when she picked her up, she held Cadenza's face near her ear. To her surprise, Cadenza brushed her whiskers against Maeve's cheek. Maeve had a sudden vision of rows of maroon velvet seats facing a stage. A gold curtain framed the front of the stage, and colorful scenery hung in the fly space above. The vision turned toward the wings and she saw a tiny dark hole below some rigging.

Whiskering indeed.

"Thank you for your trust," she said, putting Cadenza back on the grass. Maeve picked up *Magical Manhattan* and found the area Cadenza had just showed her on the map. She brushed her fingers against where Cadenza's whiskers had touched her cheek. House dragons really were amazing creatures.

Avi patted Treble's back. "I'll look after them, Maeve. They won't go hungry."

Maeve promised three more times to come back as soon as she could before the kits were content to let her go. As she pushed aside the loose board, she took a last look at the garden.

She hoped that going to the opera house wouldn't be a mistake. But if it turned out to be one, she hoped it was one worth making.

EIGHTEEN
The Bezel Opera House

Maeve

The six-story Bezel Opera House loomed like a ghost on Thirty-Ninth Street and Broadway. Its brick facade had gone ash gray during the Exing, and the domed windows stared like empty eyes. The front doors bore heavy padlocks and a printed order from the city council warning people to stay away, which the pedestrians passing by seemed happy to do. Even the motorcars seemed to speed up when they passed through the shadow the building cast across Broadway.

Maeve stopped in front of the bookstore across the street to get her bearings. The shawl Cook had given her slipped off her head and she pushed it back up. It was already quarter to eleven and the streets of Manhattan were busy. She would have to move quickly if she was going to make it back to the school before lunch and meet Cook's deadline.

After a quick consultation of the floor plan in *Magical Manhattan*, she headed for the stage door around the back. She glanced over her shoulder to make sure no one was watching and then ducked beneath a heavy chain with a sign that read KEEP OUT. Maeve walked to a nondescript black door and, to her surprise, it swung open when she pulled on the handle.

The interior of the opera house smelled like a fireplace. Not a warm, inviting fireplace, but a cold, unlit one with ashes that tickled her nose and threatened to make her sneeze. It was dark and she wished she could light a flame in her palm like she'd seen Izzy and Emma do. She tried and nothing happened. Her magic felt strange here, but familiar too, like it had in the garden before she'd brought it back to life.

The heavy gold curtain she'd seen in Cadenza's whiskering hung in gray tatters. Beyond the stage, she saw lumps of muslin and wood that had once been luxurious maroon velvet seats.

Maeve froze when she thought she heard the chain outside rattling. Her heart pounded, but when no one appeared, she let herself relax. She walked across the empty stage, feeling both very large and very small at the same time.

A board creaked behind her and Maeve spun around. "Is someone there?" And then, after a thought, she added, "Aria, is that you?"

No one answered. The hairs on the back of her neck prickled.

She tiptoed into the wings and found herself next to a

wall of ropes. The rigging went way up into the fly space, where they connected to the scenery hanging above. Even the scenery was gray and colorless, so different from what she'd seen in Cadenza's whiskering. How wondrous this place must have been before it Extinguished. Maeve hated whoever was causing the Extinguishings.

Out in the audience, someone sneezed.

Maeve stiffened. There *was* someone else here. She thought she could smell the grassy scent of the bull. *Hurry,* she told herself. *Find the cave and get out.*

Using what she'd seen in the whiskering, she picked her way through the ropes and debris to the back corner of the stage-left wings. Behind the ropes, she spotted a tiny tunnel, hidden from sight and just big enough for a small girl—or a family of house dragons.

Her heart beat an excited patter. She'd found it! The entrance was a tight fit and she had to leave her satchel hidden behind some of the ropes at the entrance. When she crawled inside, it was so dark she could barely see her hand in front of her face. There had to be some form of light in here.

Maeve thought about the whiskering. House dragon magic was strange, but there was a logic to it. It gave her an idea.

Feeling rather silly, Maeve made a purring noise. The walls around her brightened until she could see that the tunnel widened a few feet in front of her. She purred again with more confidence and crawled forward. Now she could clearly see a small space filled with soft pillows. She looked around, expecting to find diamonds or rubies. Where was the treasure?

Four iridescent scales hung in a row on the far wall. They were predominantly shades of green. Still purring, Maeve crept closer to look and discovered each scale was labeled with a name. The largest read *Aria* and the names of the kits she'd grown to love followed. On the floor below, there was a pile of mementos of a cozy family life: scraps of paper with drawings on them, well-worn toy birds, and clumps of fur. Two photographs had been placed against the wall with loving care. One was of a young Aria balancing in rafters above the stage. The other showed the tiny kits snuggled around their mother on one of the velvet audience seats.

Maeve smiled wistfully at the pile. No wonder house dragons didn't let anyone besides family into their caves. Their treasure wasn't gems or riches. It was each other.

She'd promised the kits she wouldn't touch their treasure and she didn't. Maeve turned around to look for a clue. It was lucky she was small because the cave was small too.

There was nothing besides dust under the first two pillows she tried, but then she lifted the biggest one and found two paper objects underneath. One was a program for an opera called *Les Pierres Fameuses* and the other was a newspaper article announcing the opening of the Glint Art Gallery. *Designed by popular magitect George Harris* had been circled and *Figgy Pudding* had been scrawled across the top in the same writing as the names under the scales on the wall. Maeve had no idea what to make of either of these objects. She'd been hoping the clue would be something obvious, like a map.

She checked under the rest of the pillows but only found dust and ash. Maeve glanced one last time at the family photographs before she crawled out of the cave. She felt disappointed. An opera program and a newspaper article didn't get her any closer to finding Aria.

At the entrance to the cave, Maeve froze. She'd forgotten she wasn't the only one there. A pair of boots stood directly in front of her. Very familiar boots.

"What are you doing here?" Emma Harris put her hands on her hips.

Maeve's mouth dropped open. "Me? What are *you* doing here?"

"Following you, of course." Emma gestured at the ropes. "I knew something was going on with you, but I had no idea it was this big."

Maeve realized she was still on her hands and knees. She tucked the article and program into her waiting satchel and pushed herself up to standing. "I didn't cause the Extinguishing, if that's what you're thinking."

Emma blinked at her. "Why would I think that?"

Maeve crossed her arms. "Because rich people keep saying my magic is dangerous and you're, well . . ." She gestured at Emma's fancy clothes and perfectly styled hair.

"Oh." To her surprise, Emma's expression softened. "I don't think your magic is dangerous. I think it's different and I've never seen anything like it, but it's not inherently dangerous. Besides, you haven't kindled. Any magic you do doesn't last."

Maeve remained unconvinced. "But what about plants? When I do magic with them, they keep growing. You saw what happened with the prairie roses." A part of her wanted to scare Emma off. To send her fleeing away from Maeve's dangerous magic. Maybe then she'd leave Maeve and Izzy alone. But a part of her wanted to impress Emma too.

Emma looked thoughtful. "Maybe for you, plants are like fire. You know how if you light a flame magically and it spreads, whatever you're burning doesn't stop when the magic does. Figgy says there used to be many different paths and types of magic, but people have forgotten them." Emma's eyes lit up. "That's why you were asking for books about gardening! I think I'm starting to understand everything now. You're here about the house dragon, aren't you?"

Maeve was flabbergasted. How could Emma possibly know that? She crossed her arms and started to make up an excuse. "The reward—"

But Emma was on to her. "We both know it isn't about the kits. Frankly, I suspect you've already found them. Why are you searching for Aria, Maeve?"

Maeve reeled. "Why do you think I've already found the kits?"

Emma ticked a list off on her fingers. "You're gone several days a week for hours at a time and no one knows where you go. I overheard Cook asking Miss Clementine whether she'd been breaking into her jerky—and I know from Figgy how much house dragons love jerky. For the past few weeks, you've had a sunburn on the back of your neck. And then there's the tiny detail that you're not supposed to be out of the school right now."

Maeve put a hand to the back of her neck. She hadn't thought anyone had noticed, let alone put everything together. "Are you going to report me?"

Emma shook her head. "I want to help you. I figure if you've risked leaving the school, it must be important."

"I work better alone, thanks." Maeve took a step backward and bumped into the ropes.

Emma sighed. "You and your sister are so stubborn." She gestured toward the entrance to the theater. "After Briolette, Papa tried to convince Izzy to come stay at our apartment indefinitely, but she wouldn't leave MSM while you're there. Which, by the way, how did you get out?"

Maeve felt a pang of surprise. She hadn't known that about Izzy. It made her feel warm and happy, but it also bothered her that, yet again, Emma knew things about Izzy that she didn't.

"How did you know I would be here?" she asked, hoping to distract from Emma's question so she wouldn't have to reveal that Cook was helping her.

It worked.

"I didn't. I was coming out of the bookstore when I spotted you. Then I saw where you were headed and followed you. Tell me about looking for Aria. Maybe I can help you," Emma coaxed.

Maeve felt like an animal backed up against the wall, so she lashed out.

"Why? So you can steal credit for it like you want to steal my sister?" Maeve walked away toward the audience chamber.

Emma hurried after her. "What do you mean? I'm not trying to steal your sister."

"Yes, you are." Maeve refused to look at her. She didn't want Emma to see her upset. "Izzy tells you everything first. You two are so close, you're practically sisters. You kindled together and you're basically perfect. How am I supposed to compete with that?" As she spoke, Maeve's shoulders got closer and closer to her ears and her hands rose in fists.

"Trust me, I'm far from perfect," Emma protested.

"Maybe not, but you're perfect for Izzy and her new life." Maeve swallowed. "Your dad is going to adopt her and she won't even remember her not-good-enough sister anymore."

Her words echoed around the empty theater. *Not good enough, not good enough.*

"Oh, I see." Emma stilled. "Maeve, has anyone told you the story of why your sister kindled?"

Maeve snorted. "At least a hundred times." Why was Emma bringing this up now? "You two were trapped in the attic and–"

"Not *how*. *Why*," Emma corrected.

Maeve stopped talking.

"Come here." Emma led her out into the audience chamber. She patted one of the muslin lumps to test it and a cloud of gray ash rose in the air.

"If you channel some magic into it, you might be able to restore it," Maeve suggested.

"But magical damage can't be repaired with magic." Emma gave her a strange look.

Maeve shrugged. "You don't have to believe me."

Emma's brow furrowed, but then her ruby ring flashed with magic. A rich red spread from her fingertips, inflating the chair like a balloon. Before her eyes, the ruined muslin turned to rich velvet.

Emma's eyes widened. "I want to ask you how you knew that, but first I want to tell you about your sister." She quickly magicked a second seat for Maeve, leaving a buffer seat between them, which Maeve appreciated. "When I first met Izzy, she was desperate to learn magic. I knew she wanted to kindle and get out of town, but I didn't realize it was a person she wanted to get to, not a place." Emma sat down. "She wanted to find you, Maeve. You're the whole reason that Izzy wanted her magic in the first place."

"Me?" Maeve sat down hard on the velvet seat and the springs squeaked in protest.

"Yes, you. She wanted to build the school so you could come here and learn magic too. She's trying so hard to carve out a place and a path for you. Sometimes I think she's being too hard on herself, but the point I'm trying to make is that everything she's doing is for you."

Maeve felt like someone had stepped on her stomach. "I thought she wanted me to be more like you."

"Like me?" Emma blinked in surprise. "Maeve, your sister thinks so highly of you. She loves you very much."

"Why doesn't she just say so, then?"

Emma shrugged. "Since when have we known Izzy to be good at talking about her feelings?"

Why were there tears in Maeve's eyes? She wiped them away, not wanting to cry in front of Emma. "I want her to be proud of me, you know? That's why I've been trying to do things on my own. Like how she kindled."

Emma shook her head. "Izzy didn't do that on her own. First of all, she had me. We could never have kindled without Frances and Tom, or even the kids who helped us in the Tarnish that day we went to get the flints."

It was a shock like plunging into cold water, but there was a relief in it too. "The papers make it sound like she did it on her own."

"I know." Emma rolled her eyes. "You don't have to do everything on your own, Maeve. And you don't have to be exactly like Izzy, either. The way I see it, you're both pretty great, just as you are."

"Really?" Maeve's shoulders relaxed away from her ears.

"Really," Emma said.

They smiled at each other. Maeve realized it might be the first time the two of them had shared a genuine smile. She thought again about the house dragons' treasure and how she wanted to mend things with Izzy. It was time to stop longing to be a part of Izzy's new life while also pushing it away. Izzy loved her, and Maeve made up her mind to treasure that love above all else.

Maeve sighed heavily.

"What?" Emma asked.

"I can see why Izzy likes you," she admitted.

Emma laughed. "Thanks." She took a deep breath. "If you won't let me help you, let her. But don't keep coming to places like this. It's creepy. I keep feeling like a mouse is going to run over my shoe or something."

Maeve jumped like Emma had shocked her. "Mice?"

"I know. I dislike them almost as much as Figgy does."

The light of understanding that flashed in Maeve's mind felt like the brightest thing in the burned-out room. "You would expect there to be mice in a place like this, especially once it's been abandoned, but I haven't seen a single one."

"Odd, without a house dragon," Emma added. She gasped.

"What is it?" Maeve asked. "Do you think Aria's still here?"

"No, but her magic might be." Emma pointed at their velvet seats. "How did you know how to reverse the Extinguishing?"

Maeve made a choice. Izzy trusted Emma. Maeve trusted Izzy, so she would trust Emma too. "The kits taught me. I found them two months ago, even before I knew there was a reward. I'm trying to help them find their mother."

"I thought as much." Emma nodded distractedly, like she'd heard the information that she needed. She stared at the velvet cushions. "Magical damage can't be repaired by magic . . . unless it wasn't *human* magic that caused it."

"Are you saying it's—"

"House dragon magic," they said together.

The two girls looked at each other in matching horror and wonder.

"It could be," Emma said.

Maeve shivered. "But how? And why?"

"I have no idea, but I have a feeling that Aria is connected to it." Emma stood up and brushed her skirt off, though Maeve's tip had worked and there was no ash on it. "Did you find what you needed here?"

Maeve thought about it. "I found their cave and something with Figgy's name on it. Do you think Figgy's involved in the Extinguishings? Can we trust him?"

"I would trust Figgy with my life, and in fact, I have," Emma said, very seriously. "Would you be willing to show him what you've found? I'd be happy to talk to him with you, if you'd like." A smile spread across her face. "I want to see the look on his face when you tell him that you've found the kits."

For a moment, Maeve hesitated. But then she remembered how she'd felt when she'd talked to Cook. Asking for help was a different kind of being strong, not a lesser one.

Maeve picked up her satchel. "Let's go now."

The girls headed to the stage and snuck out the back door, the way they'd come in. There was an ease between them that hadn't existed before, a friendship sparked in a place that thought it had seen the last of magic.

NINETEEN
House Dragon Magic

Maeve

They rode back to the school together in the Harrises' car, which was still waiting for Emma outside the bookstore. Maeve felt awkward when the chauffeur held the door open for her, but once inside, she forgot her discomfort. She had never been inside a motorcar before and found it wonderfully thrilling to watch the city zip by from her window.

Thanks to the quickness of the car ride, Maeve knocked on the kitchen door right before lunch.

Cook sighed with relief when she opened the door. "There you are."

"Thank you again," Maeve said, and handed her the empty red handkerchief.

"Did they like it?" Cook beamed when Maeve nodded.

"The chauffeur is going to let Papa know I'm here." Emma hurried up behind Maeve. "Hello, Cook," she said as she shut the door. "We need to speak with Figgy. Have you seen him?"

Cook looked back and forth between the two of them. "Are you in on this too?" she asked Emma.

"I have absolutely no idea what you're talking about," Emma said with a smile.

"Right," Cook said. "Figgy's in the dining room, I believe. Izzy's there too." She pointed with her thumb toward the door between the two rooms.

"Well, that's convenient," Emma said. "Ready, Maeve?"

Maeve's mouth went dry. She hadn't thought that if she were to tell Figgy everything, it would also be time to tell Izzy what she'd been up to. Would Izzy be upset with her for losing her bracelet in the first place, and for running around the city afterward? She wished she'd had some time to rehearse her story. But if their theory was right about the Exings, there was no time to spare. Maeve thanked Cook one more time and led the way to the dining room.

Izzy had several books spread out across the dining table and her head in her hands. She looked up when they entered and smiled at Maeve.

The nervous flutter in Maeve's stomach stopped. Her sister loved her. She went straight over and hugged Izzy around the shoulders.

"What was that for?" Izzy asked.

"For being you," Maeve said, pulling back. "I need to talk to you. Figgy too."

The tip of Figgy's tail curved like a question mark. "I sense the matter is of some urgency?"

"Definitely." Emma pointed at the door to the kitchen

with one hand and the door to the hall with her other. Her ruby ring flashed and both doors locked with a *click*.

Izzy looked between them. "I'm glad you two are friends now, but what's going on?"

They weren't friends . . . or were they? "It's a long story."

"Don't fidget," the figure in the fresco whispered, and Maeve stilled her hands at her sides.

For the third time in two days, Maeve recounted how she'd found the garden and the kits. She watched the concern on Izzy's face melt into wonder and astonishment, like Maeve was weaving an enchantment with her words. She told them about going back to the garden, about the kits, the magic, Avi, the produce she'd been growing, everything that came to mind and mattered.

"You did all that by yourself?" Izzy said when Maeve finished. Her eyes sparkled with tears. She stood up and threw her arms around her sister.

Maeve stiffened in surprise that Izzy wasn't angry, but then relaxed into the hug. Izzy gave the best hugs in the whole world.

"You're not mad?" Maeve asked and stepped back to look at her sister.

"Mad? I've never been prouder of anyone in my entire life!" Izzy spread her hands wide and Maeve dove into them for another hug.

Figgy finally found his voice. "I told you that opening up magic again to more people would help our numbers. Treble, Cadenza, and Forte." He said each name like he was savoring it and his eyes sparkled with the same kind of pride that Maeve felt in her heart whenever she thought about the kits. "I want to meet them. Let's go right now." He frowned. "Wait, I can't leave the house during a crisis. Can you bring them here?"

Maeve shook her head. "They won't leave the garden until Aria returns. She put some kind of protective enchantment on it that will break if they leave."

"A Safeguard Enchantment, perhaps? That's what I've been using here." Figgy rubbed his chin with a paw. He looked at Maeve. "I'm guessing the kits are too young to control their powers. Are they still steaming?"

"Frequently." Maeve sat down in the chair next to where Izzy had been sitting. "Emma and I have a theory— well, I found the facts and Emma helped figure it out at the opera house—"

"We did it together," Emma cut in, taking a seat across the table.

"You went to the opera house? The one that Extinguished?" Izzy squeaked and fell into her seat.

Maeve put her hands in her lap. She felt awkward explaining this to Figgy but didn't derail. "Our theory is that Exings are being caused by house dragon magic."

Maeve was surprised that Figgy did not seem surprised. For a heartbeat, she thought she'd made a mistake in telling him, but then he sighed and his ears drooped in sorrow.

"I've recently arrived at the same terrifying conclusion. I was chasing a theory that the Extinguishings were related to the magic-draining powers of mice when I realized that it was more akin to house dragon magic applied in reverse.

No house dragon would cause such destruction willingly, of course. Which means there must be foul play involved." He blinked his yellow eyes at Maeve and she tried not to shrink under the weight of his gaze. "I'm assuming you located their cave? Did you find any hints?"

Maeve had forgotten about the article and program. She pulled them out of her satchel and spread them on the table. "I found these but can't guess what they mean. Maybe there's a hidden message in the opera itself?"

Figgy, Emma, and Izzy leaned forward to see the program.

"*Les Pierres Fameuses.*" Emma spun the program around so she could read the title above the picture of a ballerina wearing an emerald-green tutu. "Figgy, do you know anything about the plot?"

He shook his head and flipped the program open. "The title translates to *The Famous Stones*. It says it's a world premiere. I hope we haven't missed something. The dates have already passed."

"But this hasn't and it has your name on it, Figs." Izzy passed him the article. "The Glint Art Gallery opens this weekend."

"I'd almost forgotten." Emma read it over Figgy's shoulder. "Papa invited us to the opening party on Thursday. You too, Maeve."

Maeve watched the house dragon, hoping he'd understand something she didn't. He did.

"*Glint.*" Figgy's hackles rose. "That's our clue." He stalked up and down the table. "Aria wouldn't leave her kits or her post willingly. She wanted this to reach me. Maeve, the kits said they thought someone was after their mother? That she'd been taken?"

Izzy's mouth dropped open. "Ms. Glint said she collects house dragons."

The pieces began to come together. "She's also the one who's offering the reward," Maeve pointed out with a shiver. She felt sick that she'd contemplated turning the kits in, even for a second.

Figgy nodded in affirmation.

Emma took a deep breath. "Just so I'm clear, are we saying that Ms. Glint is stealing house dragons? And she's going around the city, forcing them to use their magic to Extinguish random buildings?"

Figgy paused his pacing. "Not random. Quick, does anyone have a pen?"

Emma pulled out a hairpin as her ring flashed with magic. A moment later, she was writing as fast as Figgy could dictate a list.

"The Wigglebottoms and the Lariat Library. Patchouli Rose and Briolette." Figgy paced back and forth.

Maeve and Emma added a few sites they each remembered reading in the papers and Figgy matched them with the name of a house dragon. When they'd finished, they stared at what they'd made. They'd listed thirty-two locations along with thirty-two names.

Izzy sucked in a breath. "This is every Extinguishing."

Maeve's eyes met her sister's. "They all have house dragons."

"Or they did," Figgy said. "I wrote to the Wigglebottoms

right before the library Extinguished. If Aria's any indication, Glint must be taking the house dragons shortly before Extinguishing the buildings they protect." He scratched his head. "But how? A house dragon can only start or stop an enchantment when they're physically present. And these Extinguishings are too powerful for a single house dragon to cause."

"Figgy! Did you just explain your magic?" Emma gasped.

Figgy's whiskers quivered. "I felt it was important and pertinent information. I must stress again that I don't believe any house dragon would perform this enchantment willingly."

"But if what you said is true, that means the missing house dragons are likely on-site whenever a building Extinguishes, along with whoever is forcing them to do the Exing," Izzy summarized.

They looked at one another, comprehending that they'd uncovered something huge.

"But the papers have been following this story for weeks. Why hasn't anyone figured this out?" Emma asked.

Figgy's voice was quiet. "Possibly because no one values house dragons anymore. Many have forgotten us. We keep to ourselves too much these days. The three of you may know more about house dragon magic than any other humans."

"Or everyone's too busy looking in the wrong direction." Izzy stood up and stalked over to the window. "Mrs. Nimby's the perfect distraction."

"No slouching," the fresco figure next to the curtains whispered.

"Oh, hush up," Izzy told it.

"There's no need to be rude." The whispered reply sounded as if the figure was insulted.

"Izzy, stop arguing with the wall and tell us what you mean," Emma said. "Are you saying Mrs. Nimby and Ms. Glint are in on it together?"

Izzy stared out the window. "Not necessarily. I think Mrs. Nimby truly believes what she's saying—which is frightening for its own reasons. But while she's shouting about us stealing magic, no one's looking at Ms. Glint or the house dragons."

Maeve studied the list and a scary thought occurred to her. "Figgy, how many house dragons are left?"

Everyone went quiet and looked at Figgy. "It's hard to be certain. Several dozen, maybe. Our numbers have fallen so dramatically."

Maeve said a silent promise to herself that if they were able to stop the Extinguishings, she'd continue to do everything she could to protect the kits. Perhaps she could help house dragons thrive again.

"Let's get started," she said. "Should we tell Miss Clementine our theory? Or maybe your papa, Emma?"

"Don't make accusations you can't back up," the closest fresco figure whispered.

"Can someone please turn these things off?" Izzy huffed.

"The wall's right. We can't lower ourselves to Mrs. Nimby's level. We need to be certain before we accuse the most powerful woman in New York of being responsible for the Extinguishings. Something still doesn't make sense to me." Emma chewed on the end of her hairpin pen. "Ms. Glint donated a lot of money to open the Glint Academy. Why would she use the schools as her scapegoat for the Extinguishings and risk the license being revoked?"

The question silenced them. The wall offered no helpful tips this time.

"We can figure that part out later." Maeve stood up. "The most important thing is that we stop Ms. Glint before she Extinguishes another building or steals another house dragon." She swallowed. "Especially the kits."

"If we can catch her in the act, we'll have our proof." Izzy nodded.

A horrible wave of dread washed over Maeve. What could Ms. Glint do with the raw power of three house dragon kits? "I'll see if Cook will let me go downtown tomorrow morning. Avi should know to keep an eye out. He'll want to help."

Figgy stood. "I'll warn the remaining house dragons that I know."

"Be careful, Figgy," Emma cautioned.

"I'm as safe as I can get," Figgy reassured her. "I never leave the school, remember?" He stretched his back and hopped down from the table. "Do you mind if we adjourn? The students will be coming in for lunch momentarily and I'd like to send these Pigeon Posts." He clicked twice to emphasize his point.

"Of course," Emma agreed, and the others nodded. "We can keep brainstorming what to do. I want to search the library for any information about Ms. Glint or what landmark she might hit next—"

"You know you can't find the answer to every problem in a book, right?" Izzy teased.

"Well, I certainly don't mind trying!" Emma laughed and Maeve laughed too. It felt good to be in on the joke.

Then Maeve thought about the library book in her satchel and the chapter "Magic in the Tarnish?" What if they already had the answer? What if they knew someone connected to a secret society dedicated to helping kids from the Tarnish? Surely the Ember Society would want to help them, right?

She made up her mind to ask Avi tomorrow. A voice that sounded a lot like Mam's whispered that she shouldn't put so much stock in hope alone, but she ignored it. She could really use a little hope right about now.

After a quick lunch, Maeve, Emma, and Izzy spent the afternoon making a map of landmarks in the city and debating which ones Ms. Glint might target. Working together, Maeve felt like a weight had been lifted from her shoulders. Especially if they got the Ember Society on their side, they could stop the Extinguishings and find Aria. She went to bed that night feeling happier and more optimistic than she had in a very long time.

But Maeve woke with a start when her bedroom door flew open in the middle of the night.

"Wake up," Emma announced. "Figgy's missing."

TWENTY
In Search of Figgy Pudding

Izzy

After breakfast the next morning, Izzy pulled the dishes out of a cupboard in the kitchen and stuck her arm inside. Her hand met the back with a *thunk*.

"*Stones*," she cursed, and sat back on her heels. She rubbed her tired eyes.

Emma opened the kitchen door and frowned when she saw that Izzy had pulled everything out of the cabinets. "Izzy, we've been searching for hours. He's gone," she said.

Izzy tried to swallow the lump in her throat. She picked up a teacup. "I keep hoping I'll find him holed up in some, well, *hole*. Or I'll find his cave and he will have left us a clue too." Her lower lip wobbled. No, she wasn't going to cry, she wasn't going to—a tear slipped down her cheek.

"I don't think he knew this was coming any more than we did." Emma held out her arms and Izzy leaned into the hug. The ladle Emma had just picked up poked into Izzy's back, but Izzy didn't complain.

"I'm so worried about him," she said into Emma's shoulder.

"Me too," Emma said.

"Do you . . ." Izzy fought the constriction in her throat. "Do you think the school is going to Extinguish?"

Emma stepped back. "I think we need to tell Miss Clementine what we've discovered about the link between the missing house dragons and the Extinguishings. If we're right—"

Izzy dragged her palms down her face. "This might be the first time in my life I haven't wanted to be right. But if we are right, the school could Extinguish."

They looked at each other, both fully comprehending the terribleness of this statement.

"I'm scared," Izzy admitted.

"We'll get through this together. Maeve included."

Izzy smiled for the first time that morning. "Together."

"Shh. Do you hear that strange squeaking?" Emma tilted her ear up and looked around.

"It's coming from over here." Izzy followed the sound to the corner of the kitchen. There was a crack in the baseboards. As she watched, a tiny nose and whiskers poked out of the hole and gnawed on the wood.

"Shoo!" Emma shouted, and flapped her hands uselessly at the mouse. It ignored her and nibbled on the wallpaper.

Izzy watched with horror and understood why Extinguishings had reminded Figgy of the magic-eating powers of mice. There was no line of char, but as the mouse gnawed, the striped wallpaper faded from the ceiling downward, as if the mouse was slurping in the magic decoration like a noodle. Blank white plaster replaced the cheerful green stripes that must have been magicked on.

Izzy felt a flash of rage. She stomped her foot and the mouse scurried back inside its hole. "We have got to put a stop to this for Figgy's sake."

"And our own," Emma agreed as a thin crack appeared in the ceiling above their heads, sending down a spray of plaster dust. "Let's go."

They found the headmistress in her office, but she wasn't alone.

Mr. Rote sat in the chair across from Miss Clementine at her desk. The air in the room was tense, like it had recently been filled with angry words.

"Oh, it's you," Izzy said. She'd nearly forgotten the headmaster of Glint Kindling Academy.

Mr. Rote dipped his head in polite acknowledgment, but his mouth twisted with distaste. "I'd come to offer my school's aid, but I find my help is not appreciated." He gave a tense bow to Miss Clementine. "Good day, ma'am."

He left, and Miss Clementine exhaled loudly. "It's a struggle to keep my composure around that man. His *help*." She rolled her eyes.

"What did he say?" Emma asked.

"He said he'd consider mid-year applications from any

of our students who wanted to transfer to Glint Academy. It's clear he thinks we're shutting down." Miss Clementine scoffed. "Any luck finding Figgy?" she asked, reminding them why they'd come in here.

They told her everything they'd discovered about the missing house dragons and their theory about the Extinguishings. As they spoke, Izzy watched Miss Clementine's face go from flushed to pale.

"So what should we do now? Should we contact the police?" Emma asked when they'd finished.

Miss Clementine sighed. "I would, but their headquarters Extinguished last night." She slid a newspaper across her desk. Izzy felt nauseated. Figgy gone and another building Extinguished.

Emma skimmed the headline. "Miss Clementine, I think we need to evacuate. I'm afraid the school may be next."

Miss Clementine nodded solemnly. "You two have noticed things that adults have missed before. I'd prefer to trust your instincts and err on the side of caution." The headmistress stroked the top of her desk and looked around sadly. "I've become rather attached to this place." She stood up. "I'll make the announcement. Will you help me gather the students?"

Less than ten minutes later, the whole school crowded the table in the dining room. Miss Clementine stood at her usual place at the head of the table and struggled to keep her voice calm as she explained the situation.

Izzy watched Maeve's face as her sister listened to the headmistress. Though Maeve knew more about the situation than most of the other students at the table, she still looked disheartened by the news. Izzy realized that if the school Extinguished, it would close. Perhaps forever. What would happen to the students? Would they be able to kindle?

Up and down the table, others were clearly wondering the same thing. Miss Lawrence dabbed at her eyes with her handkerchief.

Antonia raised her hand. "When will the school reopen?"

"As soon as it's safe," Miss Clementine said.

"But when will that be?" Minnie and Ida asked in unison. They smiled sadly at each other.

The headmistress appealed to Emma and Izzy. "Any insight?"

Emma shook her head. "Most of the Extinguishings have been at night, but Briolette happened in the middle of the day."

"To be safe, I'd like everyone to be out by noon." Miss Clementine forced a smile. "I'll send telegrams to your parents to collect you. For those of you who need to go to Brooklyn and the Bronx, Miss Lawrence and I can escort you home in groups."

"But we've worked so hard," Mary protested. The students nodded their agreement.

"This will be temporary. We'll be together again soon. Keep up with your studies and I'll let you know when it's safe to come back."

A few of the students had tears running down their cheeks. Some clutched one another's arms like they couldn't bear to be separated.

"We'll do everything we can to stop it," Maeve said. A few of the girls looked at her with impressed surprise.

Miss Clementine sent everyone upstairs to pack while she went to send the telegrams to their parents. Izzy went to her room and took out her suitcase, but she couldn't focus. She sat down in the middle of the floor and stared at the wall. The room felt empty without Figgy perched on some high surface, ready to critique whatever she was doing at that moment. He'd probably know some famous person in magical history who stared at a wall once too and did something incredible. Izzy tried to smile but it came out as a sob. It felt like someone had stolen a piece of her heart. *Oh, Figgy.*

Downstairs, doors started banging open and shut and the shouts of students filled the air. The evacuation must have begun. Izzy hugged her knees. From inside the walls, she heard the scratch of even more mice. With Figgy gone, they were moving in faster than she would have expected. The school had been built with magitecture, so there would be enough magic to feed a small army of mice.

She'd worked so hard and everything was crumbling beneath her.

Emma entered with Tom right behind her. She paused when she saw Izzy on the floor.

"Izzy, it's time to go," Emma said with a glance at Izzy's empty suitcase. "I'm going to stay with Papa and I want Maeve and you to come with me."

Izzy didn't respond. She rested her head on her knees. Ms. Glint had known to take Figgy and strike them where it hurt the most. Now she might Extinguish their school and Izzy felt powerless to stop her. How were they going to stop the richest and most powerful woman in New York without any proof?

"Give her some space, Em," Tom said. Izzy silently thanked him.

Izzy heard Emma's armoire open and the sound of her suitcase being dragged from inside. Emma and Tom spoke softly while packing. She peeked when she heard a sniffle.

"Let me give you a hand with that," Tom said gently.

"Thank you. I'm so worried about Figgy. What if she hurts him?" Emma sniffled again.

"Everything will be all right, Em. We'll figure it out. We always do." Tom wrapped his arms around her, and Emma leaned her head on his shoulder.

Izzy looked away, feeling embarrassed at witnessing what felt like a private moment. But her own feelings were too immense to hold back.

"What if he's gone forever?" she asked in a voice that sounded much younger. "What if the school has to close? Everything we've worked for . . ."

"We'll find him and we'll put an end to these Exings." Emma sat down next to her and hugged her arms around Izzy's shoulders.

"How are we going to do this on our own?" Izzy wondered aloud.

"We figured out how to kindle, didn't we?" Tom said.

"And you're not on your own," Maeve said from the doorway. She clutched the cardboard suitcase she'd brought from Omaha in one hand and a beat-up leather satchel in the other. "Why are you sitting on the floor?"

Izzy ignored this question. "How did you pack already?"

"For starters, I didn't waste time sitting on the floor," Maeve said wryly. "I'm going down to the"—she cast a glance at Tom—"the place."

"You can trust him," Emma said.

Izzy was surprised when Maeve nodded in acknowledgment.

Maeve shouldered her satchel. "I need to go to the garden. If Ms. Glint knew how to get Figgy away from us, she might also know how to get the kits' location out of him. I have to protect them."

Tom looked back and forth between them, clearly hoping for more clues as to what she was talking about. "The kits? The ones in the paper?"

Izzy stood and dusted her hands. "It's not safe for you either. I'm coming with you."

"Me too," Emma said.

"And me," Tom agreed, but then whispered to Emma, "Where are we going?"

"To the Tarnish," Emma whispered back.

"Again?" Tom looked astounded. "Why?"

"That's where the garden is." Izzy pressed her lips together to keep the giggles in.

"Garden?" Tom's forehead wrinkled with confusion. "Will someone please tell me what's going on?"

"You really should keep up with the news, you know, Tom," Maeve teased.

Emma and Izzy looked at each other in delighted astonishment before bursting into laughter. Maeve joined in while Tom gaped at them.

Emma started toward the door. "Come on, Tom. We'll fill you in on the way."

TWENTY-ONE
Evacuated and Evicted

Maeve

The Tarnish was as bustling as usual when Maeve and Izzy got off the subway at Grand Street. There was a street fair happening and the market street was packed, so they took the long way to reach the garden.

Though clouds gathered overhead, Maeve's smile was as bright as the sun.

After some discussion, they'd decided that it made more sense for Emma and Tom to take their suitcases to Mr. Harris's apartment in the motorcar instead of dragging everything down to the garden. They'd join the sisters shortly, but for now, Maeve had Izzy all to herself. Though she was excited to show them all the garden, Maeve was pleased that Izzy would get to see it first.

Maeve didn't realize what street they were on until they passed Anoush and Nareg perched on their pushcart outside East Side Carpets.

"Maeve! You haven't come to an Ember Society meeting in a long time!" Anoush shouted.

Maeve felt guilty that she'd forgotten. "I'm so sorry. I've been busy."

"Or we could come visit you and see your garden," Nareg suggested. Maeve was still struggling with how to answer this when he turned to look at Izzy. "Is that your sister?"

Maeve nodded in confirmation.

"Hi, Maeve's sister!" Anoush waved at them with her whole arm. She hopped off the pushcart and scooped up two of the potatoes inside. "Here, you can each take a wish."

Izzy raised a questioning eyebrow at Maeve.

"Thank you," Maeve said very seriously with a bow of her head.

Anoush bowed her head back. "Of course. In addition to saving all the kids in the Tarnish, we Embers have to look out for each other."

Maeve tucked the small potato into her satchel. *I wish the real Ember Society would get here soon and fix everything*, she thought. Her heart fluttered with the thought that, if she was right about Avi's uncle, her wish could come true.

Maeve promised Anoush and Nareg she'd come back soon—for real this time—and she and Izzy continued on to the garden. As they walked, Maeve thought about kids like Anoush and Nareg, growing up in the Tarnish with so much love for their magic. She wished there was something she could do to help them.

She didn't realize she was walking so fast until Izzy hurried to catch up. "How do you know them?"

Maeve pushed a strand of hair behind her ear. "They helped me find seeds for the garden. I hope you're not mad that I came back here."

"I'm not mad," Izzy said, and in fact, she seemed far from it. "I'd forgotten about the garden, honestly. I'm glad you didn't."

As Maeve pushed aside the board and led Izzy into the garden, she thought how far they'd come since that first day they found it. They'd both grown like two different branches on the same tree, grounded by their shared roots. Maeve looked at the leaves and vines she'd tended so carefully over the past months and hoped that with the right care, her relationship with Izzy could also flourish.

Izzy stood with her arms straight at her sides and her mouth open. Maeve watched as her sister took in the vegetable garden with the produce as colorful as gems. She held her breath as Izzy beheld the rose-lined pathway to the back of the garden, the blooming azaleas, and the trees filled with ripe red fruit.

"Are those real apples?" Izzy pointed.

"Have one—they're delicious," Maeve offered. "Avi and I made them."

Her big sister reached up and picked a low-hanging apple. She took a bite. Maeve's heart thumped anxiously, *Please love it,* which really meant, *Please love me.*

"That's the best apple I've ever had." Izzy stared at her sister. "Maeve, this place is incredible." She pointed at the bountiful vegetable garden. "Look at those zucchinis! Does Cook know you're growing those? She loves them."

Though it was still cloudy, Maeve felt like she was standing in the sun. "I'll bring her some. I owe her at least that much."

Izzy peered deeper into the garden. "Will you show me around, please? I want to meet Avi and the kits."

"The kits are probably watching us." Maeve cupped a hand to her mouth and called to the kits. "You can come out. This is my sister."

"I was right!" Forte bragged, charging out of the azaleas.

Cadenza rolled her eyes as she followed him. "The color of her head-fur made it obvious."

Maeve brimmed with excitement as she introduced each of the kits to her sister. Little puffs of steam rose between their ears, which she took to mean they were happy too.

Like a cloud passing in front of the sun, a thought crossed her mind. Soon the kits would live with their mother and she wouldn't see them in the garden anymore. But her sister's smile made her believe that if she could have Izzy and Avi here, she'd be all right. The kits could visit, of course.

Speaking of which, she looked around for the missing member of their group. "Where's Avi?"

Forte shook his head. "We haven't seen him today."

"He's probably ironing his shirt or something. I'll go get him."

Maeve tried to act calm, but her heart was pounding. This was perfect. She'd have a moment alone with Avi to tell him that she'd figured out his uncle's connection to the

Ember Society. She couldn't wait to see the expression on his face.

"I know your mother's cousin, Figgy Pudding," Maeve heard Izzy say as she hurried toward the front of the garden.

When she was on the sidewalk, she paused under Avi's fire escape. The window was open and a corner of the paisley curtain was draped outside the sill.

"Avi, come out!" Maeve shouted up at the open window.

Avi stuck his well-combed head out the window. "Shh. I can't come down today."

Maeve was too excited to notice that his hands were again wrapped in rags.

"My sister's here and we need your help," Maeve insisted. "I have something really important to ask you about your uncle Benjamin."

Avi's eyes widened and he glanced over his shoulder. The reason for his tension became clear a moment later when a second head joined his in the window.

Maeve knew immediately this was Avi's mameh. She looked younger than Mr. Harris but her face had more lines. A black-and-white headscarf covered her hair. She and Avi had the same shape of eyes, though his were darker. Her lips were pursed in the concerned way that Maeve had imagined whenever Avi talked about his mother and magic.

"Benjamin?" Mrs. Sigal gripped the windowsill and stared down at Maeve. She turned to her son and asked a question in Yiddish. As she spoke, Mrs. Sigal pointed at Maeve, and Avi pointed at Maeve again when he replied, also in Yiddish. Maeve stood there, her fears mounting. She didn't know if his mother spoke any English. How was she going to talk to Avi about the kits and the garden with her right there?

Mrs. Sigal pointed at Maeve. "You come upstairs."

Then she disappeared through the window again.

"You should leave. Now," Avi suggested.

Maeve didn't move. This wasn't going according to plan at all. "Why isn't she at work?"

"Because we're moving. We have until sunup tomorrow morning to get out." His voice constricted and he glanced over his shoulder. "Mameh, don't lift that yourself—" he said before switching to Yiddish again.

The sound of someone shouting behind her made Maeve turn. Across the street, a couple carrying a rolled-up carpet out the front door of their tenement building had knocked a chair off someone else's wagon. Up and down the block, residents were carrying furniture or wrapped bundles out of the buildings to waiting carts.

"Everyone is leaving," Maeve said as the realization struck her. She'd been so excited to show Izzy the garden, she hadn't noticed before.

"They have to," Avi said. "Gladys Glint bought the whole block."

Maeve felt like the city had jolted beneath her feet. "What does she want a bunch of old buildings for?"

"They're tearing them down." Avi gripped the windowsill like he alone could keep it standing. "You know what this means, right? They're going to find the garden. Or they'll destroy it with the buildings."

Maeve reeled from this news. If Ms. Glint had purchased the block, she clearly knew where the kits were. Maybe she'd already tried to get into the garden, but Aria's protection had been enough to keep her out. Avi was right—if Ms. Glint tore down the buildings, she'd either destroy the garden or expose it. Either way, it would be lost to Maeve forever.

Maeve could practically hear the scrape of the bull's hooves. She felt trapped and alone.

She made up her mind. "I'm coming upstairs." They had to find the Ember Society. It had never been more important.

To get through the front door, she had to squeeze past two other tenants moving a table. Inside, the building was even more poorly maintained than the one she'd grown up in. It was dim, cramped, and filled with too many smells that didn't go particularly well together. The steep and narrow wooden stairs continued up three more flights, but Avi stuck his head out the door on the second floor and waved her inside.

The door opened into a small kitchen dominated by an iron stove. She could see the corner of a bed peeking around the doorway of a dark room on her left. Clean laundry hung on lines zigzagging across the room and Maeve had to duck under a woman's blouse to follow Avi into the living room on the right. The first thing she noticed was the window that Avi always climbed out of to get to the fire escape. A few crates packed with odds and ends sat beside it, along with bundles of linens tied with strings.

"Did you already find another apartment?" she asked.

"We're leaving New York," Avi said. "We're moving to Baltimore to be near my sister."

Maeve was stunned. "But that's too far."

The school . . . the garden . . . Avi . . . was she going to lose everything in a single day?

Avi's voice cracked. "I don't want to go. I want to stay here with the garden and you—"

"You know Benjamin?" Mrs. Sigal came out of the bedroom carrying a stack of folded blankets.

Maeve shook her head. "No, ma'am. I know Avi." She was still reeling from his news.

Avi introduced the two of them. "We talk through the window," he admitted, saying it first in Yiddish and then in English.

At this, Mrs. Sigal's shoulders relaxed. "Avi is a good boy." The pride in Mrs. Sigal's voice was evident. Avi blushed.

Maeve's mind raced. How could she ask about the Ember Society without alerting Avi's mother that her son had been doing magic? She hoped coming upstairs hadn't been a mistake.

"Mameh wants you to sit," Avi said, sweeping his hand to indicate four wooden chairs in the living room. Maeve was about to protest that she didn't want to be in the way, but Avi said, "I told her you came to say goodbye."

The word settled in Maeve's gut like a stone. She sat in the closest wooden chair.

"I need to talk to you about the . . . you know," Maeve said when Mrs. Sigal resumed her packing. "It's the only way to save *the place*." Choosing her words carefully, she explained that Figgy had gone missing and that they feared the school would be next to Extinguish. "Izzy's worked so hard for it and now the garden might be getting destroyed and don't you see? I know you said it's a secret but I figured it out. Your uncle was part of the Ember Society, wasn't he?"

"The Emb—Maeve, he wasn't . . ." Avi's brow creased. He shifted in his seat and his voice softened. "I don't think so. Playing Ember Society is a game. It's not real, right?"

"But it has to be," she said lamely. "I don't know what else to do. Someone has to save the garden."

"I'm sorry." Avi exhaled. "Mameh said it was a neighbor who taught him, someone who had kindled before they immigrated here. Neighbors used to help neighbors, apparently, but it's too dangerous now with the Registry. Maybe she was wrong, but I don't know."

Maeve felt like she'd been punched in the gut. Mam had warned her and she'd still been counting on the Ember Society to swoop in and rescue everything. Her hands brushed against her skirt and she felt a lump in her pocket. She reached inside and pulled out Anoush's old potato.

"What's that?" Avi asked.

"A long story," Maeve said.

She felt like she had a hundred wishes all mashed together, but she was tired of wishes, tired of hoping for things that wouldn't come true.

"I need to get back," she said. She didn't want to say

goodbye, but Izzy and the kits were waiting. "Will you come to the garden one last time?"

Avi bit his lip. "I want to, but I can't sneak around right now."

"Then don't sneak. Tell her what the garden means to you."

"She wouldn't understand, Maeve. She's afraid of magic." Avi shook his head.

Maeve's head and heart both ached. "So was I, but I just didn't understand it. I'm terrified of kindling, but that doesn't mean I'm not going to try. The garden taught me that I could be afraid and brave at the same time." Maeve swallowed and set the potato down on the table. "Talk to her, Avi. Maybe you can make her understand too."

Mrs. Sigal bustled into the room, struggling under the weight of a crate of kitchen items. Avi hurried over to help her. Maeve watched them and wished things didn't have to be so complicated. She wished there was an easy way for Avi to be honest with his mother about his magic. She understood now that not all secrets were created equal. Some protected something important or vulnerable like the kits, but others succeeded in driving a wedge between people.

Avi set down the crate. "I should get back to packing." He crossed his arms. "I guess this is goodbye?"

Everything in Maeve railed against it. She wanted to drag him back to the garden where they could play with the kits and their magic forever. Everything was falling apart and no one was coming to rescue her.

"Come to the garden if you can," Maeve said, but he looked away. "Goodbye, Avi," she said.

For the first time in weeks, she longed for her prairie rose sachet. This was why she had tried so hard to be alone. If she was already alone, there was no one who could leave her behind. Forgetting the potato on the table, she left with a broken heart.

TWENTY-TWO

When Things Get Dark

Izzy

Izzy was waiting when her sister returned to the garden alone. Maeve's smile was as absent as Avi.

"What's wrong?" Izzy asked. "Where's your friend?"

"He's not coming." Maeve crossed her arms and looked away.

Izzy listened with growing shock as her sister told her about Ms. Glint buying the block and Maeve's suspicion that she was tearing down the buildings to get to the garden.

"What's going to happen to us?" Cadenza asked tearfully. "Mother isn't back yet."

"Whatever happens, we'll be together, right?" Treble's ears drooped. "Avi wouldn't really leave without saying goodbye to us."

"Sunup tomorrow doesn't give him much time. It doesn't give us much time either," Forte pointed out, and Izzy secretly agreed.

"There has to be something we can do." Maeve looked to Izzy. "You're here. You have kindled magic. Can't you do something to protect the garden?"

Maeve already looked so disappointed that Izzy didn't want to let her down further. But she had to be honest.

"I—I can't sear enchantments," Izzy said. "I've been working on it and Miss Clementine said to give it time, but it's just not happening."

Maeve's mouth opened in surprise. "Why didn't you tell me before?"

"I was embarrassed. I want you to be proud of me." Izzy buried her face in her hands. Gentle hands pushed her arms back down.

"I am proud of you," Maeve said. "You're my big sister. I'll always look up to you."

Though it was still cloudy, Izzy felt as warm and happy as if she'd been standing in the sun.

The kits' ears swiveled to the front of the garden.

"Someone's here," Cadenza announced, jumping to her feet.

"It must be Emma and Tom," Maeve said. "I'll go."

She strode away before Izzy had time to object. The kits slipped into the undergrowth behind her, leaving Izzy alone in the garden. She sat down on the stone bench and watched the gently blowing leaves. It was truly incredible what Maeve had accomplished with her magic. Izzy had never felt prouder of her sister, or more frustrated with herself. She wished there was something she could do to stop the destruction of the school and the garden. She understood then that perfecting her magic wasn't just about getting into a school. It was about making real changes in the world. There were people that her magic could help.

Forte burst out of the undergrowth. "Everything's fine! Maeve knows them."

A moment later, Maeve rounded the bend with Tom and Emma behind her. Cadenza and Treble trotted at their heels.

Tom stared at the trees, openmouthed. "This place is incredible."

Emma clasped her hands under her chin in delight. "This is so much better than how I imagined it. What? Why do you both look so sad?" she asked when she saw Izzy's and Maeve's response.

Izzy quickly filled them in on Ms. Glint's latest move.

"Why don't more people know about this?" Tom sputtered. "She shouldn't be able to evict hundreds of people on a whim!"

"Do you think people uptown care about some Tarnish residents being evicted?" Maeve scoffed. "Those buildings are in terrible shape. They'd probably say it was good for them to be torn down."

"They should care. These are people's homes. If they knew about the garden, they'd want to protect it too," Emma said softly. "There's something incredibly special about this place. It deserves to be preserved."

"We can't tell anyone about the garden until the kits are safe, but by then—" Izzy started.

"It might be too late," Maeve finished. "That's it, then,

isn't it? We've lost. We have no way to find Figgy and Aria, the school is going to Extinguish, and Ms. Glint's going to tear down the garden." A single tear slipped down her cheek. "It's so stupid, but I thought someone was going to swoop in and help us."

"Who?" Izzy asked gently.

Maeve wiped her cheek. "You'll laugh. The Ember Society. But it was silly of me to hope they were real."

Laughing was the furthest thing from Izzy's mind. She hadn't thought about the Ember Society in a long time, but she remembered the way she'd longed for it to be real. She could understand why Maeve would want it to be too.

Maeve's voice broke. "No one's coming. Not even Avi."

She sniffled and began to cry. The sight of her sister in tears made Izzy want to burn the world down. For the first time, Izzy truly understood what Miss Clementine had meant about needing to burn brighter when things got dark.

She had a voice and it was time she learned to use it.

"You're not alone. I'm here." She stepped toward Maeve. "So are Emma and Tom. And that counts for something, right?"

Maeve cracked a watery smile. The sight of it gave Izzy the courage to continue. "We don't need rescuing. We built the school and the garden and we can save them ourselves. I'm not giving up until Figgy is safely back at the school, curled up in front of the fire in Miss Clementine's office and gorging himself on gravy."

"I like the sound of that," Treble said.

"Hear! Hear!" Emma agreed.

"We'll be our own Ember Society." Maeve stood up straighter. "No. We'll be better than the Ember Society, because we'll be real."

Izzy nodded. "Exactly. We just need to make a plan." She held out a hand to Emma. "Pen, please."

"I'm going to need to get some new hairpins." Emma sighed, but she grinned as she magicked a pen one more time.

Izzy made a quick list. "The first thing we need to do is figure out where Ms. Glint is. Do we have any idea of her whereabouts?"

Emma's eyes widened. "We do. She'll be at the Glint Art Gallery opening tomorrow. If we're there, we can follow her. She's bound to lead us to the house dragons that she's kidnapped."

Izzy checked *Find Glint* off her list.

"What if she tries to Extinguish the school tonight?" Maeve pointed out.

"Then we'll be ready for her." Tom cracked his knuckles. Everyone stared at him in surprise. "What? My hand just hurt. I'm not going to punch her. But we will be waiting and ready to defend the school."

"How?" Maeve asked.

"Newsie style." He winked. "Sheer numbers. I have some friends who owe me a favor."

"All right." Izzy added *Set Up Guard at School*. She thought about the tearful faces of the students forced to leave. "I bet your sister and some of the other students would help."

Maeve nodded. "Antonia is good friends with them. She'll know how to find them." She looked at the group. "We should tell them everything. They deserve to know what we're up against."

"Is that who has Mother?" Cadenza asked. "Glint?"

"We think so." Maeve leaned down. "Does the name sound familiar?"

The kits shook their heads.

"We should take the kits uptown. Papa wouldn't mind a few more guests," Emma suggested.

"No," Cadenza insisted. "We're not leaving the garden until Mother gets back." Her whiskers trembled. "Or until we have to."

Maeve nodded. "Then I'll stay with them."

"And I'll stay with you," Izzy added. "I'm not leaving you alone."

"Thank you." Maeve hugged Izzy tightly around the middle.

"Yeah, yeah, let's keep working," Izzy said, though she was smiling.

When Maeve let go, Izzy was surprised by the new-found resolve in her sister's eyes. She felt like the fire of her own determination had lit her sister's as well.

Emma looked at the stone bench and the blankets coiled underneath that the kits had been sleeping in. "If you're staying here tonight, you'll need a better place to sleep. Do you mind if I use that?" She pointed at the birdbath underneath the apple tree and Maeve shook her head. "Tom, will you help, please?"

They positioned the birdbath in the clearing near the stone bench. Izzy watched as Emma's diamond bracelet glowed with magic. The birdbath expanded out and up. She watched as the cupped top flipped. The pedestal opened and filled with holes like a large lace doily. When Emma had finished, a lovely beige gazebo stood where the birdbath had been moments before.

"And seared." Emma made a tying gesture with her hands. Little beads of sweat had appeared on Emma's forehead and her cheeks were flushed with the heat of the magic.

"Well done, Em." Tom brought over the blankets and shook them. "What if I just . . ." His glass ring flashed with magic and the blankets fluffed out into clean, cushy down comforters.

"Thanks. I wish I could do that," Izzy said.

"No more wishes, Izzy." Maeve put her hands on her hips. "You're learning to sear. Tonight."

TWENTY-THREE

Aria's Clues

Maeve

As the sun set over the garden, Maeve and Izzy did magic together. Izzy showed Maeve how to manifest a flame in her palm and they whooped and cheered as their excitement made the flames brighter. Maeve grinned until her face hurt as a vine of morning glories unfurled their petals and turned toward the glow of their magic. The kits hummed and purred and they all danced through the garden. Izzy practiced searing enchantment after enchantment until they had a feast of roasted eggplant, baked zucchini, bread, and cheese—because a feast should always include cheese, Izzy argued. They sat on the grass with their shoulders pressed together while they ate and watched the kits chase fireflies.

After they ate, they were both tired but couldn't sleep. They curled up in the gazebo and talked until the stars blinked brightly overhead. Now that they'd shared the secrets of the garden and Izzy's struggles with searing, there was an ease between them that had been absent for too long. Izzy told Maeve everything about her life at Miss Posterity's and how hard it had been. Maeve told Izzy about her loneliness out West and the constant fear of making a mistake and showing her magic. Neither remembered falling asleep, but eventually they did. Izzy draped an arm over her sister's side, just like she used to when they were younger. The kits coiled around them, purring. Small puffs of steam rose from the kits' fur as they slept, warming the inside of the gazebo.

They slept late and the sun was high overhead by the time Maeve opened her eyes. She felt the sun on her face and watched the way light shone on the magically ripened fruits and vegetables in their tidy garden rows. For a moment she forgot that her world was falling apart.

"Figgy?" Izzy whispered in her sleep.

Instantly, it came crashing back. They had to find the house dragons today and stop the Extinguishings. It was their only option.

Maeve sat up. Awakened by her movement, the kits stood and stretched. Izzy snored and rolled over so her back was facing them.

"The last day." Forte arched his back and yawned. "Should I go get it?"

"I suppose it's time," Cadenza said, and Forte trotted out of the gazebo.

Maeve wasn't sure what they were talking about until Forte returned a moment later with her gold bracelet dangling from his mouth. He sat in front of Maeve and she took the bracelet from him. There was dirt encrusting the three diamonds, but they still shone.

"We can't keep it for you any longer," Forte said. "We'll all be leaving today, one way or another."

Maeve stared at the thin gold chain. Had she really thought it too heavy a burden to wear? She fastened the clasp and pulled her sleeve down over it. She wanted to try to see if she could get used to it before she showed anyone else.

Footsteps from the front of the garden made her jump. For a moment, she thought Ms. Glint had found a way inside, but her shoulders relaxed when she saw it was Emma. Maeve went to meet her. In the gazebo, Izzy began to stir.

"Cook sent lunch for you and bacon for the kits," Emma said. She set a tin pail on the stone bench. Maeve had never seen Emma look so worn out. She had dark circles under her eyes and her curls hung limp. "Sorry I'm here so late. I had to take a nap this morning. Tom and I were at the school all night with Miss Clementine, Cook, Tom's newsie friends, and most of the students."

Maeve's heart thumped as she pictured everyone standing strong, defending the school. "Did the school Extinguish?" she asked.

"No, but the mice have done so much damage it's hard to tell. I don't know how Papa will fix it, if he even can." Emma sat down hard on the bench. "We found an open box with a bunch of air holes in the closet near Miss Clementine's office. It appears that someone planted the mice."

Maeve was horrified. "But the mice arrived while we were still there. How did someone get inside?"

Emma sighed and rubbed her eyes. "I don't know. I feel like I'm staring at the puzzle but the pieces aren't coming together."

"Hey, look," Forte interrupted. He pointed a paw up at the apple tree and Maeve followed it to see a small flock of pigeons roosting in the branches. Forte clicked at them and one of the birds flew down and saluted him. "It works!" Forte preened. "You know, if you don't want to be a squirrel you could always be a pigeon, Treble."

Treble stuck out his lower lip. "Ha ha, very funny."

"Don't you dare scare him up a tree again," Maeve scolded.

"You can go," Forte said to the pigeon. "I don't have any messages right now."

"Morning. Or should I say afternoon?" Izzy yawned and stretched as she strolled over to them. "I'm sore. The ground is softer than that old bed in Miss Posterity's attic, but not by much." She wrapped her arms around Maeve's shoulders. "You still snore, by the way."

"So do you," Maeve countered, and Emma laughed. "Emma brought us breakfast," Maeve said, embarrassed but pleased by her sister's display of affection. Out of habit, she glanced up at Avi's fire escape but found it empty. She gulped when she realized it was long after sunup. He'd left without saying goodbye.

She ate the muffin that Emma offered, but she barely tasted it. Avi was gone and the garden had already changed from what she knew. But they had a plan to stop it from changing any more.

"The gallery opening is in a few hours, so we need to get going, Izzy. We've got a lot to do," Emma said. "Frances is going to be there too and I'm sure she'll help us." She turned to Maeve. "You're sure you don't want to come?"

Maeve shook her head. "The kits are determined to stay and I'll stay to guard them."

"Remember, if they show up to start demolition, meet at our apartment like we planned," Emma said.

"We'll keep an eye on Ms. Glint. She can't bother the garden if she's at the gallery opening," Izzy reiterated, and Maeve wondered who her sister was trying to reassure. Izzy bit her lip. "But I'll stay if you need me."

Hearing that Izzy would have stayed made all the difference in the world. Maeve took a deep breath. "Go. You need to follow Ms. Glint. It's the only way to stop everything."

"I'm afraid it's too late for our home. I heard what Emma said about the mice." Izzy's shoulders slumped.

"You mean the school? We can rebuild it," Maeve vowed. "*Home* is wherever our family is."

"Well said, Maeve," Emma agreed. Maeve smiled at Emma, but before she could say anything, the kits jumped in.

"We're part of your family now," Cadenza announced, strolling over with her tail in the air.

"I love my family," Treble announced. He sniffed the air. "Especially when my family has bacon."

Maeve scooped him up and gave him a kiss between the ears. His whiskers trembled with pride.

Emma cleared her throat gently. "I hate to do this, but Izzy, we really have to go. We need to change and get ready. Maeve, we'll send word with Tom if we find anything."

"I'll be all right," Maeve promised them.

Izzy and Emma departed. Maeve stood for a long moment in the dappled sunlight under the apple tree and let the quiet of the garden wash over her. Until the pigeons in the apple tree started cooing loudly, that was. After eyeing them to let them know she was annoyed, she headed to the vegetable patch. She might as well pack up the produce while she had the chance.

As she'd done so many times now, Maeve went down the row, channeling magic into each plant. Each touch carried a sense of finality. Within ten minutes, she was hot and sweaty, and the plants drooped under the weight of bright gems of fruits and vegetables. She couldn't wait to see the looks on Anoush's and Nareg's faces when she brought them a big pile of vegetables.

She looked around. It was quiet. Too quiet. Where were the kits?

Maeve called their names as she hurried through the garden. She arrived at the stone bench in time to see a gray tail poking out of her satchel. Treble tried to back up but tripped over the strap and knocked the whole satchel off the bench. Its contents spread across the ground.

"I told him to leave it alone," Cadenza tattled.

"I found a piece of jerky," Treble said with his teeth clamped down around his prize.

Maeve sighed and bent to clean up the contents of her

satchel. When she picked up the book about plants that Emma had given her, the newspaper article about the Glint Art Gallery opening and the opera program fell out. She'd forgotten she was still carrying around the things that she'd found in the cave.

Cadenza spotted the opera program. "Oh! That's from home! May I see it, please?" Her tail swished back and forth as Maeve set the program in front of her. "I loved watching the operas every night." The kit flipped it open with a claw. "I never got to see this one. It was supposed to open the night after Mother brought us here."

Maeve froze. "You mean it never opened because the opera house Extinguished?"

Cadenza nodded, not realizing the significance of what she'd just said. "Pity. The rehearsals were excellent."

Maeve felt like someone had channeled magic through her. That was the clue and Aria had left them an article about another opening.

Maeve stood up. "The Glint Art Gallery is going to Extinguish at the opening later today." With a growing sense of horror, she realized what this meant. "And everyone is going to be there."

"What are we going to do?" Treble asked.

Maeve considered the pigeons in the apple tree. "How fast do you think those things can fly?"

TWENTY-FOUR

The Glint Art Gallery

Izzy

Izzy ran her palm down her fine silk skirt and scanned the lobby of the Glint Art Gallery. Following Ms. Glint was harder than she'd expected. The hostess knew everyone and kept stopping to talk to clusters of people.

Izzy leaned against a column and pretended to survey the lobby. The crème de la crème of magical society had arrived for the affair, and the Glint Art Gallery was living up to its shiny name. Over one hundred guests strolled across the marble floors. On the other side of the room, Beatrice Scorn was watching a trio of musicians channeling their magic into their flute, piano, and cello. The air smelled like expensive perfume and the spun-sugar confections from Foxglove's on the refreshment tables. Guests wandered in and out of the exhibitions, holding glowing glasses of wine and cider. The theme of the party was Glint and Glimmer—rather obvious, Izzy thought—and everyone and everything sparkled with magic.

A few months ago, Izzy would have given anything to be invited to a party like this, but now her thoughts kept straying to the garden in the Tarnish. She knew that with Ms. Glint here, Maeve was safe, but she still had a horrible feeling about leaving her sister alone.

Ms. Glint was wrapping up her conversation with two women wearing *Votes for Women* sashes. Izzy leaned out from behind a potted plant, getting ready to move again.

Frances came up behind her. "Any sign of Ms. Glint?"

Izzy jumped. "Don't scare me like that." When she looked back, Ms. Glint was gone. "I lost her."

They scanned the room. "There she is." Frances pointed to where a long line was waiting to ride the relevator.

Izzy turned in time to hear the *ding* and see the relevator doors open. She spotted a shimmering gold dress entering the relevator amid the dizzy and delighted guests pouring out. Izzy's heart thumped. She had to get there before those doors closed, or Ms. Glint could get to any room in the multistory gallery. She threaded her way through the crowd as fast as she could.

The relevator doors dinged and slid shut while she was still a good twenty feet away. Izzy cursed, a little louder than she meant to.

Someone coughed awkwardly and Izzy discovered she'd stopped in front of the refreshment table. The teenage clerk stood with his hands clasped in front of his crisp Foxglove's apron.

"Would you like anything?" he asked, gesturing toward a bite-size lemon tart with a glazed raspberry in the center.

The tart looked perfect, but Izzy knew now that looks weren't the only thing that mattered. Wearing a fancy outfit didn't make her any more or less herself.

Izzy stared him right in the eye. "No, thanks."

"Just for the record, I support your school." He shrugged like it wasn't a big deal.

Izzy took a step toward him. "*Just for the record*, your support means nothing if you don't speak up."

Feeling rather stunned at her own daring, Izzy turned on her heel. Emma and Frances had joined Tom and Mr. Harris next to the dais, so she headed in that direction. A lump formed in Izzy's throat. Figgy had been the one who told her she had a voice, and she desperately wanted to tell him that she was finally starting to understand.

A hush fell over the crowd as Mr. Harris ascended the dais. He leaned toward a small megaphone that had been magicked to amplify his voice through the room.

"Welcome, everyone. I'd like to open the festivities by thanking my three muses. One is here beside me." He gestured at Emma, who waved daintily to the crowd. "Another couldn't be with us today. But where is Izzy?" He scanned the room and a delighted smile spread across his face when he spotted her. "Come join me, my dear."

Mr. Harris continued his speech as the crowd parted around Izzy. Her cheeks flushed and she kept her head down.

"The girls brighten my every day. This gallery both literally and figuratively wouldn't exist without them—as well as Ms. Glint, who seems to have disappeared for the moment. Perhaps she's riding my relevator? How do you like it?"

The crowd cheered and clapped in appreciation. Izzy hesitated as she reached the ramp of the dais, suddenly nervous. Wasn't this what she wanted? To be recognized and appreciated by magical society? Emma beckoned Izzy up to the stage, where Mr. Harris was still addressing the crowd. Izzy took a deep breath and stepped up to take her place next to them.

As Mr. Harris spoke about the design work and thanked the construction team, Izzy scanned the faces peering up at her. A terrible thought occurred to her. If Ms. Glint wasn't here, she might have gone to the garden to get the kits.

No sooner had Izzy thought this than the relevator dinged and Mr. Harris said, "Ah! There she is!"

Ms. Glint exited the relevator. Her dress reflected the light of the chandeliers back onto the ceiling. She put her hands on her hips, striking a pose, and camera flashes popped. When they'd finished, Ms. Glint spread her arms wide to receive the applause. "Thank you, George Harris, for helping me make such a dramatic entrance—though I almost left my lunch behind!"

Those who had ridden the relevator laughed. Izzy wasn't charmed. This was the woman stealing the house dragons, the woman who had taken Figgy. She was sure of it. She narrowed her eyes at Ms. Glint and received an elbow in the side from Emma.

Mr. Harris glanced over his shoulder at them, his brow knitted with concern. "Is everything all right back there?"

Before Izzy could speak, someone by the front door screamed.

Six pigeons flew in through the open lobby doors. They circled the chandeliers while the squealing guests below covered their heads.

"Get them out!" Mayor Slight waved his arm toward the ceiling, but the birds of New York did not respect his authority.

Izzy and Emma had spotted what no one else had. One of the pigeons clutched a scrap of paper between its toes.

"They're Pigeon Post!" Izzy gasped. "Did Figgy send them?"

"Click!" Emma said.

"What?" Izzy turned to her.

"They're searching for someone. Click!" Emma insisted.

They clicked their tongues, trying to sound like Figgy.

"What the—?" Mr. Harris wheeled his chair out of the way as the pigeons veered toward the dais.

The pigeons landed at Izzy's feet, bobbing their heads and puffing out their chests self-importantly. The pigeon with the message held out its scaly foot and Izzy took the paper. She recognized her sister's handwriting at once.

Behind her, she heard the mayor demand someone get the birds out, but Izzy was too busy staring at the message Maeve had sent. It was on a torn scrap of the article about this event and written in what appeared to be beet juice.

The gallery is going to Ex.

Emma leaned over to look and gasped when she saw what Maeve had written. "How? Ms. Glint is right here!"

"She must have been setting it up! That's where she came from." Izzy pointed at the relevator. "We have to get everyone out now."

"If we say something, they're going to think you caused it."

"It's too dangerous not to." There were at least a hundred people in the crowd. Why would they listen to Izzy? She heard Figgy in her ear. *You have a voice and you must learn to use it.*

"Excuse me, Mr. Harris," she said, pushing in front of him to the podium. She leaned to speak into the magicked megaphone. "The building is about to Extinguish. You're all in terrible danger and have to get out."

The people in the crowd regarded one another like they thought this was the strangest speech ever. Her eyes found Ms. Glint, who appeared equally confused.

Someone gasped, and Izzy thought her words were finally sinking in. Then, in the back corner, several hands pointed at the line of red char that was slowly spreading across the ceiling.

People screamed and pushed toward the exit.

"We have to go!" Emma tugged Izzy's sleeve.

"No!" Izzy pointed toward the stairs at the back of the gallery. "A house dragon can only start or stop an enchantment when they're physically present. If the building is Exing, Figgy and the house dragons are here."

"Never mind! We've got house dragons to save!" Emma agreed, turning around.

When they reached the bottom of the stairs, Izzy realized Tom and Frances were following them.

"You two need to get out!" Izzy spun around to face them. "The building is about to—"

"Extinguish. We know," Tom said.

"We're Figgy's friends too, and we're not letting you do this without us," Frances insisted.

Izzy decided she was very lucky to have such wonderful friends. She turned back to the stairs but someone was blocking her path. She stared in surprise at Beatrice Scorn.

"Beatrice, get out of the way," Izzy started. "We—"

"You've got house dragons to save. I heard you. You're really loud." Beatrice pointed up the stairs. "Whoever took the house dragons Exed my school and stole Patchouli Rose. I want to get her back and make sure they pay."

"Fair enough. Let's go," Izzy said.

They raced up the stairs. At the top, a number of signs pointed to different exhibits within the gallery. This part of the building didn't show any sign of Exing yet. But the closest thing to a house dragon was a brown cat admiring a fish in one of the paintings.

"Does anyone know where Ms. Glint came from? Did she give a hint?" Emma asked.

"Ms. Glint?" Beatrice raised her eyebrows.

"We'll catch you up." Frances patted her shoulder.

"Where are you, Figs?" Izzy whispered. He was here somewhere, she just had to find him.

"What's that sound?" Beatrice asked.

Izzy closed her eyes and listened. In the distance, she could hear a low hum, like the whir of machinery.

No. Not a hum. A purr.

"That way," she announced, pointing to a doorway on their right.

The acrid scent of the Extinguishing filled Izzy's nose as they ran past paintings and sculptures. She looked back and saw a line of red char following them, turning the marble into concrete in its wake.

Emma saw it too. "Don't stop."

Izzy took a corner too fast. She skidded, but Frances caught her arm. Izzy wished she had on her trusty boots instead of these dainty party shoes. How was anyone supposed to run in these things?

They reached the end of the hall. A large sign that said EXHIBIT CLOSED blocked the doorway. Izzy peered around the sign, but the lights were off.

"This has to be it," she said between panting breaths. "Will someone help me move this sign?"

It was heavier than it looked, or maybe it had been magicked to stay put, but either way, Izzy and Tom managed to rotate it enough so they could all squeeze into the darkened gallery.

"Ms. Glint, are you there? We've come for Figgy," Izzy said, and then ducked, just in case. But only silence answered.

"There's no one here," Emma said, sounding as relieved as Izzy felt.

"Is it hot or is it just me?" Frances whispered.

"It's hot," Izzy agreed, wiping her forehead with the back of her hand. Maybe the room had already Exed. What happened to people trapped inside an Extinguishing? They might be the first to find out. She had a feeling it wasn't a good thing.

Tom flipped his palm toward the ceiling and a tiny flame appeared. "Lights, everyone."

They each raised a palm. One by one, their gems flashed and flickering flames appeared in their palms, casting a warm yellow glow around the room.

"*What in the stones*," Emma whispered in horror.

The exhibit space was smaller than the others, but no less impressive. On the walls, hammered gold jewelry and gold artwork reflected back the light, but Izzy barely glanced at the finery. The air in the center of the room rippled like an invisible bonfire burned beneath it. The invisible fire sucked the flames from their palms into it and began to give off light, casting the room in a strange, silver glow.

At least two dozen small metal cages were stacked on top of each other in a circle around the fire. A coiled house dragon slumbered in each cage.

Izzy's heart pounded as she searched them, every beat whispering, *Please be here*. She spotted him on the far side of the room. His glossy black side rose and fell in an unnatural deep sleep.

Figgy was here.

TWENTY-FIVE
Shine Brighter

Izzy

Izzy started to run straight to Figgy, but Emma grabbed her by the hand. "Izzy, don't!"

The hem of Izzy's skirt brushed against the closest cage. With a burning smell, the bottom six inches of her skirt turned into unhemmed muslin. The magic had been pulled right out of it.

Izzy gulped and stopped to take stock of the situation.

The house dragons' cages filled the entire small gallery. There were tabbies and tortoiseshells, spots, stripes, long-hair, short-hair: more house dragons than Izzy had ever seen.

The strange silver fire cast shadows on the wall, revealing the not-at-all-feline true forms of the slumbering house dragons. Long, scaled tails curled around massive, armored bodies. One of them rolled over and stretched in its sleep, revealing huge talons.

This was the epicenter of the Extinguishing. Whatever enchantment those house dragons were doing was pulling the magic out of the building.

Izzy had to stop it.

Beatrice crouched down next to the house dragon in the closest cage. She tucked her hair behind her ear and inspected the long-haired Persian with a grumpy face. "It's Patchouli Rose," Beatrice said with obvious affection. "They're in some kind of trance."

"If we wake them up, it might be enough to end the enchantment," Frances guessed.

Beatrice stood. "I hate whoever did this."

Izzy did too, but she had to use her anger to fuel her actions, not let it stop her. "It was Ms. Glint, we told you," she said, without taking her eyes off Figgy. There was no way to get to him without getting close to the cages or going through the fire in the center.

"But that doesn't make sense," Beatrice said. "Why would Ms. Glint Ex her own buildings?"

"Maybe to make herself look innocent?" Emma guessed.

Izzy gestured at the cages. "We don't have time to get into this right now. We have to wake them up." She clapped her hands like she was holding invisible cymbals. "Be as loud as you can!"

Emma yelled and stomped her feet. Tom cupped his hands around his mouth and shouted at the top of his lungs. Frances found a golden gong on display and rang it with the heel of her shoe. Even Beatrice joined in, crouching and shrieking near the tortoiseshell. The house dragons shifted restlessly in their cages and the fire dipped, but the second they stopped making noise, it rose again.

Emma stopped yelling and gasped for air. "It's not enough."

The others quieted around her.

"We could pour some water on them," Beatrice suggested. "Our cat at home hates it when my little sister does that, but it wakes her up."

"When we were trying to kindle, Figgy used to brag that house dragons were masters of flame. I'd be afraid pouring water on them would be like snuffing," Frances said.

The mention of snuffing made the room feel hotter. Izzy rubbed her hands on the remaining silk of her skirt. What were they going to do?

The line of char crept steadily down the hall toward the exhibit where the house dragons slept. Not all the artwork was magicked, but even the real paint became gray and dusted with ash. What would happen when the line of char reached them? Would the Extinguishing be complete?

Anger rose within Izzy. Clever, cultured Figgy would hate that his magic was being used to destroy beautiful artwork and buildings. She had to wake him up. Something about what Frances had said clicked in her brain.

"They're masters of flame." Izzy clapped her hands over her mouth as the realization hit her. No one understood fire the way house dragons did and no one understood house dragon magic. She couldn't fix this, but she could help the house dragons find their own way out.

You have a voice and you must learn to use it, Figgy

had told her. What if it wasn't about fancy speeches, but about knowing the right thing to say at the right time? To the right person?

Or to the right house dragon.

Izzy channeled her magic into her diamond bracelet. Each of the three stones glowed with magic. She reached out her hand toward the flames.

Emma jumped up, seeing what she intended.

"Izzy, you can't! It pulls the magic out of everything. What if it hurts *your* magic?" Emma protested.

Izzy pointed at Figgy, asleep in his cage across the room. "I have to get to Figgy, Em. It's our only way to stop this." She swallowed, summoning her courage. "Keep making noise. You have to wake them up enough to let me though."

To her relief, Emma began stomping her feet and shouting. The gray house dragon in the closest cage stretched a paw in the air like he was trying to wake. Tom joined in, yelling and clapping, and Frances took up banging the gong again. Beatrice knocked over the EXHIBIT CLOSED sign and beat it like a drum.

Now was her chance. Izzy steeled herself.

"Wake up," she said, stepping into the circle. "Wake up," she said over and over. The house dragon magic thrummed against her like loud purring. She took one step and then another toward Figgy.

Magic swirled around her, reminding her of the way she'd felt she was both flying and falling when she kindled. The house dragons' flames danced higher than her head. It was so hot she could barely breathe, but still she walked forward.

"I'm coming, Figgy," she promised.

A line of char spread upward from her toes, reversing the magic in the rest of her fancy dress. It stung, but the house dragons didn't burn her. They didn't want to be doing this.

"Fight it," she whispered. She could feel the strength of their magic surrounding her. How could anyone ever underestimate house dragons?

The fire lowered to her shoulders.

Her hair came loose from her ringlets and hung limp around her face. Izzy didn't care about any of it. Her only thought was for her friend, lying prone in the cage in front of her.

One step and then another. As she walked, she wove an enchantment of her own. She felt for the heat of the fire and, using the opposite of the expanding enchantments she'd practiced with Figgy, condensed it. The house dragons around the circle stirred, ears and paws twitching, like they sensed what she was doing. A Siamese near Beatrice yawned and rolled over.

Izzy pushed more magic into her bracelet until she was sweating with the effort. The fire shrank with every step she took toward Figgy.

When Izzy looked back, she saw the char in the distance. As she watched, it receded.

It's working, she realized.

Izzy took another step and then one more. She was only

a few feet away from Figgy, but it was so hot she could barely stand. *One more step*, she urged herself. Her legs buckled and she fell to the floor. The calico in the cage below Figgy rolled over in her sleep.

Izzy pushed herself up to her knees and stretched her hand toward Figgy's cage. She screamed, feeling like her hand was burning as she reached her fingertips through the bars of the cage. "I'm here, Figgy. I'm here."

Her fingers touched Figgy's soft fur, and his magic rose to meet hers. It was the final push she needed. Izzy found the loose ends of the house dragons' enchantment and seared them to her own.

A swirling wind filled the gallery. Her friends were shouting, but it was all Izzy could do to hang on to Figgy's cage. She gripped the bars, refusing to let go, even as the wind pulled her toward the center of the circle.

At once, the wind stopped. The silence rang in her ears.

Figgy's yellow eyes fluttered open. "Izzy?"

Tears sprang to Izzy's eyes. "Hi, Figs. I missed you."

The room cooled as the house dragons awakened. Tom and Frances worked at one of the locks on the cages, trying to free the lanky tabby within. Beatrice already had the door of Patchouli Rose's cage open.

Emma hurried over and knelt beside Izzy. "Figgy, we're so glad we found you. We'll get you out of there in a moment."

Figgy looked between them, ears and tail at attention. "Wait, if you're here, that means he's already gone."

"He?" Izzy exchanged a look with Emma. "Don't you mean Ms. Glint?"

The elegant calico in the cage below Figgy sat up. "Cousin, he's going for my kits, I know he is."

"Aria?" Izzy guessed, and the house dragon dipped her head in acknowledgment. "My sister's with the kits now, protecting them. But if it's not Glint, who's been doing this?" She waved her hand, gesturing at the cages.

Figgy shook his head. "Oh, Izzy. We were so wrong."

TWENTY-SIX

The Bull Charges

Maeve

Maeve curled and uncurled her fingertips, watching the green sparks flicker between them. She hoped Izzy had gotten her message about the Exing. It was hard to be here by herself, with no way of knowing what was happening uptown.

It was quiet but not peaceful in the garden. Every time she looked at the flowers blowing softly in the wind, she pictured them crushed beneath debris from a wrecking ball. How soon would Glint's wrecking crew start tearing things down now that the residents had left? She turned to the vegetable garden. *This place could help so many people,* she thought. What would Ms. Glint build? Another fancy building for the rich?

Boom.

Cadenza yelped and leaped off the stone bench. "What was that?"

"It sounded like a sledgehammer against the fence."

Forte scampered up the branch of the closest apple tree and craned his neck.

Boom.

Maeve swallowed. "I think it *is* a sledgehammer against the fence."

She helped the kittens down from the tree. They raced to the path in time to see the fence shudder as a third *boom* pounded the boards.

Maeve felt dizzy. It was too soon. She wasn't ready.

Cadenza pawed at Maeve's ankle. "The garden's defenses won't let them in, right? Mother's enchantment will hold?"

Another *boom* and one of the boards splintered in the middle. Maeve could hear voices and the sound of demolition outside. Her shoulders tensed. She had never heard outside noises in here before. The garden's defenses must be cracking with the boards.

Treble joined his siblings at her feet, rubbing the sleep from his eyes. "Did they just say *kits*? Are they talking about us?"

"It has to be Ms. Glint." Maeve's mouth was dry. "But she should be at the opening uptown." Had she been wrong about Aria's warning? No, she knew she hadn't been. Ms. Glint must have thought no one would be protecting the garden. But Maeve was here.

Her leg twinged where she'd broken it when the bull threw her high in the air.

"I'm scared," Forte whimpered, and drew close to Maeve.

"I'm scared too," Maeve admitted. She squared her shoulders. "You need to hide. I'll tell you if it's safe to come out. If it's not, you need to make a run for it while I distract Ms. Glint."

The undergrowth rustled as the kits scurried into it.

Resisting the urge to hide herself, Maeve faced the fence. She took one step forward and then another. The scrape of tools against the fence sounded like the scrape of the bull's hooves. Her nightmare was coming true and she would have to face it alone.

"Hurry up," a man said. "I'm not paying you to take breaks."

His cold voice was familiar, but Maeve couldn't place it.

Two metal crowbars poked through the gap and tugged at the boards. They were coming inside the garden.

Maeve stood in front of the fence and prepared for the bull to charge. This time, she wouldn't be caught unawares.

With a crack, the first fence board splintered and fell. A great gust of wind whooshed from behind Maeve, flipping the leaves of the plants upside down. There was a shout from outside. Then the wind died, the leaves settled, and she could hear the voices clearly.

"What was that noise?" the man on the other side of the fence demanded, but Maeve knew what it was. One of the garden's magical protections, gone. She could feel it, like a faint tingling on her skin. The air felt different in here already.

"It's easier now." The crowbars appeared again and the boards on either side of the hole fell away.

Maeve gasped as a tall, thin man stepped into the garden.

Mr. Rote's hair looked even whiter against the bright green plants. The headmaster of Glint Kindling Academy beheld the garden with disdain. "This can't be right. The cat said she'd Extinguished it."

Two white men holding sledgehammers stepped inside behind him. They both had closely cropped hair, huge muscles, and the square shoulders of local dockworkers. The shorter one looked like he might have taken a sledgehammer to the teeth at some point.

Maeve felt like running away, but she didn't. She took a deep breath and stood her ground.

"Well, this is unexpected," Mr. Rote said with a sneer. Izzy had said something about Mr. Rote having a talent with ice, and indeed his manner was just as cold. He raised an eyebrow in Maeve's direction and then turned back to his sledgehammer-wielding lackeys. "Find the kits. She's not going to be a problem."

Her hands curled into fists. He did not get to dismiss her. Not here in her garden. She planned on being a very big problem.

Her eyes landed on the gaping hole in the fence. If she could distract him, the kits could sneak away.

Maeve raised her voice. "The kits *ran away*." She hoped they would take the hint. Maeve took a step to the side, hoping to draw his attention away from the fence. "Why are you working for Glint? What does she want with the kits anyway?"

"Gladys Glint?" Mr. Rote scoffed. "I doubt she even knows I'm here. She offered that reward to improve her image, though she doesn't understand what these kits truly mean. But I don't have time for you." He reached his hands out like he intended to grab her. Ice crystals formed on his fingertips. He took a step forward but his feet stuck fast. "What the . . . ?"

Maeve's heart fluttered with hope. It was the last of Aria's enchantment, protecting her and the kits from anyone with bad intentions. He couldn't go any farther.

But his lackeys wanted to get paid, which apparently wasn't ill-intentioned enough for Aria's enchantment to stop them. Mr. Rote pointed behind Maeve. "Boys, search the garden. The kits are here somewhere, I know it."

The muscled men swung their sledgehammers indiscriminately as they made their way through the garden. *Crash.* The trellis that Avi had built splintered. With another swing, an azalea bush exploded in a shower of leaves and petals. Maeve tried to tell herself it didn't matter, the garden was slated for demolition anyway, but she hadn't expected to see her beloved plants destroyed with her own eyes.

"Stop, please," she begged. "I told you they're not here."

The shorter man lumbered toward the apple trees with the sledgehammer raised over his shoulder. "Come out, come out, little kitties."

"Be careful," Mr. Rote shouted. "I want the kits alive." He shaded his eyes with his hand and scanned the underbrush.

"Why do you want the kits so badly?" she shouted. "Is it because you want a house dragon at your school?"

"What are you stalling for, girl? No one is coming to help you," Mr. Rote taunted. Maeve cringed. "Your friends are uptown and that gaudy gallery should be finished Extinguishing by now. They'll have their hands full." A slow, terrifying smile spread across his face. "Do you know how much raw power a house dragon kit has? No, I don't suppose you do. Tell me where the kits are so I can put their powers to use."

A cold, hard knot of realization tightened in Maeve's gut. She felt like she couldn't breathe from the horror of it. "You're the one causing the Extinguishings."

Mr. Rote sighed. "So much work and still no respect. *I* am saving this city from itself. Do you know what would happen if we let magic go unchecked?" He made an explosion gesture with his hands. "Chaos, that's what! Everyone reaching for the next rung of the social ladder, climbing willy-nilly." He grunted. "No, I'm doing this city a favor. You see, I set a little trap for your sister tonight at the gallery opening. Your house dragon, Banana Pudding—"

"*Figgy* Pudding," Maeve interrupted.

"I don't care what his name is." Mr. Rote raised his eyebrows at the vehemence of her response. "Your sister's affection for him was pitifully obvious and I knew she'd attempt to rescue him. That will put her squarely at the scene of the crime. Do you know what happens after that?"

The taller henchman swinging his sledgehammer paused. "No. What happens?" he shouted from the bushes.

"I'm not talking to you!" Mr. Rote's face turned red with anger.

There was a blur of calico as Cadenza darted behind Mr. Rote's ankles from the underbrush to the pumpkin vines. Forte followed a second later. Maeve swallowed. Where was Treble?

Focus. Keep the bull's attention.

"What happens?" Maeve asked, though she didn't think she wanted to hear this.

Mr. Rote lifted his chin and squared his shoulders like he was teaching a class. "Excellent question. The papers will print that your sister was tied to the site of another Exing—this time with hundreds of witnesses. She'll be arrested and then, lo and behold, the Exings will stop. Your ridiculous excuse of a school will close and mine will carry on. From now on, only those with actual worth will kindle—and I will be the one to determine their worth. Too bad a very small number of children from neighborhoods like this will qualify." His smile was so cold Maeve expected to see ice crystals on it too. "I will make sure magic stays in the right hands where it belongs."

"But what about my kids?" the tall henchman interrupted again.

"Shut up and keep searching for those kits." Mr. Rote grumbled something else under his breath.

Maeve wasn't listening to any of this. It wasn't just Mr. Rote's vision of the future that had frozen her with fear. No, she'd finally spotted Treble. He wasn't following his siblings like they'd planned. He was slowly climbing the fence on the other side of Mr. Rote. Maeve's fingers clawed at the air at her sides in frustration. Any moment now, Rote's goons would spot him. She watched with horror as Mr. Rote turned toward the kit.

Maeve stepped toward Mr. Rote and waved her arms to

draw his attention back. "You'll never get away with this. I'll go to the papers—"

"And who will they believe? You or me? A penniless student from a shuttered school or one of the most influential voices in magical education?" Mr. Rote scoffed. "We'll have to do something about you, though. My friends at the Gemstone Society for Orphan Welfare should be able to help."

Not them. Hearing the name of the society caused a visceral response in Maeve's stomach. She wrapped her arms around her middle, feeling small and alone. No one was coming to help her now, like no one had come then. "Just because you have money and magic doesn't mean you can control everyone's lives," she said. She took a step toward him and tried to raise her chin in defiance, but her voice quivered and betrayed her fear.

"Want to bet?" Mr. Rote leaned forward and grabbed her by the wrist. Maeve screamed. She hadn't meant to get so close.

Treble sprang off the fence, a whirlwind of flailing claws. "Leave my Maeve alone!"

"Treble, don't!" Maeve shouted, but it was too late.

Treble collided with the side of Mr. Rote's face. The headmaster screamed and tried to wave away the furry projectile, but Treble had sunk his claws into his collar. Golden sparks shot from Mr. Rote's hands as he struggled against the raging furball. Maeve thought they were burning Treble's fur until she saw that where each spark landed, it revealed a shiny green scale.

"No!" Maeve lunged toward them, but one of Mr. Rote's henchmen pulled her back by the collar of her dress.

Mr. Rote thrashed around like an injured animal. He managed to grab Treble by the scruff of his neck. His wristwatch flashed with magic and a collar of ice appeared around the house dragon's neck. Treble let out a scared squeak and flopped across Rote's arm with his eyes closed.

"Works every time," Mr. Rote bragged.

"What have you done to him?" Maeve yanked herself out of the henchman's grip and lunged toward Mr. Rote. But the other goon nearly grabbed her and she had to dodge.

Maeve wasn't afraid anymore. The sight of Treble's still body draped across Mr. Rote's arm lit a fire within her and her rage became courage. She reached down inside herself and felt her magic burning bright. The three diamonds on her wrist glowed with magic as she crouched down and plunged her hands into the soil.

The hum of magic filled her veins as the garden rose to defend itself. Pumpkin and zucchini vines surged forward, tangling themselves around the henchmen's ankles. One of them tripped and his sledgehammer flew through the air to land at Mr. Rote's feet. The grass grew higher until it shielded the fallen henchman from view. Ripe tomatoes expanded to the size of balloons and then exploded. The second henchman screamed and wiped the pulp from his eyes.

Like the prairie roses before them, the azaleas and rosebushes in the garden swelled and stretched their branches toward Mr. Rote.

"You little brat," Mr. Rote shouted as the thorns tore through the legs of his pants.

Before he had time to recover, Maeve leaped over the branches and grabbed the still-unconscious Treble right out of his hands. The green scales that Mr. Rote's fire had revealed had already been covered over with downy fur again, but Treble was hot to the touch.

"Let's go!" she shouted to the other kits.

Cadenza and Forte came sprinting out of the undergrowth to race alongside her. Clutching Treble to her chest, Maeve ran through the hole in the fence. Treble let out a little mew and shuddered as they crossed the line of the fence but didn't wake. His ice collar was still tight around his neck.

The tomato-faced henchman was right behind her. He reached toward her.

"Maeve! Duck!" a voice shouted from in front of her.

Maeve leaned forward and Avi threw the wrinkled potato with all his might. It hit the henchman square in the nose and he fell back with a cry.

"What are you doing here? I thought you left." Maeve panted. She couldn't tell Avi how happy she was to see him.

"I came back. I realized I couldn't leave without saying goodbye." Avi grinned at her. "Who was that chasing you?"

"No time to explain. We have to get the kits out of here."

She turned toward the end of the block and let out a cry of despair. Ms. Glint's crew must have gotten there early because the whole street was walled off. They were trapped—

Wait.

It wasn't a wall, it was *people*. Hundreds of them, marching toward the garden. They spanned from storefront to storefront across the street, and as far back as she could see. Their faces were every shade of color and their clothes ranged from department-store finery to tattered shawls, but they all wore the same look of determination as they marched.

Emma, Tom, and Antonia walked in the front. Mr. Harris was right beside them, with Figgy Pudding riding on his lap. A policeman in a bell-shaped hat marched alongside them with a tough-looking tabby house dragon draped over his shoulders. Maeve spotted Miss Clementine's orange hair amid a group of women wearing *Votes for Women* sashes. Maeve's classmates waved when they saw her and pointed her out to several kids in the frilly uniforms of Glint Kindling Academy. There was Frances Slight and her mustached father, the mayor. Ms. Glint herself was there—and her photographer, naturally—along with several other fancy-dressed people from the gallery opening. Shoulder to shoulder with them were the people she'd seen around the neighborhood. The shopkeepers who had sold her the tools, the pushcart vendors she'd passed on her way to the garden, and Anoush and Nareg, waving at her.

There at the very front of the crowd was Izzy, her beloved Izzy, with a calico house dragon trotting at her heels.

Maeve looked at Avi beside her. He had come back.

She had never been less alone in her entire life.

"Mother!" Cadenza and Forte shouted with joy and raced toward the calico.

Maeve stood panting in the street, her heart pounding. She'd faced the bull and survived. She hugged Treble. "Wake up, it's over," she whispered.

But it wasn't.

"Maeve, look out!" Avi shouted.

Mr. Rote climbed though the gap in the fence with a sledgehammer in his hands, and his gaze locked on Maeve. She stumbled back a step. Her sister and the others were still too far away. Izzy shouted and broke into a run.

Mr. Rote shouldered the sledgehammer and Maeve's knees went weak. "I will not be foiled by an insignificant little girl. If I can't have the kits, no one will have them."

He turned around and drove his sledgehammer into the fence. She saw the flash of his watch and knew this was no ordinary blow.

There was a booming crash as the garden's final protective enchantment broke. A crack appeared in the air above the fence, like a giant invisible piece of glass breaking. As Maeve watched in mute horror, a spiderweb of cracks stretched out in a dome over the garden.

Arms encircled Maeve, pulling her down into a crouch. There was a loud *whoosh*, like a long-held seal had broken, and air rushed toward them as the fence teetered. Maeve screamed, but the sound was drowned out by the crash of the garden's invisibility raining down in sharp shards to the street below. Then everything disappeared in a hailstorm of sparkling pieces of sky.

TWENTY-SEVEN

Diamonds in the Rough

Izzy

For a moment, everything was so bright that Izzy didn't know where she was. As the glittering pieces of the garden's invisibility fell around her, the world seemed to stretch out and blur. The greens of the garden blended with the brown bricks of the Tarnish.

Then, all at once, the crashing stopped. The sudden silence rang in her ears. Izzy looked out at the astonished faces of the crowd in front of her.

Sharp shards of shattered magic covered the street, except for a perfect circle around her and Maeve and the boy she assumed must be Avi, who was crouched behind them. What had happened? She should have been sliced to bits.

"How?" Izzy sputtered, turning to Maeve. That was when she spotted the tiny gray furball tucked in her sister's elbow.

Maeve snuggled him under her chin. "Treble! You saved us!"

Treble purred and his whiskers trembled with unrestrained pride. He had a ring of wet fur around his neck, but his golden eyes were wide and alert. "I did magic! I don't have to be a squirrel!"

"You are a wonderful house dragon." Maeve hugged him tightly.

"Are you all right?" Emma called. Twenty feet of glittering shards covered the ground between her and the O'Donnells.

"Can we go see Mother now?" Treble asked, peering at his family. Cadenza and Forte were bouncing around, talking to their mother while she alternated giving them each a bath.

Izzy inched closer to the shards. "I think we're stuck for the moment."

"Hang tight and don't touch it. We're coming," Mr. Harris shouted.

"This is so weird," the boy behind them said, and the sisters turned toward him. "Hi, I'm Avi. You must be Izzy."

Maeve grinned at both of them. "I was afraid you two would never meet."

Across the shards, Emma cupped her hands around her mouth. "Figgy says not to use more magic on the broken enchantment. People are fetching brooms."

Izzy waited as patiently as she could. After the flurry of activity in racing out of the gallery and speeding downtown, it felt odd to be standing so still.

Maeve stared at her sister. "Izzy, what are you wearing?"

Izzy still had on the dress that the house dragons' magic had reduced to its pre-magicked form. Rough cut, plain muslin hung from her shoulders like a sack. "It's a long story," she said.

"You're all here. You came back for me." Maeve smiled and hugged Treble again. Then her eyes widened. "Wait, what happened to Mr. Rote? He was right behind us."

Avi pointed to a large, unmoving lump beneath the shards.

Treble winced. "That doesn't look comfortable."

A *swoosh plink* noise from behind them made Izzy spin back around. Several shopkeepers and locals had returned with brooms and were sweeping up the shards. Emma and Tom took the brooms that were offered to them and swept a path toward Izzy, Maeve, and Avi.

"Oh no," Maeve said quietly.

Izzy followed her gaze to the garden and her happiness deflated.

The fence had come down and the garden was visible to everyone. But it was in rough shape. Some of the plants looked like they'd had sledgehammers driven through them—which they probably had. But that wasn't the worst of it. Shards of magic an inch deep covered every surface, making it look like the garden was covered in snow.

"Avi, I'm so sorry." Maeve's voice cracked.

Avi stared at the garden. "It isn't your fault, Maeve. I know you love it as much as I do." His lips quirked up in a smile. "In a strange way, I'm happy. Now everyone will get to see how wonderful the garden is before the block gets torn down."

"Almost there!" Emma announced from a few feet away. When she was within arm's reach, Treble leaped from Maeve's arms onto Emma's shoulder, somersaulted down her back, and sprinted down the path.

"Mother!" he cried as he ran. "I did magic!"

Izzy couldn't help but smile as she watched him snuggle against his mother's side.

Tom held up his broom. "Does anyone else enjoy the irony that we rescued you from magic with the most mundane thing possible?"

Emma pushed her hair away from her sweaty forehead. Her curls had come loose, but her smile had gotten bigger. "You saved us, Maeve. Figgy says you thought like a true house dragon. I'm pretty sure that's a compliment of the highest order."

"I'll take it," Maeve said, with the start of a smile. "Everyone, this is Avi."

As Izzy watched Maeve introducing Avi to Emma, Izzy's heart felt whole.

"You look pretty happy for someone who just survived a magical catastrophe, Iz. Whatcha thinking?" Tom asked her as he leaned on his broom handle.

"I was thinking about family." Izzy would have said more, but she was interrupted by a loud groan from behind them.

Mr. Rote pushed himself up to sit. Shards of magic plinked off him to the ground below. His face was bloodied and bruised, but somehow he'd survived the destruction intact . . . well, relatively.

"This is a lovely place," he said. His gaze was unfocused and dreamy. "How did I get here?"

Izzy exchanged a look with her friends. "Anyone else in favor of getting as far away from him as possible?"

"I know he's evil, but we should probably send someone to check on him," Emma suggested as Mr. Rote rocked back and forth, making soft meowing noises.

"Yeah, and to arrest him," Maeve added.

"We'll take care of that." The Chief of Police marched up the path. The grizzled house dragon on the chief's shoulders growled at Mr. Rote. "Mr. Cupcake has told me the whole story about this cad. He'll be going away for a long, long time."

"The police house dragon is named *Mr. Cupcake?*" Izzy whispered to Maeve, unable to keep the glee out of her voice. Maeve's shoulders bounced with laughter.

The hard knot in Izzy's chest relaxed. If Maeve was laughing, they could get through this.

"Mind if I borrow that broom, miss?" The chief extended his hand toward Emma, who relinquished her broom. He swept his way toward Mr. Rote, who was now arching his back and making clicking noises at the pigeons on Avi's fire escape.

"He thinks he's a house dragon." Avi winced.

Mr. Rote hissed as the Chief of Police handcuffed him.

"Let's give them some space," Emma suggested. They

headed back down the path that Emma and Tom had swept. Izzy stuck firmly to her sister's side.

"I can't wait to read the newspapers' accounts about this tomorrow," Tom said as they walked. "What do you think the headline will be? 'Headmaster's Career Extinguished?' Hm, or maybe 'House Dragons and Schoolgirls in Epic Showdown at the Tarnished Garden.'" He spread his arms wide, enraptured by the invisible headlines. Izzy lunged to grab his broom handle before he dropped it.

"'The Tarnished Garden' has a real ring to it," Maeve said with a sad look over her shoulder.

Izzy hugged her with the arm that wasn't holding Tom's broom. "Either way, I hope they get it right."

"They'd better." Tom nodded in agreement.

"You should write the article, Tom. After all, who could write it more accurately than you?" Emma suggested.

Tom stopped in his tracks. "I could! *I could write it.*" His face fell. "But the papers aren't going to let me. I'm a kid."

Emma squeezed his arm. "So? Tom, *kids* stopped the Extinguishings. *Kids* found the kits and saved the house dragons. Besides, you were actually there and you're a really good writer." Tom blushed so hard his ears turned pink. Emma pointed. "There's Ms. Glint's photographer. I'm sure he knows people at the papers. Go talk to him."

Tom started to protest, so Izzy gave him a shove. "Go. Get the story right."

Still blushing, Tom hurried toward the photographer.

"I'll be right back," Avi said to Maeve. "There's something I have to do." He pushed his way into the crowd.

Izzy, Emma, and Maeve headed toward Mr. Harris, who was waiting for them at the end of the path.

"Are you all right, girls?" he asked.

Izzy opened her mouth to answer, but Maeve beat her to it.

"I can't believe you came here for me," Maeve said, looking between Mr. Harris and Emma.

"I wish we'd been here sooner. He didn't hurt you, did he?" Mr. Harris asked without taking his eyes off Maeve. His forehead was creased with worry, and his normally impeccable hair looked like he'd run his fingers through it more than once.

Maeve shook her head. "I'll be fine. He only hurt the garden."

"I wish there was something I could do," Mr. Harris said.

To Izzy's surprise, Maeve smiled.

"Thank you," Maeve said. "I know you mean that."

"I do." Mr. Harris gestured to the side of the street. "Would you like to see what Figgy is doing over there? He's gathered quite an audience."

Maeve smiled shyly. "Probably telling his harrowing tale. Would you like a push?"

Mr. Harris folded his hands in his lap. "That would be lovely, thank you."

As Maeve reached for the handles of his wheelchair, Izzy spotted a thin gold bracelet sparkling beneath her sister's sleeve.

"Well, that was unexpected," Izzy whispered to Emma.

"Unexpected, but not unhoped-for," Emma agreed with a smile.

They found Figgy perched on the side of a pushcart, talking to a rapt crowd. At the front, some local kids, including Maeve's friends Anoush and Nareg, and a few of the Manhattan School students sat cross-legged on the ground with house dragons on their laps. Aria stood beside the pushcart while her kits stared up at Figgy in awe.

Figgy was not recounting his harrowing tale as Maeve had guessed, but rather was in the middle of a history lesson.

"There was a similar occurrence in Boston in March of 1770. A group of British soldiers shattered a protective enchantment over a town square when they opened fire. Of course, there was snow on the ground so many accounts do not include the shattered enchantment—" Figgy cut off as he saw them approaching. "Here they come now."

The crowd broke into applause.

"I have a question." Anoush pointed toward the garden. "Are those big plants in there from the seeds we helped you find? How'd they get so big so fast?"

"They are, Anoush." Maeve shrugged modestly. "I grew them with my magic."

"That's incredible!" Anoush threw her hands in the air, upending the tortoiseshell house dragon in her lap. The house dragon flicked his ears in annoyance and settled into the lap of Nareg, who looked delighted.

"Excuse me. Coming through," Mayor Slight announced, and the people at the back stepped aside. Izzy recognized

Frances's father both from his very serious mustache and his daughter's presence at his side. "Well, Isabelle O'Donnell. You've done it again." He paused. "But how?"

Ms. Glint appeared beside the mayor. "Yes. I want to hear about the children who saved my art gallery."

Everyone looked at Izzy, but Izzy looked at Maeve. "I couldn't have done any of it without my sister." Izzy explained how Maeve had figured out Aria's clue and sent the pigeons to warn them.

"But how did you know?" Mayor Slight turned to Maeve.

Maeve waved to Aria and the kits. "I had some help from a few good house dragons."

"Very powerful and magical house dragons." Treble preened, and his mother gave him a lick between the ears.

"We want to hear the whole story!" someone in the back shouted.

"Come on up," Figgy suggested, scooting over.

Izzy climbed onto the pushcart and helped Maeve up behind her.

Both sisters offered their hands to Emma, but she demurred with a shake of her head. "You tell it. It's your story."

So the whole story came pouring out, with Izzy telling bits about the school, and Maeve sharing about how she'd found the garden and cultivated it while searching for information about Aria. The house dragon kits jumped in to add details of what had happened in the garden, and Figgy and Aria recounted the dreamless sleep they'd been kept in while being carted from place to place to cause the Extinguishings.

While they spoke, the crowd around them grew. Izzy looked out at the faces, familiar and not, of children from the Tarnish, listening to two kids from their neighborhood who had gone uptown and come back again.

When they were done, Mr. Harris put his head in his hands. "I haven't decided whether to ground you all or request a medal in your honor."

"But you're children! Surely you had help from an adult," Mayor Slight insisted.

"Does Figgy count as an adult?" Izzy asked.

"I should hope not," Figgy said, ears swiveling.

Mayor Slight shook his head in disbelief. "I had my best people working on the Extinguishings and they couldn't figure it out."

"Kids are good at noticing things," Maeve said with a smile.

"Speaking of which." Mr. Harris looked thoughtful. He stroked his chin and glanced toward the garden. "Maeve, you were able to restore the garden after it Extinguished. Do you think you could teach us how you did it? Perhaps we can restore the other buildings."

"That would be wonderful. I would so love to go home to the opera house," Cadenza said. Forte nodded.

"The garden Extinguished overnight, but repairing it took a long time," Maeve cautioned. "We did it little by little, day by day." She looked around at the crowd. "I'll teach you, but it will take all of us working together if we want to fix every building that Extinguished. We'll need people to clear away the debris and damage, and we'll need magic to rebuild."

"I'll help." Emma raised her hand.

Frances waved with her whole arm from the back of the crowd. "Me too!"

Shouts of "I'll help too" filled the street as, side by side, the residents of uptown and the Tarnish raised their hands and pledged their aid to fix the city. Maeve nodded in thanks and acknowledgment at each new offer of help. Izzy watched her sister with a growing sense of pride. Perhaps Izzy hadn't been the only one to find her voice and learn how to use it.

"And where is the boy, this Avi you mentioned? Will he help us too?" Mr. Harris asked.

Maeve looked around. "I don't know where he went." But then she spotted him.

In the back of the crowd, Avi led his mother by the hand toward the garden.

The golden sparks of surprise that shot from Maeve's fingertips were as bright as the joy on her face.

TWENTY-EIGHT

The O'Donnell Sisters

Maeve

Maeve hopped off the pushcart and wove through the crowd to her friend. When she reached Avi and Mrs. Sigal, she paused.

"Hi," Avi said.

"Hi," Maeve said back.

His hands weren't wrapped in rags. She realized they hadn't been when he'd thrown the potato that hit Mr. Rote, either. Her heart beat faster in her chest.

"Why did you come back for real?" Maeve asked.

Avi shifted. "We were on our way to Grand Central when I found that potato of yours in my bag. It made me want to turn around, so I told Mameh I had to go back to say goodbye to someone—and something—important." His smile grew as he spoke. "Tateh's waiting with our bags, but I asked Mameh to come with me."

Mrs. Sigal had her hands over her mouth and tears in her eyes as she stared at the garden.

"I'm sorry. I didn't mean to destroy your brother's garden," Maeve started before she remembered that Mrs. Sigal didn't speak English very well. She looked to Avi. "Please tell her."

"It's not that, Maeve." Avi swallowed, looking close to tears himself. "She's never seen the garden before. It's always been invisible to her before now."

Mrs. Sigal murmured something, and Maeve didn't need a common language to understand the joy, awe, and sadness in her words.

"I wish you could both stay and enjoy it," Maeve said, half to Avi and half to herself.

"We're still moving." Avi sounded glum. "Tateh and Mameh can get jobs at the factory where my sister works and it's less crowded there. But I hate to leave the garden alone and undefended."

"It's not alone anymore. Look." Maeve pointed at the garden.

Someone had pulled apart the boards from the fence and laid them end to end to create a path over the shards. Maeve watched people stopping to admire the plants and found she didn't mind at all. In fact, her heart soared when she saw Anoush and Nareg prancing along the boards and jumping up to swing from the lowest branches of the apple trees. It was better this way, open and no longer a secret. Maeve wished she could sear joy like an enchantment, to make it last forever.

Mrs. Sigal spoke without taking her eyes off the garden.

Avi's shoulders tensed. "She wants to go inside."

"Go," Maeve urged him. "Show her what you made."

Avi gently took his mother's arm. Maeve watched how Mrs. Sigal lowered her head closer to her son's as they walked together into the garden she'd known existed for so long but had never seen.

Maeve stood alone, but she wasn't lonely. She thought again that these people had come to her aid and was astonished all over again.

"Miss O'Donnell? I'd like a word with you, please." Ms. Glint stepped out of the crowd. The woman lived up to her name. Her dress shimmered so brightly it hurt Maeve's eyes.

Maeve took a deep breath. "I'm really sorry about the mess on your new property."

"She's not angry," Mr. Harris said, coming up alongside them.

Maeve's shoulders relaxed, but only a fraction.

"I wanted to thank you for your quick thinking and for saving my gallery." Ms. Glint stilled. "I also wanted to apologize for the behavior of my colleagues. I'm firing Mr. Rote from his position as headmaster. I also spoke to Mayor Slight and he just left for his office to remove Mrs. Nimby as the Acting Commissioner on the Board of Magical Education. She won't bother you anymore." Ms. Glint sighed regretfully. "I'm sorry. I truly want to help children."

Maeve was grateful to hear this news, but another

worry still plagued her mind. She shifted her weight. "Are you still going to tear the block down?"

Ms. Glint shook her head. "Mr. Harris and I were just discussing how I would have preferred to purchase more land uptown. I bought this block at Mr. Rote's insistence. He said he was going to open another school, but now I think he only wanted into that garden of yours." She looked around the block. "Now I'm not sure what to do with this. Maybe I'll rent out these apartments until I decide."

Mr. Harris raised an eyebrow. Maeve wondered if he was thinking the same thing she was. She doubted it, but she'd say it anyway. "What if *we* opened the school?"

To her surprise, Mr. Harris smiled and gave her an encouraging nod.

Ms. Glint tilted her head. "Go on."

Maeve swallowed. "I grew up here. So did Izzy." She took a deep breath. "This community needs magic. The school uptown is destroyed. What if we traded you that property for this one? We could build a school for magic in the Tarnish with a garden that everyone could enjoy?"

Izzy, Emma, and Figgy joined their circle in time to hear Maeve's suggestion.

"I always wanted a school like that when we were growing up." Izzy grinned.

Maeve turned to Mr. Harris. "I'm sorry. I got carried away. You own the property uptown so—"

"I love this idea, Maeve." Mr. Harris smiled. "Gladys? What do you think?"

Ms. Glint paused thoughtfully, but there was a joyful gleam in her eye. "It's an interesting business proposition, though you're selling yourself short. Land uptown is much more expensive than land down here. I'd have to throw in some extra to make it worth your while." Ms. Glint headed off toward her photographer. "George, why don't we meet for lunch tomorrow to discuss the details?"

"Splendid," Mr. Harris agreed.

"But what about the shards?" Emma pointed to the ground by the fence where it still looked as if it had snowed in large, sharp fragments. "How could we build when the street is covered with raw magic?"

"Ahem." Figgy cleared his throat. "This is exactly what I'd been about to say when my history lesson was interrupted." He pointed at the shards with a paw. "It's called *translucence*. This is what happens when an invisibility spell is interrupted."

"Of course!" Izzy smacked her forehead. "I read about that. But doesn't translucence mean it will disappear?"

"Not exactly, but an excellent question, Isabelle." Figgy was in his element. He didn't notice that Treble had crouched behind him, wriggling his rear end as he prepared to pounce on Figgy's swishing tail. "It is indeed raw magic, but that means over time—and with a little sunlight—it will absorb into the surrounding area."

Maeve could hardly speak, she was so happy. "How long will it take to absorb?"

Figgy pondered this. "About as long as it takes to obtain

a deed and construction permit, I'd guess. *Ah!*" He leaped in the air as Treble pounced. "Little scamp," he said, and batted Treble's head affectionately with his paw.

"Uncle Figgy, do you think I could come guard the new school with you when I'm old enough, please?" Treble asked. "It sounds so very exciting and I don't like opera very much." He licked his lips. "Plus, I hear Cook makes the best gravy."

Maeve had never seen such a look of delight on Figgy's face before.

"I would be honored! I've always wanted to be a mentor." Figgy's voice was choked with emotion.

Treble nuzzled Figgy's side and both house dragons purred. Everyone *awwed*.

Anoush ran over and tugged Maeve by the arm. "Maeve, come play in the garden with us!"

"Anoushjan, it looks like Maeve is busy." Mrs. Kalfayan walked up, holding Nareg by the hand. "Let her finish her conversation."

Maeve had an idea. "Mrs. Kalfayan, has your husband found work yet?"

When Mrs. Kalfayan shook her head, Maeve quickly told her about the school and explained to Mr. Harris that Mr. Kalfayan was a construction foreman. Anoush grabbed her brother's hands and began dancing him around when she heard about the school.

Mr. Harris nodded. "I'd very much like to speak with your husband, if he's here. It would be good to have someone who knows the community leading the project."

"I agree, and thank you. I'll go find him." Mrs. Kalfayan pointed down the block. As she turned, Mrs. Kalfayan leaned in close and whispered so that only Maeve could hear. "The Ember Society will be here to help with the school when you need us. Benjamin would have loved your plan for the garden."

With a wink, Mrs. Kalfayan headed into the crowd. Anoush and Nareg followed, still skipping with joy. Maeve stared after them, feeling stunned. A slow smile crept across her face as what she'd just heard sank in. She couldn't wait to tell Avi.

Izzy came up behind Maeve and squeezed her shoulder. Her diamond bracelet sparkled in the sunlight. "I love your idea for the school. Mam and Da would have been proud."

Maeve smiled, knowing her sister was right.

"Speaking of schools, Isabelle, there's something you should know." Figgy stilled. "Aria told me that Mr. Rote Extinguished Briolette because they are planning to offer you admission and a scholarship for next year."

Izzy covered her mouth with her hands. Happy tears shone in her eyes. "They're accepting me? I haven't even applied yet."

Figgy winked. "Apparently the headmistress has been keeping an eye on you and is a fan."

Emma squeaked with excitement. "You'll get to go to school with Frances and me! We'll be classmates, Izzy!"

"This is wonderful news!" Mr. Harris beamed at Izzy.

Maeve hugged her sister. "I'm so happy for you, Izzy," she said, and she meant it.

When they broke apart again, Izzy's face was serious. "Emma, Mr. Harris, I've been thinking. I really appreciate the offer to join your family, but I have to turn you down." She took Maeve's hand. "I've wrestled with this decision for a long time, but I'm already part of a family and I don't want to change my name or who I am."

Maeve stared at her sister in shock. Had she heard Izzy correctly?

"Oh, Izzy." Mr. Harris put his hand to his heart. "I never would have asked if I'd known it would cause you anguish. That's the last thing in the world I would want."

Izzy turned to Emma. "I'm sorry. I know you're disappointed we won't be real sisters."

Emma shook her head and her tangled blond curls bounced. "We're already sisters, Iz."

Maeve was surprised by how disappointed she felt. "Izzy, she's right. They're our family too."

Everyone looked at her. Maeve didn't shrink under their gaze.

Mr. Harris smiled. "I have an alternate suggestion. I can be your legal guardian. No name changes, no paternity, just our friendship, a home, and the ability to sign a legal document when you need it. It's like being extended family."

Izzy inhaled and Maeve could hear the hope in her breath. "Maeve? What do you think?"

Maeve paused. No one could ever replace her real family, but no one was trying to. "I think that sounds wonderful."

The three girls wrapped their arms around one another.

"I have never seen a group of people who hug as much as you girls do," Mr. Harris teased, but he was clearly thrilled when they pulled him into the circle too.

They were still hugging when someone tapped Maeve on the shoulder. She turned to find Avi and his mother waiting a few paces behind him.

Mrs. Sigal rushed up to Maeve and squeezed her hands. Her gaze held only joy.

"I love it," she said in English, followed by a long stretch of Yiddish.

"She says the garden is beautiful," Avi translated. "She wishes there was a way for me to have my magic safely because now she understands what magic can do."

Happy pink sparks flickered at Avi's fingertips. Mrs. Sigal let go of Maeve's hands and patted her son's arm proudly.

"I'm glad you told her about your magic," Maeve said.

"Me too." Avi smiled shyly. "Speaking of magic, I hear you're opening a kindling school here?"

Maeve blinked. "Wow, word travels fast."

"It's the Tarnish. You know." Avi shrugged and smiled. "Any chance you're admitting boys? And boarding students? Say, for example, boys from Baltimore?"

Maeve looked to Izzy, Emma, and Mr. Harris. They nodded. "We'll take anyone who wants to learn," Maeve announced proudly.

"I want to learn magic. I want to kindle," Avi said. He quickly translated for his mother, stumbling over his words in excitement.

Maeve's heart soared when Mrs. Sigal nodded.

"My boy is magic," she said, which everyone understood to mean yes.

Maeve hugged Avi, who blushed until he was as red as the brick buildings.

After that, the cleanup took on the atmosphere of a festival. More brooms were procured, and even Ms. Glint took a turn sweeping the shards of magic into piles—though she posed for several photos with the broom, of course.

When the street had been cleared, some of the neighbors brought out fiddles, drums, and other instruments and threw an impromptu dance party in the middle of the street. Maeve was distributing the produce they'd been able to salvage from the shards when Izzy skipped over. Her big sister took her by the hands and lead Maeve into the dance.

Caught up in the joy of the music, they linked elbows like they had when they were younger and laughed and laughed as they twirled past Tom and Emma, Antonia and the other girls from the school, and Anoush and Nareg. Treble, Cadenza, and Forte took turns pouncing on Figgy's tail and he grinned at them like a proud uncle. Miss Clementine spun Mr. Harris around in his chair while the two of them laughed, already deep in plans for moving the school downtown. Maeve felt a rush of affection for all of them.

"Now this is a party," Izzy said breathlessly.

Maeve couldn't have agreed more. There was nowhere else in the world she'd rather be.

Epilogue

Maeve and Izzy shared the guest room at the Harrises' apartment that night with Aria and the kits. Maeve slept long and hard, and when she went downstairs to breakfast, she found Aria, the kits, Figgy, Izzy, Tom, Antonia, and the Harrises already gathered around the dining table. The table normally sat four, so it was a tight squeeze, but no one looked unhappy about it. A stack of pancakes taller than Treble sat in the middle of the table, but everyone was focused on the newspaper.

The headline spanned the width of the page:

THE O'DONNELL SISTERS SAVE THE DAY
BY TOM SABETTI

Maeve stood behind Izzy and hugged her. "Don't you want to read it?" Izzy asked.

"I will later." Maeve shook her head. She already knew what it would say. "Right now, I want to enjoy the morning.

"I love you," she said to Izzy.

"I love you too." Izzy pulled out the empty chair next to her and patted it. "Join us. Papa Harris, can you scoot over, please?"

"Make room for Maeve, everyone," Mr. Harris commanded, and there was a clatter of plates and forks as everyone shifted their chairs to let her in.

Maeve sat down and put her napkin in her lap. "Will someone pass the butter, please? These pancakes smell amazing."

"Figgy made them." Emma raised her fork and her eyebrows at the same time.

Maeve's eyes widened. "More house dragon magic?"

Figgy laughed. "No. A cookbook and some help."

Cook and Miss Clementine carried two more stacks of pancakes out from the kitchen. "Everyone here? Let's eat!" Cook announced.

Tom raised his orange juice. "To the O'Donnell sisters."

Everyone cheered. Then Maeve and Izzy settled in to enjoy their breakfast with the rest of their magical family.

ACKNOWLEDGMENTS

Thank you to my readers for embracing this book and *The Gilded Girl* so warmly. Releasing my first book during a global pandemic was daunting, but it turned out to be a wonderful, life-affirming experience. Thank you for joining me for this second adventure and I hope many more.

I have to start by thanking the dream team at Farrar, Straus and Giroux and Macmillan Children's Publishing Group. Janine O'Malley, editor extraordinaire: In addition to your brilliant notes, thank you for being my advocate, brainstorm buddy, and sounding board. I count my lucky stars every day that I get to work with you. Thank you to the incomparable Melissa Warten, whose keen editorial eye saved me from myself more than once and who always knew the answers to my questions. Brittany Pearlman and Jordin Streeter, thank you for your hard work and out-of-the-box thinking to help the book reach readers and for having the best taste in graphics. Aurora Parlagreco, thank you for sharing your incredible talent and designing the books of my dreams. Thank you to production editor Lelia Mander, production manager Susan Doran, copyeditor Chandra Wohleber, and proofreader Annie McDonnell.

Thank you to Geneviève Godbout for bringing Maeve and the kits to life with her beautiful illustration. I couldn't love my covers more.

Thank you to Sarah Landis, who appeared in my life like the Ember Society when I needed help. Working with you is a dream come true! Thanks also go to Mary Pender-Coplan for her enthusiasm and continued support.

Many thanks, Brooks Sherman, for believing in these books from the start and for helping me find the perfect home for them.

Thank you to Julie Abe, Sam Farkas, Kalyn Josephson, and Melissa Seymour for reading early drafts of this book. Your sharp eyes and kind feedback were the magic that helped this story grow.

Thank you so much to those who helped me keep my history and facts straight: Anush A., Anne-Sophie Jouhanneau (Gemmes! Ha!), and Danielle Ball and the research librarians at the Los Angeles Public Library.

To the Guillotine Queens, a writing and support group with some of the kindest people in publishing: Brittney Arena, Tracy Badua, Rae Castor, Kat Enright, Sam Farkas, Jenn Gruenke, Jessica James, Kalyn Josephson, and Ashley Northup. Thank you to Wes, Zuko, El & Snags, Wes & Cress, Mochi, Paprika, and Snow & Mango for all the house dragon inspiration.

To Lorelei Savaryn and Felicity: Thank you for your joy, support, and enthusiasm. I will treasure it always.

Anne Ursu, thank you for being my writing fairy godmother and for all your support and wisdom.

Thank you to Professor James A. Wilson, who reminded me every day that I live in the world and should know what is happening in it.

Sending a big hug to my writer community for the check-ins, shout-outs, love, and support. I'm so lucky to know these talented and wonderful humans: Kate Albus, Nicole Bross, Stephanie Brubaker, Yvette Clark, Erika Cruz, Alexa Donne, Kristin Dwyer, Karina Evans, Jessica Kim, Erika Lewis, Brian Palmer, Bill Povletich, Gretchen Schreiber, Austin Siegemund-Broka, Emily Skrutskie, Melanie Thorne, Victoria Van Vleet, Whitney Vendt, Emily Wibberly, Alysa Wishingrad, and Adrienne Young.

On a personal level, thank you to the doctors and nurses at Cedars-Sinai who kept every member of my immediate family alive at one point or another during the course of writing this book. Thank you to my strong mom, who did the night shift without a single complaint, and my incredible dad, who stepped in to help for the long haul. Thank you to Jessie and Zac, who always arrived just in time and gave me room to breathe. I don't know what I would have done without you.

Thank you to my Wake Forest crew: Cainna, Nelson, Alex, Mitchell, Matt G., Zach, Ben, and Matt Z. You showed me the true meaning of burning brighter when things were dark.

This book wouldn't exist without the support, kindness, generosity, and enthusiasm from wonderful people: Julie C., Caroline T., Dave K., Lindsay W., Jane S., Emily S., Patrick S., Lindsey M., Michele H., Annette A., TheOGTwinMom group (Ana, Ashley, Christine, Clare, Rosalind, and Taryn), Teddie M., Cat F., Melissa G., Lauren V., Steve V., Kathleen S., Whitney W., Elizabeth C., and Peter R.

Last but certainly not least, thank you to Dan, Cora, and Maggie for making every day magical. You are my inspiration and my joy.